OPAL

Elvi Rhodes

CORGI BOOKS

OPAL
A CORGI BOOK : 0 552 12367 6

Originally published in Great Britain by
Century Publishing Co. Ltd

PRINTING HISTORY
Century edition published 1984
Corgi edition published 1984

15 17 19 20 18 16 14

Set in 10/11pt Plantin

Corgi Books are published by Transworld Publishers,
61–63 Uxbridge Road, London W5 5SA,
a division of The Random House Group Ltd,
in Australia by Random House Australia (Pty) Ltd,
20 Alfred Street, Milsons Point, Sydney, NSW 2061, Australia,
and in New Zealand by Random House New Zealand Ltd,
18 Poland Road, Glenfield, Auckland 10, New Zealand
and in South Africa by Random House (Pty) Ltd,
Endulini, 5a Jubilee Road, Parktown 2193, South Africa.

Printed and bound in Great Britain by
Mackays of Chatham plc, Chatham, Kent

For my daughters-in-law,
Christine and Margaret

Chapter One

Opal, carrying the child in one arm and a canvas bag over the other, came into the house and kicked the door to with her foot, but not quickly enough to keep out the thin cloud of powdery snowflakes which followed her. They settled on the doormat and, though the room was bitterly cold, were quickly melted and absorbed. The child started to cry, a thin, miserable sound.

'I know son. You're cold,' Opal said. 'Just let me set you down and we'll soon get things warmed up.'

She sat him on the black horsehair sofa which was partly covered by a large square of knitted patchwork.

'There!' she said gently. 'Now wait on. I'll be as quick as I can.'

The light had almost gone from the short February day. She found the box of matches on the mantelpiece and lit the gas, standing on tiptoe and stretching out her arm to the bracket, for she was only five feet tall. The gas popped and spluttered, seeming reluctant to settle down to its usual steady hiss. Its soft glow lit the centre of the room, enhancing the ruby-red plush tablecloth, picking out the odd patches of colour in the rag rugs on the stone floor, but not penetrating into the corners of even so small a room. The rugs were made from old clothes cut into strips, or 'tabs'. Everyone's clothes seemed to have been made in dark, serviceable colours, but whenever she had been able to get hold of something brighter, Opal had worked it into the rug in the rough shape of a flower. She loved colour, and nowhere in her life was there enough of it.

'We need a new gas mantle,' she said, kneeling down to be on a level with her small son. His cry had changed to an intermittent whimper.

'Now' she went on 'Mam'll blow on your hands for a minute to warm them, then she'll light the fire.' She cupped his small hands in her own, though hers were scarcely less cold, and blew her warm breath over them, gently chafing his fingers until he was comforted.

'There!' she said. 'Isn't that better?'

She took food from the canvas bag and put it into the oven, which always retained a vestige of heat. Then she pulled down the window blind and drew the heavy chenille curtain against the back of the street door. The door leading to the stairs was similarly curtained, for the house was full of draughts.

'When the wind blows from the north,' she observed, 'when it's blowing straight from the moor, nothing'll keep it out!'

The fire was laid. She took a taper from the jar on the shelf – for not even a match must be wasted – lit it from the gas and put it to the kindling.

'We'll soon have you warmed up,' she promised the child. 'See the smoke curling up the chimney? And the pretty orange flames, though you must never go near them. Now if you sit there and watch you'll see the black coals turn red and then we'll be really warm. But perhaps you'd better keep your coat and scarf on a bit longer.'

She talked to Daniel most of the time when they were alone together but, being not quite two years old, he seldom answered her. In any case he was a quiet

8

child. He was dark, like herself, with large, solemn eyes which watched everything. She wondered what went on in his mind.

'I had hoped your dad might have been home before us, got the fire going,' she said. 'I wonder where he's got to?'

At this time of the year the fire should be lit in the morning and be warming the house all day; but coal cost money and they had none. To be precise, she had twopence in her purse, which had to see her through until Friday morning. It was Wednesday today.

Every Wednesday she visited her mother-in-law, arriving before the midday dinner and leaving in time to have Edgar's tea ready when he came in from work. Though it was now six months since he had worked she kept to the same routine. No need to rub it in that time was no longer important to him. He could have gone with her, enjoyed a good meal, but he seldom did. Perhaps to visit his mother in the middle of the day was to underline his position and Opal did not press him. She enjoyed Sarah Carson's company. Her mother-in-law was a warm, fat, cheerful woman. Her house was warm too because her husband, Percy, was the local baker. Today's overheated kitchen, right next to the bakehouse, had felt like heaven.

Opal heard her husband at the door and went to ease back the curtain. He entered, bringing a gust of cold air and more snowflakes with him. Edgar Carson was not especially tall, but he seemed at once to fill the space in the small room, perhaps because of the breadth of his shoulders and the set of his handsome head, but really more because of some indefinable inner quality. Whatever it was it never failed to quicken Opal's pulse, to enliven her. Even when things were going badly his magnetism for her never lessened. He removed his cap, shaking the snow on to the floor, and revealed tightly-curled, light brown hair in need of cutting.

'My word!' he said. 'It's bitter out there! I'm perished!'

He looked it. The tip of his nose glowed as red as a beacon in his white face and a few snowflakes had caught and stayed, too icy to melt, in his thick, fair moustache and heavy eyebrows.

'It's cold in here,' Opal said. 'I've only just lit the fire. We went early to your mother's – just after you'd left for the Labour Exchange – so as not to have to light it. Why didn't you come home for your dinner, love? We had a lovely steak and kidney pie.'

'They sent me after a job.'

'And?' But she didn't need to ask.

The years immediately after the war had been good ones. Trade had picked up quickly and there had been an air of optimism everywhere. But it didn't last long. Edgar knew he was only one of thousands who'd been laid off in 1922, and prospects for 1923 seemed no brighter. Hope for a new kind of world, which was what had kept him going in the filth of the trenches, for he had hated every minute of being a soldier, had already died in him.

'There were twenty of us after it. There's a lot of weavers out of work, as well you know,' he said defensively.

'Oh I know all right,' Opal said. 'I know!'

She pushed past him to fill the kettle at the scullery tap, and then back again to place it on the hob. Hunger and cold had so numbed him that he seemed not to have the wit to get out of her way.

'Lloyd George promised us a land fit for heroes to live in,' he said. 'We believed him, simple folk like me. Well, he's out of it now, and serve him right I say. But I see nothing better from this lot.'

Opal sighed. 'Politics! Politics won't fill our bellies! See to Daniel, will you love?'

Edgar moved to the sofa and took his son on his lap. There were days when his insides seemed to turn to stone, when his broad shoulders seemed unable to bear the almost physical weight of his depression. Opal, though he knew she tried, didn't understand how a man in his position felt.

'Don't take Daniel's coat off yet,' she said. 'Not until the house has warmed up.'

'All the same, you're wrong about politics,' Edgar said. 'They matter all right. It's Governments decide the way we live, you and me.'

'Don't forget there was a war,' Opal said.

'I'm not likely to,' he said grimly. 'But who caused that lot if it wasn't the politicians? Answer me that!'

'I can't.'

She sighed. He was in bad mood again, working himself up to no purpose. She *did* sympathize with him, ached at his inability to get a job. Yet as the months went by a cold voice inside her too often asked why, whenever there was a job going, it never went to Edgar? His appearance was good. He was a competent workman. But the months of idleness were dulling him, resentment was taking hold. At a time when even good workmen were without jobs he lacked the spark which would have given him the edge in an interview with a prospective employer. She could see all that so plainly, but how could she tell him without hurting him further?

'Kettle's boiling,' Edgar said.

Opal made the tea and set it aside to brew. The longer it stood the more strength they would get from the spoonful of tea. She wondered if life was to go on like this for ever. And to crown it all she was pregnant again, though see had not yet told Edgar, or indeed anyone. People who were better off preached that it was wrong and improvident of the unemployed to have children. Well, she wasn't overjoyed about the child she was carrying, either. She had no idea how they would manage. But what the well-off didn't understand – how could they? – was that sex was the only pleasure left which didn't need money in the purse; that in the warmth and darkness of the bed it blotted out reality. And that while it lasted, the coupling of the poorest man and woman could equal that of the rich.

But at its conclusion the worry always started again. Supposing I've been caught? We should have been more careful, stopped before the climax. 'Always take a towel to bed with you,' the women advised each other. 'Let him come on that!'

Easier said than done, so that after the earliest possible douching, uncomfortably carried out in the kitchen with a bucket of water and an arrangement of rubber tubing, one waited and prayed daily for the menstrual blood to flow again. And if the blood did not flow, then it was the large measure of gin, the raspberry-leaf tea, the repeated jumping off the kitchen table – all advised to bring on an early miscarriage.

Opal had done none of that, nor would she. She was too afraid that if she tampered with Nature, then Nature might take its revenge and give her a deformed child. But she was three months gone now and she would have to tell Edgar, as well as his parents and hers. Also, she had this other matter in mind. Both subjects would have to be broached. But better wait until they'd eaten. Food might raise Edgar's spirits.

'Your mother gave me a couple of meat pasties today,' she said. 'And currant teacakes to finish off with. I don't know where we'd be without your mother. My Mam's well-intentioned enough, and I know she'd help if she were asked, but somehow she doesn't think of the little things like your mother does.'

Perhaps, Opal thought, because her mother had been a servant in a house where there were no shortages, and since her marriage had lived on farms, where basic foods were more easily come by, it had never occurred to her that her daughter might be hungry. And Opal would not have hinted at it. She did not see her mother often and in her heart she knew that she neglected her.

She served the pasties, one each for herself and Edgar.

'I'll give Daniel a bit of mine if he fancies it,' she said. 'But he ate well at his grandma's today.'

She must visit her mother soon. The small sheep farm to which her parents had moved from Grandpa Derwent's place was four miles away across the moors, and it was a bad time for walking, but see her mother she must. She had a favour to ask of her.

'I'd like you to look after Daniel on Saturday,' she said to Edgar. I want to go to Highcliffe. He's a weight to carry and it's too far for him to walk.'

'Whatever do you want to go for in this weather?' Edgar asked. 'There's snow on the ground. It might not clear by the weekend.'

'It might not clear all winter,' Opal said. 'I can't wait until the Spring comes.'

She went to the kettle and poured more water over the tea leaves.

'I can squeeze another cup,' she said. 'There's no sugar. You'll have to manage without.'

'What is there that can't wait, for Heaven's sake?'

Opal sipped her tea. She felt better now. The room was warming up and the food had done her good. She was always ravenous these days.

'Well . . .' she began hesitantly. 'There's two things I have to tell you, love. I reckon you won't like either of them.'

He stared at her. 'Well, what is it then?'

'The first is, I'm three months pregnant. The second is . . . I'm going to open up a house shop!'

'A house shop? What on earth do you mean?'

It was clear, Opal thought, which announcement had upset him the most.

'What else can I mean, Edgar,' she replied patiently, 'than a little shop right here in the house? It's not uncommon. Other people have done it.'

'But why? Why you?'

'Why me?'

And then it was as if the poison of every bad feeling – of frustration, of hunger, of fear for the future – which for Edgar's sake she had striven to hide over the last few months, churned in her stomach, rose chokingly into her throat, and had to be spat out.

'Why me?' she snapped. 'Because I want sugar in my tea and butter on my bread! I want more to live on every Thursday than a twopenny packet of soup! And Daniel's growing out of his clothes and your boots let in the water!' Her voice rose to a shout and Daniel, frightened, began to cry. 'I can think of several other reasons, but will those do to be going on with?'

Edgar's hurt eyes met hers. To her horror she saw the tears rise in them and spill over. She felt as though she had taken a whip to him. But if crying was any good, she thought wearily, she'd have solved all their problems long ago. She never cried nowadays. As for a man doing so, as for Edgar doing so, that was weakness, and frightening. Now even more than ever they needed each other's strength.

She picked up Daniel and held him in her lap, burying her face in the warm nape of his neck. Then eventually she stretched out her hand and took Edgar's.

'I'm sorry, love,' she said. 'I know you want to get work. I know you deserve to have a job. But it might be a long time before you do and we can't go on like this. Twenty-one shillings a week was bad enough for the three of us, but now you've run out of benefit and what the Board of Guardians allows us won't feed a cat. And another thing – I'm sick of Food Vouchers! Some Jack-in-Office telling me what I can buy and what I can't buy! Do you know there's a list as long as my arm of foods I *can't* get on the vouchers because *they* think they're luxuries? Not for the likes of us! No, Edgar, if I can make just a bit extra, a shilling or two a week, it'll make all the difference. I'm going to need new things for the baby, too.'

She was babbling. She knew it. But anything to wipe that look from his face.

Edgar wiped his eyes with the back of his hand. She was always so logical, so right. When they were court-ing and in the early days of their marriage he had admired her strengths, though they were different from his own. She was a wife who would help a husband to get on, spur his ambitions. He was a man who would work for his family, strive to do all that was expected of him, given the chance. But sometimes now, though she did not know it, Opal's strength seemed to diminish him. Sometimes he longed for a glimpse of some frailty in her which would excuse the weakness he knew in himself.

'You must see it's reasonable,' Opal said more quietly. She saw by the look in his eyes, the all-too-familiar look of defeat, that she had won. She would have her house shop. But the victory itself gave her no pleasure. How much better if the idea has been his!

'We don't have much room here,' Edgar said in a dull voice. 'Where will you put everything?'

'I thought I'd clear the top of the sideboard and set up shop there, and perhaps on a bit of the table. I could empty the sideboard cupboards, too. God knows there's not much in them. You could take the doors off for me and it would be like display shelves.'

'But what about the other shops in the village? Won't they object?'

'No,' she said. 'What little bit of trade I do won't affect them. I'll sell a variety of things so it'll be a very little from each.' In any case she did not care. She had her own family to look out for.

'Where will you get money to buy stock?' Edgar asked. 'You'll need cash on the nail.'

'I know. That's why I want to go to Highcliffe. I'm sure Mam has a bit put by. Her egg money from the market and suchlike. If she'd lend me five pounds I could make a start.'

Edgar sighed. 'Well, you seem to have it all worked out.'

'Oh I have,' Opal agreed. 'And I'll make it pay. You'll see. But you've not said anything to me about the baby!'

'What do you want me to say? These things happen. Of course I'm pleased. We didn't want Daniel to be our only bairn, did we? But it'll be harder for you than for me. Are you sure you'll be able to manage the shop as well?'

It was strange, Opal thought, that it never occurred to him that he might run the shop while she looked after their children and kept house. While he might not forbid her to go ahead with the scheme it would not enter his head to contribute. Running a house shop – selling needles and thread and sweets and groceries was, like housework, cooking, and bringing up children, women's work. It was beside the point that he had nothing else to do except sign on at the Labour Exchange and attend a decreasing number of interviews.

But having told Edgar she felt the project was as good as launched. She was sure she could get the loan. For the first time in many weeks excitement stirred in her and with it came that other, more familiar feeling. It ran like fire through her body and tingled in her breasts. She wanted, needed, to make love now, urgently. If it had not been for Daniel she would have liked to have lain with Edgar on the hearthrug, naked in the light from the fire, now glowing red, instead of in the dark, chilly bedroom. But, though he knew how much she loved him, such desires of the body were not ones which she could put into words to Edgar. It was shaming enough that she, a woman, should have them.

'I'll put Daniel to bed and we'll have an early night,' she said. 'It'll save the gas.'

She began to undress Daniel. There was one thing to be said in favour of being pregnant; you could make love whenever you wanted to. When Daniel was in his nightshift she put him down gently on the rug. Then she began to remove the pins from her hair. It cascaded around her shoulders, thick, jet black, gleaming in the light from the fire. Edgar had always like to see her hair loose. When they were first married he would take out the pins himself, slowly, one by one, watching the hair fall.

She lifted Daniel from the rug and went up to the bedroom, leaving the stairs door open behind her.

The main street of Milton ran down to the railway bridge, and just beyond that to the bridge over the river. The mill which gave the village its reason for being there (for it had not grown from early beginnings like other villages, but had been built all in one go) stood on a strip of land between two bridges. Sir Henry Milton, in the nineteenth century, had carefully calculated the advantages of this position: the soft river water to wash the wool, the railway (in which he was a shareholder) to bear it away; spun, woven and dyed into the finest cloth.

Though the village was dominated by the mill and could not have existed without it, Sir Henry was a philanthropic businessman and had also built a school, a public washhouse, a chapel (in the grounds of which he now rested in his ornate tomb), a cottage hospital and several streets of small, terraced houses for his millhands, with a few larger ones for the managers. It was because he once worked at the mill that Edgar had been able, on his marriage, to rent the house in Acer Street.

This morning groups of men stood on the railway bridge. One of them called out to Opal as she passed.

'Good morning Mrs Carson!'

'Good morning Mr Holroyd. Cold weather we're having!'

They were standing there, she knew, because Saturday was a working day and they had been used to rising early and going to the mill. Though for most of them there was now no work, they felt better getting up, getting out of the house, meeting with their mates.

Beyond the river the cobbled street ended and the track through the woods up to the moor began, rising steeply from the valley. Opal enjoyed the climb. On the top of the moor the air was clear and dry, the sky unusually high for February. She was glad to get away from Milton for a few hours and was looking forward to seeing her family and hearing the news of the farm.

She had not always thought that way. When Edgar Carson had first called at the farm – he was returning over the moors from Ilkley with two friends and enquired if a ham and egg tea could be provided – Opal had answered the door to him. She knew at once that here was the man she had been waiting for to carry her away. And after that first Sunday he had returned often, sometimes with his friends and then, as time went on, more often on his own.

'It's clear what *he's* coming for,' Opal's mother said. 'Plain as a pikestaff!'

'Well, I like him,' Opal said. She loved him, but that was too extravagant a feeling to express out loud, to her mother.

'So do we all,' her mother replied. 'He's an agreeable lad. And he did his bit in the war, there's no denying that.'

'So what have you got against him?' Opal demanded.

'Not against *him*. Not personally. It's just that . . .

well, your Dad and me thought of something better for you. A farmer or a schoolteacher.'

'But not a weaver,' Opal said. 'Well, he'll not always be a weaver. He means to get on. And I don't see any farmers or schoolteachers queueing up for me, do you?'

'There's plenty of time,' Mrs Derwent said. 'Why is it you can never wait for anything?'

Then in the June of 1920 Edgar had come one weekend to give a hand with the haymaking, working all day beside Opal, forking the hay stooks into the cart. The day's toil, the hot sun, the clover-scented, newly-cut grass, were powerful aphrodisiacs for both of them (had they needed such aids). Before nightfall, in the stone barn where they had stacked the new hay, Daniel was conceived. Benjamin and Hannah Derwent said goodbye to their dreams for Opal and in September the couple were married in the tiny Methodist chapel at Highcliffe.

Opal climbed the last short steep rise before the summit of the moor. From now on it was all downhill. The countryside, its contours softened by the deep covering of snow, reminded her of a picture of Switzerland she had once seen on a calender. A mile down the hill she could see the hamlet which was Highcliffe, and on the edge of it her father's farm. The sheep, which in the summer were allowed to roam the hill, were now folded in the small field close to the farmhouse, where they were handy for winter feeding. They huddled together against the cold. In a couple of months from now the fields would be freshly green and the low pastures would be dotted with new lambs.

She began to hurry down the slope, sliding and slipping in the snow. In spite of being pregnant she felt incredibly fit and healthy. She had no morning sickness and wouldn't have now. But she was terribly hungry and hoped that by the time she reached the farm, dinner would be on the table. They didn't know she was coming but there was always enough for an extra person. The way she felt she could eat two men's dinners.

She was not disappointed. When she reached the farm and walked into the big kitchen the warm air was filled with the delicious smell of food. Everyone was there, including her brother Mark and his bride-to-be, Queenie Stone, and Opal's Aunt Garnet. They were at the table, already starting on the meal. Mary jumped up from her chair and rushed to embrace her sister. Only Mary would ever dream of giving such an effusive greeting, but they all looked up from their heaped plates, pleased enough to see her.

'Come and sit down, love,' her mother said. 'Mary, lay another place. You've not brought Daniel nor Edgar, then?'

'No. I thought the weather might turn bad. And Daniel has a bit of a cold.'

As her mother rose to fetch the meat pie which she had returned to the oven to keep hot, Opal thought how thin she was looking. But she sounded well enough. Her voice was strong.

'I'm starving!' Opal said. 'I could eat a huge helping!'

'You always could,' her father said. 'I don't know where you put it. You not the size of two pennorth of copper!'

'Well, you know what they say,' Opal retorted. 'They don't make diamonds as big as bricks.'

'She's like me,' Aunt Garnet mumbled through a mouthful of pie. Aunt Garnet was the middle one of Opal's father's three sisters. The three were named

Pearl, Garnet and Ruby because Grandpa Derwent said they were his jewels. When his first granddaughter was born he expected the tradition to be followed, favouring Diamond or Emerald, but Hannah was against it and Benjamin reckoned it was the mother's privilege to name the baby. In the end, Hannah compromised on Opal. Her own mother said that that was worse because everyone knew that opals were for tears. When it came to her second daughter and last child she chose the name Mary as being the most straightforward she could think of.

'I didn't expect to find you here, Aunt Garnet,' Opal said.

'No you wouldn't,' her aunt replied. 'But as you know, there's less to do on the farm in winter, so I gave myself a holiday. Father wasn't too pleased, of course.'

Aunt Garnet must be in her forties, Opal thought, and Aunt Pearl was older still. Unlike Ruby, they had never married but had remained at home on the dales farm, where Grandfather Derwent treated them like children.

Opal turned to Queenie and Mark, who were seated side by side and were so much in love that they held hands between mouthfuls.

'Have you fixed the date yet?' she asked.

'Saturday the second of June,' Queenie said happily. 'Only sixteen weeks to go! And I have a favour to ask you, Opal. Will you make the wedding hats? Mine and the bridesmaids? You're so clever at it.'

'You can do mine as well,' Aunt Garnet said.

'You're not having a white wedding, then?' Opal enquired.

'No. With Mother gone and Father rather poorly, it seems best not.'

'Well of course I'll do them.'

'Our Opal was always gifted with her needle,' Hannah Derwent said. 'When she was little she didn't really play with dolls like other children do. She just made hats and dresses for them, and always in the latest style.'

'I'll make you a new hat, too, Mother,' Opal said.

'Nay lass,' her mother answered. 'The one I had for your wedding's as good as new. I've hardly worn it since, except to Harvest Thanksgiving and Whitsundays to chapel. It'll do me nicely.'

'You'll have to go with me to buy the material, Queenie,' Opal said. There was no way she could lay out a penny. She would earn a bit in the end, but not much since it was for family.

'Oh we'll arrange all that,' Queenie said. 'Shall we have a trip to Leasfield? Or Leeds or Bradford?'

Queenie's father was a prosperous wool merchant and none of his family was ever short of money, but Queenie was sensitive to other people's needs and perfectly understood Opal's remark.

When the meal was over Opal contrived to get her mother to accompany her upstairs so that they could speak alone.

'I wanted you to know before the others,' Opal said. 'I'm expecting. It'll be in August.'

There was a barely felt pause, a fleeting look of pain on her mother's face, but swiftly followed by a pleased smile.

'Well that's good news, Opal love!' She patted her daughter's hand, the nearest she ever came to a caress. 'It's best for Daniel not to be an only child. But don't have a quiverful as the Good Book says. It's too big a burden. Oh I don't mean that any of you lot were,' she added quickly. 'Nothing like that. But with jobs so hard to come by . . . I suppose Edgar hasn't heard anything yet?'

'No,' Opal said. 'Which brings me to the next thing.'

She explained to her mother what she had in mind about the shop and asked for the loan of five pounds.

'I'll pay it back as soon as I can. A bit at a time, but you'll get it all,' Opal promised.

'Well if you're sure it's what you want to do, you can have the money and welcome,' Mrs Derwent said. She crossed to the walnut chest and took out a small bag from the back of a drawer.

'Here you are love,' she said. 'And ten gold sovereigns, not five. You'll do better with a good start. I don't want it back. It's yours to keep. Only don't you go telling anyone – not your father nor anyone. What's mine is my own and it's up to me what I do with it!'

'Oh Mam! I don't know how to thank you!'

'Then don't! And now we'd best get back downstairs. There's a mountain of washing-up.'

Downstairs, Mary shooed her mother out of the kitchen.

'You go and sit in the parlour and talk weddings with Queenie,' she said.

'Mam's not well,' Mary told Opal when their mother had left the room. 'But she won't rest. That's why Aunt Garnet's here, only Mam doesn't know it.'

'What's wrong with her?' Opal asked. 'I thought she looked thinner. Why didn't you let me know? I'd have come sooner.'

'I was going to if you hadn't come today. I don't know what's wrong and she won't see a doctor. She says it's simply the end of the winter and she'll be better in the spring. Of course we both know that she's never been the same since George was killed. More than six years now, but she doesn't get over it. George was more to her than you and me put together!'

It was not to be wondered at, Opal thought. She, too, had worshipped her brother. A light had gone out for all of them when George had been killed on the Somme. For their mother it had never been rekindled.

'I'm having another baby,' she announced.

'Oh Opal, you're not! Oh you are lucky! I do envy you. Sometimes I think I'll never get married and have babies, yet it's all I ever want.'

Opal laughed. 'What *do* you mean. Of course you will. You're only eighteen. There's all the time in the world.'

'I never meet anyone,' Mary said.

'You will,' Opal assured her. 'Perhaps someone will come knocking on the door, like Edgar did.'

Too soon it was time to leave. Opal would have liked to have stayed longer, wouldn't have minded in the least walking back across the moor in the dark, but Edgar would expect her back and Daniel would no doubt be waiting for his tea.

'I'll walk along the bottom path with you,' her mother said. It was an unusual gesture, and even more strange that she should wave Mary aside, wanting to have Opal to herself. Yet as they walked she had nothing of significance to say. At the end of the level path where Opal must turn to start the walk up to the moor, she took both her daughter's hands in hers.

'You've always been a good lass to me,' she said. 'I don't forget it. Now get on and take care of yourself.'

'And you do the same, Mam,' Opal answered.

She wondered about her mother as she climbed the hill. Was she perhaps trying to say that she was sorry for her concentration on her dead son and the exclusion of her living children? When she reached the top of the hill she turned and looked back. Her mother was still standing there. The two women raised their hands in a final gesture of farewell. But when Opal started on the downward slope her thoughts turned at once to her house shop. She began to plan what she would buty with the ten gold sovereigns in her purse.

On the Monday following her visit to Highcliffe she did the family wash; starching, blueing, mangling, drying, ironing – so that by bedtime everything had been aired off on the clothes horse by the fire and could be put away. On Tuesday she cleaned the living-room, polished the sideboard, scrubbing the table top with coarse salt, blackleading the range until Daniel could see his face in the oven door.

'Why all the fuss?' Edgar enquired. 'If somebody wants a packet of pins in a hurry they won't care a tinker's curse whether the firegrate's clean or not.'

'Oh yes they will,' Opal contradicted. 'They may not realize it, but everything about the surroundings matters when you're trying to sell something.'

Edgar looked at her in astonishment.

'How do you know? You've never sold anything.'

'I just do, that's all. I know I'm right. I wish I had a few flowers to brighten up the place. When I'm rich I shall have fresh flowers every day.'

On Wednesday she made her usual visit to her mother-in-law and gave her the news. Mrs Carson was delighted about the baby. 'It was great sorrow to Percy and me' she said 'that Edgar was the only one.' About the shop she was dubious but resigned, even a little guilty that her son might have brought this upon his family.

'I'm sure our Edgar tries to get work,' she defended him. 'These are hard times we live in. We can't even afford to take a man on in the bakery, or there'd be a job for Edgar there. I just wish we could help you more.'

'No-one's been more helpful than you have,' Opal said. 'You've been a Godsend.'

'I daresay you'll make a go of it,' Mrs Carson said more cheerfully. She could never be downhearted for long. 'Though I'm sorry you won't be able to come here on a Wednesday any more.'

'With Wednesday being half-day closing around here,' Opal said, 'it's a good time for me to be open.'

The next day she was up early. Immediately after breakfast she set off for Shepton, pushing Daniel's empty perambulator. Ridley's was the wholesaler she intended visiting. She had seen the advertisement in the *Argus* and it looked as though they might supply everything she needed. She hoped for as many lines as possible, reckoning that by stocking all the different goods her capital would allow, she might attract more customers. A woman who came for a reel of thread might be tempted by a chocolate bar if it was under her nose. 'You can get it at Opal's' was to be her slogan.

The wholesaler's was situated over a newsagent and tobacconist, in the middle of a row of dismal-looking shops. 'Keenist prices, highest quality' the advertisement had said. Well, that was what she was after. She propped the pram against the wall outside the newsagent's and hoped it would be there when she returned.

'K. Ridley, General Wholesaler' the door on the first landing proclaimed. And below that a notice said 'Please do not ask for Credit since a Refusal may cause

Offence.' She knocked and entered. The warehouse was larger than she had expected. The walls were shelved and crammed with goods from floor to ceiling. The man who greeted her was a wisp of a man; scarcely bigger than she herself.

'Ken Ridley, Esquire, at your service,' he announced.

His voice was inappropriately deep and strong. 'I don't know you, do I?'

'Mrs Opal Carson.'

'So what can I do for a pretty lady like you?' he asked.

Opal explained her errand.

'Well then,' he said. 'You'd best look around and see what takes your fancy! It's all here somewhere!'

It was difficult to know where to start and even more difficult to know when to stop. She chose reels of cotton, reluctantly confining herself to black and white; cards of white linen shirt buttons, pins, sewing and darning needles, knicker elastic, grey darning wool. From the confectionary shelves she selected small items which children could buy with a halfpenny: toffee bars, aniseed balls, sherbert fountains, liquorice chews, fruit gums, dolly mixtures, jelly babies, pear drops and acid drops. And to tempt the mothers with a copper or two to spare and a treat in mind, Fry's cream bars and Rowntree's whipped cream walnuts.

'You'll find sweets a good line,' Mr Ridley advised. 'The less money people have, the more they seem to want to suck sweets. But save enough money for a few packets of groceries. Baking powder, tea. And a few medicinal items for the sudden upset. All obtainable in handy sizes. Daisy headache powders, senna pods, epsom salts, syrup of figs – if you'll pardon me for mentioning them. And Doctor Cassell's tablets.

Magical for shell-shock, nervous debility, stomach pains. Take the one-and-threepenny box and sell them a couple at a time. You'll make a penny or two there.'

'I think I must have reached the limit,' Opal said eventually. She had been trying to add up in her head but had long ago lost count. 'But what I *would* like, even if I have to put something else back on the shelf, is a jar of Fortune's Whispers.'

'Ah!' Mr. Ridley said. 'You're a romantic, like all the ladies!'

'No,' Opal said. 'I'm a realist. It's my intention to allow every customer for the first month to pick out a Fortune's Whisper, free. I'm relying on everyone else to be romantic, you see. To want to see into the future.'

Mr Ridley clapped his hands. 'Well I'll be blowed if you don't take the biscuit,' he chuckled. 'I'll tell you what, I'll do something which is against the rules of a lifetime. You can have the Fortune's Whispers on credit! Pay me when you have given them all away! And while you're at it, pick one for yourself. Go on! Let's see what *your* future's going to be! Come on, dip in. Close your eyes first!'

Opal put her hand into the sweet jar and extracted the small, flat, pastel-coloured sugar sweet, with its message printed on one surface.

'Well, what does it say?' Mr Ridley was all eagerness. She read the words aloud.

'This could be your lucky day.'

'There you are!' cried Mr Ridley. 'I knew it!'

So did Opal. She felt it in her bones and was at once elated and awed.

Amazingly, the goods came to sixpence short of ten pounds. She would be able to eat.

'And I'll throw in a few little cards which might be

useful,' Mr Ridley said. 'You'll find the customers appreciate them' He gave here three oblong cards, threaded with string to hang on the wall. 'We Aim To Please', 'If You Don't See What You Require, Please Ask', and 'Thank You, Please Call Again'.

Before leaving Shepton she bought a plain teacake filled with boiled ham and spread with mustard, for fourpence, and an Eccles cake for a penny. Walking along the road, pushing the laden pram, she ate them greedily.

On Friday morning when Edgar had left for the Labour Exchange she spread her best tablecloth on top of the sideboard and arranged her stock. She placed an empty Oxo tin on the corner of the sideboard and hoped that no-one would require change. She had a float of one penny. Then she sat back, too excited to engage in any activity, and waited for customers. She had put the word around among the neighbours and there was nothing more she could do.

It was a quarter before midday when the door opened and her first customer appeared – a small boy, the son of a neighbour.

'What can I do for you, Thomas?' she asked.

'Mam says do you sell Oxo cubes?'

'I do,' Opal said. 'How many would you like?'

'One.'

When he had paid her she proffered the jar of Fortune's Whispers. 'There's one for every customer who buys,' she told him. 'A lucky dip. Be sure to tell your friends, won't you? And because you're my very first customer, Thomas, you can choose something from amongst the sweets. Anything you like as long as it costs a halfpenny!'

She was in business.

Chapter Two

Opal cleared the breakfast table quickly, then opened the door and shook the crumbs from the tablecloth to the sparrows waiting in the street. She glanced up at the sky; blue, with fleecy white clouds hurrying before a breeze. A perfect May morning. Earlier she had taken a cup of tea to Edgar but he had not yet come down. Well then, he must fend for himself when he did get up – which she hoped would be soon because she was going out and both Daniel and the shop were to be left in his care.

Each day now she made an early start with the shop so that she could catch the children's custom on their way to school. How, in these hard times, parents could afford to give their children a halfpenny two or three times a week, she just didn't know. But so long as they did, she wanted it to come to her. Mr Ridley had been right; the less money some people had, the more they spent on sweets.

She wished Edgar would get a move on. These last few weeks, except on his signing-on mornings, he'd taken to sleeping late every day, sometimes not coming down until after eleven. It seemed that the harder she tried, the less he co-operated. She went to the bottom of the stairs and called out to him.

'Edgar! It's time you were up! Don't forget I'm going to Queenie's.'

A grunt confirmed that he had heard her, but it was

another quarter of an hour before he shuffled downstairs, rubbing the sleep from his eyes.

'I don't know how you can loll in bed the way you do,' Opal said.

'You wouldn't,' he replied.

Even after all this time he still wakened at six, forgetting for a moment, then remembering. Why couldn't Opal understand that to rise early only made the day longer. There was no purpose to it. Better to turn over and go to sleep again.

'You know perfectly well I have to take the hats,' Opal said.

'I'd forgotten. What about my breakfast?'

'I've left you some porridge. It's in the pan on the side. Don't use the milk. Daniel needs it.'

She ought to be drinking milk herself, being pregnant, but most of the half-pint a day which she bought went to Daniel. Perhaps before long she could order extra. She was now making a regular two or three shillings a week profit on the shop. A proportion of this was regularly put aside to invest in more stock, but some she did spend on food. Twice a week she bought fresh herrings, which were cheap and tasty. Every Saturday night she bought 'pie bits' or a rabbit from the butcher, so that they always had a good Sunday dinner. But also, though she had no clear idea why, she was trying to save a few coppers each week, in a toffee tin. One day she would know why she wanted them, and they would be there. Meanwhile the sight of the toffee tin gave her a feeling of security.

'How long will you be gone?' Edgar asked.

'I don't know. It'll be dinner-time before I get to the other side of Leasfield. After dinner I have to set to and do the final bits on the hats. Mary and the other bridesmaid will be there and Mary's taking Aunt Garnet's hat back with her.'

'Aunt Garnet's not back at Highcliffe, is she?' Edgar asked.

'No. But they'll be stopping there on their way to the wedding.'

She wished her aunt could have been at Highcliffe, since her mother was no better. She had walked over to the farm a fortnight ago and had been concerned to see her thinner than ever, and breathless after the slightest exertion.

Opal tried to fasten her jacket and found that it would no longer meet over her increasing girth.

'It's a good thing it's cut to hang straight from the shoulders,' she said. 'I can leave it undone and it'll help to hide me.'

She looked at herself critically in the mirror over the sideboard, adjusting her hat. It was a cream-coloured straw with a deep brim, the crown trimmed with green ribbon finishing in a large bow at the side. However little she had in her purse she tried never to show poverty in her appearance. Her clothes were always clean and well pressed and by clever alterations and small touches here and there she kept in fashion. Never, ever, would she be seen like the other women in Milton, with a shawl over her head to slip to the local shops. And when she went out she always wore gloves.

She gave a final adjustment to her hat and turned to face Edgar.

'Will I do then?' she asked.

'You look grand,' he said. 'Good enough to eat!'

She smiled happily, her good humour restored by his praise.

'What in *my* condition? Well I'll be off then.'

She gathered up her bulky parcels and bent to kiss Daniel.

'Now don't forget Edgar,' she said. 'There's some soup in the pan for your dinner and Daniel's. See that he has his afternoon sleep. I've set out the shop, as you can see. Try not to use paper bags, but if you really must, then use the smallest. Wrapping paper costs money. And don't forget—'

'All right, all right!' Edgar interrupted. 'Are you sure you wouldn't like me to do the washing and blacklead the fireplace in my spare time?'

'Well, if you were me you might have to,' Opal quipped. 'Ta-ta then!'

It was generally supposed that the tram ran from Leasfield to a point quite close to Milton because Sir Henry and his descendants held so much power in both places. Also because when Milton was in full work the Miltonians flocked to Leasfield to spend their wages. In Leasfield there were large shops, two markets, two theatres, three cinemas and countless public houses. Opal took the tram into the centre of the town, then boarded another tram outside the smoke-blackened town hall, destination Barton, where the well-to-do lived.

Queenie's father, Henry Stone, had made his money in wool. His wife had died, leaving Queenie to look after her father and, when the time came, to inherit his wealth. Mr Stone would never have let Mark Derwent come near Queenie if Mark hadn't saved her life, Opal thought, climbing the steps of the large stone house, ringing the bell. He had seen her in difficulties in the river, near Milton, and as her boat capsized he jumped in and rescued her. It was love at first sight for both of them. Queenie would look at no-one else and her father could hardly turn away the man but for whom, his daughter assured him, she might not *be* there.

A maid showed Opal into the large, comfortable sitting-room where Queenie stood with outstretched hands to greet her.

'Opal, how lovely to see you! Oh, how exciting your parcels look! I can hardly wait. But I must, and you must have a cup of tea after your journey. Or better still a glass of sherry. That's it! We'll both be quite wicked and have a glass of sherry! Come over here and sit on the sofa.'

Opal sank into the soft, springy comfort of the sofa, pushing one of the several down-filled cushions into the small of her back. Intent on getting here, she hadn't noticed until now how tired she was.

'There you are!' Queenie said. 'Finest Amontillac'! It will put new life into you. Now tell me how you are. Oh, I can't wait to be pregnant!' She blushed. 'After I'm married of course.'

'I'm fine,' Opal said. 'And this May weather is perfect for me. Selfishly, I hope we don't have a hot summer.'

'As long as you'll allow me a fine wedding day,' Queenie said.

'You shall have a beautiful wedding day,' Opal promised. 'Now, do you want to take a peek at the hats before dinner?'

'Oh yes please. I can hardly wait. But bring them upstairs and I'll show you the dresses. Mrs Bassett has almost finished them. By the way, how is Edgar?'

'He's a bit low,' Opal replied. 'I suppose it's to be expected and I do feel sorry for him, but sometimes I think he should make an effort to snap out of it.'

'Poor Edgar!' Queenie said sympathetically.

In the bedroom Queenie opened the large mahogany wardrobe and took out her wedding dress, holding it with reverence.

'I know it's extravagant to have crepe georgette when so many people are poor' she apologized. 'But it's the only wedding I'll ever have. I'm not beautiful like you, but I want to look my very best for Mark.'

'It's quite perfect,' Opal assured her. 'And so will you be. This soft lavender with your fair colouring is exactly right. And Mrs Bassett's made a marvellous job of the silver beading.' She touched the georgette lovingly. She had a feeling for fine materials.

'Hasn't she just! She still has to turn up the hem. The last few stitches won't be put in until the day, and I mustn't try it on, once it's finished, until I'm ready to wear it because that might bring bad luck.'

Opal laughed. 'Don't be silly!'

'I know it's silly,' Queenie confessed. 'But I daren't risk it.'

'Well, don't let Mrs Bassett make it too long. Seven inches from the ground is quite long enough. Skirts are getting shorter all the time. Now, here's your hat, my lady!'

She unwrapped the hat carefully and held it out to Queenie. The crown was deep, the brim wide, but narrowing towards the centre and dipping at the sides. The whole shape was covered in fine silk velvet in intermingling, finely-graded shades of pale mauve, deep lilac and cream. Queenie, eyes shining, cried out with pleasure.

'Oh it's beautiful, Opal! It's beautiful! Don't you think it's the loveliest thing you've ever made?'

'I think it might be,' Opal admitted. 'Especially when

I've finished the trimming. I thought I'd use a little of the material left over from your dress to make the band, and embroider it with some of those silver beads. What do you think?'

'I think that would be perfect.'

'And here are the bridesmaids' hats. Lilac straw, trimmed with the rose-coloured velvet we found in Leasfield. They're smaller in the brim than yours because yours must be the most important; but don't you think they'll be pretty with the pale grey dresses?'

'Oh I do, I do Opal! Mary will look lovely with her dark colouring. And even dear Cousin Maud . . .' she giggled '. . . will be enhanced. Oh I'm so grateful to you, dear Opal!'

'There's no need,' Opal said.

It was true. She would do almost anything in the world for Queenie. Although the Stones were well-to-do, Queenie had treated her like a sister from their very first meeting. Her love for Mark had spread out and embraced his whole family. Even Edgar fell under her spell and on the few occasions he was with her he became at once brighter and more cheerful.

'Will your father be well enough to attend the wedding?' she asked.

Queenie's face clouded. 'I don't know. He's not at all well and the doctor has advised him to take things very quietly. It will be sad for me if I have no parents at my wedding. But yours will be there and they are always so nice to me. Even your grandparents are coming, which is wonderful.'

'Which reminds me,' Opal said. 'I have to tell you that I can't come.'

Queenie stared at her.

'*You* not come? But Opal, why?'

'Well,' Opal said, 'I'll be seven months pregnant. I shouldn't really be appearing in public. But the truth is I shan't have a single garment which will fit me. Things are difficult right now. I haven't been able to make anything.'

Tears filled Queenie's eyes.

'Oh Opal, how selfish I've been! I never thought . . . I expect because you always look so smart. But you must let me buy you something. Some nice material.'

'Thank you, Queenie, but I couldn't,' Opal said firmly. 'I really couldn't.'

'Then there must be something in my mother's wardrobe' Queenie said. 'I haven't been able to bear to give away all her things. She wore voluminous clothes so there's sure to be something with plenty of material for you to make over. You couldn't refuse to have something of my mother's.'

'No,' Opal agreed, 'I couldn't refuse that.'

'Then we'll go and choose it before Mary and Maud arrive. No-one else need know.'

'It's a fine day,' Opal remarked. 'I knew it would be.'

She got out of bed slowly. If she moved too fast she might go dizzy again and have to rest, and today there was no time for that. She looked out of the window. In one way they were lucky. Acer Street ran north and south so that, though the street itself with its long rows of dark stone houses on either side was uniformly drab, from the bedroom window it was possible to see beyond the village to the moors on the horizon.

Every morning of her life now, Opal's first act after getting out of bed was to look towards the moors. When she'd married and come to live in Acer Street she had thought she was gaining her freedom. 'In any case we shan't be in Acer Street long,' she'd said to Edgar. 'I just know you'll be a Mill Manager one of these days and then we'll live in Park Road.'

Now it seemed as though she had simply flown into another cage; a smaller one with a heavier lock on the door. She felt trapped by poverty, by Edgar's failure to find work; by Daniel who needed her all the time; by the child she was carrying. Between them they imprisoned her here, and she knew she was born for something better. She was born to go somewhere, be somebody.

'It's time we were up and doing,' she said.

'Why? The wedding's not until two o'clock.' Edgar's voice came muffled from under the bedclothes.

'There's plenty to do,' Opal said. 'We're all to get ready. I've got to set out the shop and then clear it away again before we leave, or the mice will have it.'

Edgar sat up slowly, yawning. Daniel, wide awake, climbed from his cot on to his parents' bed, which he much preferred to his own. Edgar took his son in his arms and ruffled his soft, dark hair.

'You're surely not going to open the shop today, Opal?'

'For an hour or two this morning, of course I am. Whyever not?'

'I would have thought you could have given yourself one day off,' he said. 'It can't make all that much difference.'

'Oh yes it can,' Opal replied. 'That's just where you're wrong. People don't have all that much loyalty. It only needs a shop to be closed one day for them to take their custom elsewhere. I can't afford to risk that.'

'Then I wonder you haven't got someone to look after it while we're at the wedding.'

39

'I thought about it,' Opal admitted. 'But I'm not keen on neighbours knowing my business. So I'll keep open for most of the morning and if we're not too late back I'll open up again in the evening.'

Edgar said nothing more. He might as well keep his mouth shut, he thought, for all the weight his opinions carried.

After breakfast Opal took the kettle of hot water from the fire to the kitchen, closed the door and, standing at the sink, gave herself a good wash from top to toe. She had treated herself to a small tablet of scented soap especially for this day and she used it lavishly. As she rinsed and dried her swollen stomach, hating the sight of it, she felt the baby kick, and then saw the ripple of its movement across her flesh. She ought, she supposed, to feel pleasure, tenderness, but such feelings did not come as they had when she was pregnant with Daniel.

She dressed, for the time being, in a clean blouse and the navy wrap-around skirt which was all that would fit her. She would not put on her new dress until the last minute for fear of accidents.

She was pleased with the new dress and looked forward to wearing it. In the end, from the late Mrs Stone's wardrobe, she had chosen a long skirt in fine, cream gabardine, with a matching coat. There was so much material in it that she had been able to contrive a dress with plenty of fullness, and from the clippings she had made small flowers which she had appliqued on to her brown hat.

'I dread to think what it's like up at Highcliffe, with Grandfather and Grandma and the aunts there and everybody getting ready at once,' she said, coming back into the living-room. 'A good thing they had a bath put in. I'd like to live in a house with a bathroom. They say the new council houses in Leasfield have them.'

'If all we lack is a bathroom we shan't do so badly,' Edgar said.

'Well one day we shall have a house with a bathroom, hot and cold water, electric light and a garden,' Opal said pleasantly. 'And it won't be a council house either.'

She made him feel, Edgar thought, that it was his fault that she didn't have these things. That if only *he* was different, then everything would be all right. But they weren't the only people in their present straits, not by a long chalk.

'And what'll you use for rent money?' he asked. 'Shall you use monkey nuts?'

Opal smiled. 'Oh we won't rent the house. We'll buy it,' she teased.

And then suddenly her mood changed. In the act of setting out the shop, the children's sweets well to the fore because with luck they'd be coming in with their Saturday pennies, she paused, and looked at Edgar.

'Can't you see, can't you *see*, Edgar, that the only way I can bear this rotten present is to look forward to the future. Oh I know it's not your fault, love – and I know my dreams are a bit fanciful, but can't you understand that?'

'I try,' he said quietly. 'I do try to understand, but I can't always share your feelings about the future. You leave me behind, Opal. I wasn't born with your imagination.'

'I know,' she spoke gently. 'Mam always said I had too much imagination and I dare say she was right. But sometimes it's what keeps me going, even if I don't believe every bit of it myself. I wish I could give a bit of it to you, love!'

She recognized, with a deep feeling of sadness, that what she missed most in Edgar, what more and more came between them even though she truly loved him, was not their poverty, not his lack of a job, but his refusal, his inability, to share her dreams. That was what mattered. That was what lay at the root of the loneliness she increasingly felt.

Shortly before noon they had a slice or two of bread to keep them going until the wedding reception, at which there would be a spread. They were ready for off when the door opened and a girl of about twelve walked in. It slightly irritated Opal that no-one around here ever knocked before entering, though she knew it was an irrational feeling in one who had set herself up as a shopkeeper.

'Oh Mrs Carson, you do look lovely!' the girl said.

'We're off to a wedding, Milly,' Edgar told her. 'Mrs Carson's brother. In fact we've just shut up shop.'

'Never mind that,' Opal said quickly. 'If there's something you want I'll be pleased to get it out for you.'

'It's me mam,' Milly said. 'She says have you got a Daisy headache powder. Her head's splitting.'

'I'm sorry to hear that, Milly,' Opal said. 'Yes, I always keep them. Tell your mother I hope she'll soon feel better but should she need another powder I'll be back this evening.'

They reached the church in the nick of time. It was not possible to greet anyone for as they settled into their seats the organ music announced the arrival of the bride. How radiant and lovely Queenie looked! How clearly and eagerly she made her responses.

Insofar as she ever addressed God, Opal prayed that marriage would not rob her new sister-in-law of that radiance and eagerness. But marriage changed people.

After the ceremony everyone except the bridal couple and the bridesmaids walked back to the house. Opal fell into step beside her mother. Hannah's pace was slow and her breathing difficult. She took her daughter's arm and though to Opal her mother looked slighter than ever, as if a strong wind on the top of the moor would blow her away, she leaned heavily upon her daughter. Opal, bearing the weight of her own pregnancy, found it difficult to support her mother, though not for the world would she have showed it.

'You should have gone in the motor car,' she said. 'This is quite a hill. In fact, should you have come at all, Mother?'

'Of course I should. I wanted to see Mark married.'

They were the last to arrive at the house. Queenie, standing beside her new husband, her eyes shining, cheeks glowing, embraced them in turn.

'Come and sit down, Mother!' She blushed prettily at her first use of the new title. 'You know, you *are* my mother now!'

'And pleased to be,' Hannah Derwent said. 'You're looking very bonny, isn't she Opal?'

'She looks beautiful!'

'Well it's partly due to Opal if I do. Everyone's been admiring my hat, and the bridesmaids'. In fact, Opal, one of the guests is the sister of a lady who has a milliner's shop. She says you're just the person her sister's looking for.'

Opal glanced down at her figure. 'Not in this state,' she said ruefully.

43

'That's what I told her,' Queenie replied. 'And that you also had another child and a husband to look after.'

'Now that everyone's here,' Mark broke in, 'we can have the toast and then we can all eat. I'm starving!'

'We're to drink champagne,' Queenie said. 'Father insisted, though *he's* not supposed to touch it.'

'Is he feeling better?' Opal asked.

'Not really, though he's determined to get through the reception. He's over there, sitting in the armchair by the screen. Do go and have a word with him, Opal. He enjoys talking to you. He thinks you're much cleverer and more sensible than I am.'

'Rubbish,' Opal said. 'He thinks the sun shines on you.' All the same, she was pleased by Queenie's remark.

She moved to where her grandparents, parents and aunts stood in a tight group. Champagne was handed round and the toast was drunk to the newly-weds.

'Mmm! It's delicious!' Opal cried. 'I've never tasted champagne before!'

'Nor have I, and I'm seventy-three,' her grandfather said. 'And I reckon nothing to it. Here you are, Opal. You can have mine. I'd sooner have a glass of beer any day.'

'Oh, but Father, do you think Opal should? In her condition?' Aunt Pearl said doubtfully. 'Alcohol!'

'Nay, it's more like fizzy lemonade,' her father said. 'What can that do except give you belly-ache?'

'Abraham! Do mind your words!' His wife's quiet whisper was anguished. 'You're not on the farm now. You're in a drawing-room, and a very lovely one it is, too.' She gazed appreciatively at the green flock wallpaper, the rosewood grand piano, the embossed velvet upholstery and the crystal chandelier. 'Fancy our Mark marrying into a home like this!'

Opal laughed. 'He's married Queenie, not the piano!'

As for her grandfather, she thought, though his warm personality made him welcome wherever he went, the background of his farm suited him better than this room. It was a long time now since she had been up to Langstrothdale. Her grandfather was the fourth generation of Derwents to farm there and her own earliest memories were of the dale where she had spent the first five years of her life, before her father had moved to his own farm in the West Riding. It was a small, wild dale which saw the beginnings of the River Wharfe. The river was always the clearest thing in her memories of childhood.

'Do you remember, Grandma, that afternoon when you showed me how to dam a bit of the river with stones?' she asked. Her grandmother, in spite of the hard work of the farm, had always had time to spare for her.

'Aye, I do that,' her grandmother said. 'I mind it well. You enjoyed that bit of power, didn't you? You thought you had it in you to change the whole course of the river!'

So I did, Opal thought. 'I'm going to talk to Mr Stone,' she said. 'I promised Queenie.'

Mr Stone seemed pleased to see her, though she thought how strained and tired he looked.

'Queenie talks a lot about you,' he said. 'She's very fond of you, you know.'

'And I of her,' Opal said. 'I hope she'll be very happy with my brother.'

'Young Mark'll have me to answer to if she's not,'

Mr Stone said. 'But I wouldn't have offered him a job in my Company, let alone give him my daughter, if I hadn't thought highly of him – once I got to know him. I hope you'll come and see them often when they're living here.'

'I will,' Opal promised.

She would have liked to have talked to him longer but other guests came and claimed his attention and she could see that he was weary. She left him and found herself a seat. She was desperate to sit down. Besides, food was being handed round; ham and tongue sand-wiches, salmon patties, savoury things on toast – and on the table she could see cream trifles and iced fancies flanking the two-tier wedding cake. She was tremend-ously hungry. She took several items of food from the tray a waitress offered and settled down to eat in earnest. Daniel was being looked after by his Aunt Mary; Edgar was talking, with unusual animation, to Queenie. When she had eaten her fill she went over to join them.

'We must go soon,' she said. 'If we stay too long Daniel will get too tired, and then he'll be fractious. He's fine now, but it won't last.'

'I understand,' Queenie said. 'We're going to cut the cake now, and then Mark and I must leave.' The colour rose in her face again at the thought of the honeymoon. 'I hope you won't take it amiss, Opal, but I've asked Jane to pack you a basket to take home. It will be waiting in the hall for you and no-one will see it. There's so much food here and if someone doesn't take it it will go to waste. So you'll be doing me a favour.'

'I'm grateful,' Opal said quietly. It would probably feed them through the weekend and beyond. 'It's been a lovely wedding. I hope you have a wonderful honeymoon.'

Queenie and Mark looked at each other, their faces alight with love.

'Oh we shall,' Mark said. 'We shall.'

'Your mother looks none too good,' Edgar said when they were home. After the double tram ride they were hungry again and when Daniel, who had fallen asleep on the tram and had had to be carried home in his father's arms, had been put to bed, and the shop set out afresh, Opal spread some of the contents of Queenie's basket on the table.

'I agree,' she said. 'I'm worried about her. Well, best come and eat.'

'Bits and pieces,' Edgar said. 'Bits and pieces. Not what I call solid food.'

'It's all delicious,' Opal said. 'I'd like to eat like this every day. And drink champagne!'

'You've got ideas above your station,' Edgar said, but not unkindly. Something, perhaps the champagne which he affected not to like, had put him in a good mood.

Only two people came to buy from the shop; a small boy for a sherbert fountain and a woman for a whipped cream walnut. 'As it's Saturday night,' she said. At nine o'clock, though it was still daylight, Opal said, 'It's been a long day. Why don't we go to bed?'

She was nearing the end of the Monday wash when she heard the knock at the door. The whites, having been rubbed, boiled and starched, with a squeeze of Dolly blue in the starch water for added whiteness, were already drying in the sun, on the line which stretched across the street. On Monday mornings the whole length of every street in Milton was strung with

47

laundry, like a village *en fête*. No cart of any kind could pass and even a pedestrian must dodge between sheets and shirts, shifts and blouses.

Opal straightened her body as she heard the knock. Pounding and twisting the peggy stick, in her condition, was painful. Thank goodness Edgar would help her with the mangle.

'See who's at the door, Edgar,' she called out. 'If it's a hawker he's out of luck, poor devil!'

'Why, Sam, whatever brings you here?' she heard Edgar say. Her stomach lurched at the greeting. Sam worked for her father on the farm and in the middle of Monday morning he could only be bringing bad news.

'What is it' she asked, coming to the door. 'What's amiss?'

'It's Mrs Derwent,' the boy said. 'She's been took real bad. The Maister thinks you'd best come.'

Opal grasped Edgar's arm, trying to steady the world which had started to spin. And yet it was no surprise. She had seen it in her mother's face at the wedding, only two days ago. She had felt it in her mother's weight on her arm and heard it in her weakened voice.

'Steady on,' Edgar said. 'Sit down and I'll make you a cup of tea. Sam, you'll have a drink of tea?'

'Nay, I mun get back. Shall I tell the Maister you're coming, then?'

'Yes,' Opal answered. 'I'll be there as quickly as ever I can.'

'You'd best have a few minutes rest before you go,' Edgar advised when Sam had gone. 'It's a tidy walk. Do you want me to come with you, take Daniel to Ma's?'

'No. You stay here and look after him. I'll be all

right. But I might not be back tonight. If there's nursing to be done I shall want to take my share. I won't wait for a cup of tea right now. Fetch my clean nightdress in from the line, will you. Quickly!'

Climbing the hillside, though there was some shade from the trees, was warm work. Sweat ran down Opal's face and around the collar of her blouse, which clung damply to her back. She would have liked to have taken a short rest but there was no time. In spite of the awkwardness of her body she walked quickly. On the top of the moor, away from the trees, it was hotter than ever. The sun, almost at its zenith now, beat down on her head. There was no shade anywhere and the outcroppings of rock seemed to reflect the sun's rays, bouncing them back into the air to heat it still further. But she kept up her pace, trying not to notice her fatigue.

She had neglected her mother. She knew it only too well. 'Dear God,' she prayed. 'Only let my mother live and I'll be better!' But would God make a bargain with someone who most of the time ignored him? The pain in her back was worsening. She wanted more than anything in the world to lie down, but there was no question of doing so.

She was almost at the top of the moor now. The downhill journey would be easier. When she reached the crest of the hill and saw Highcliffe down below she felt a new rush of strength to match her urgency, and started to run. She never knew what tripped her up, perhaps a bramble root, perhaps a stone on the track. She fell to the ground and rolled over and over down the hill until a narrow, shelving plateau stopped her. There, for a second or two, she lay on the ground, her whole body shaking. But there were no bones broken and she must get on. She must hurry, hurry! She got to her feet and started down the hill again as quickly as her trembling legs would take her.

When she reached the farm the door was open. She passed through the empty kitchen and, with great difficulty, for she had neither breath nor strength left, went upstairs to her mother's bedroom. Her father, Aunt Garnet and Mary stood by the bed. It was Mary who turned towards her, the tears streaming down her white face.

'Oh Opal!' she sobbed 'You're too late! It's all over! She died not five minutes ago. You're too late!'

And then her sister and her aunt moved forward quickly as Opal, the pain searing her back and now embracing her belly with hands of red-hot iron, screamed as the world grew dark and she dropped to the floor.

It was almost a month before the doctor declared Opal fit to return to her own home.

'You'll be glad to get back to your husband and your little boy,' he said. 'But go carefully, my dear. You're not completely strong yet.'

In her heart she knew she was not, and never would be, ready to return to Acer Street. Though it contained those she held most dear, Edgar and Daniel, the doctor's words sounded in her ears like a prison sentence. 'I condemn you to penal servitude for life!' If only they could get away! If only they could make a fresh start. But she said nothing of these feelings; not to her father, sunk in his own world of grief; not to Aunt Garnet or to Mary; not to Edgar when he came to visit her.

Her baby daughter, born before Hannah Derwent was in her coffin, had died less than twenty-four hours after the grandmother who never saw her. Aunt Garnet said they would meet in heaven and know each other.

'She was quite perfect,' Mary wept – though whether for the baby or her mother she was not sure. 'Such a darling little girl!'

'But too small to survive,' Aunt Garnet said. 'Our Opal's small herself, so at seven months what chance did the bairn have? And a rough passage into the world at that.'

It had been clear to all except Opal, to whom because of her pain nothing was real except the pain itself, that the child could not live, and the same clergyman who was in the house because of Mrs Derwent's passing, baptized the infant. Opal, rallying for a moment, chose the name Judith. Then the milk which Nature sent so liberally to Opal's breasts turned against her. When the small coffin followed the larger one out of the house, to be buried in the graveyard on the side of the moor, Opal was raging with milk fever, too delirious to know anything. For a while it seemed as though a third funeral must follow.

But as the days went by the fever subsided. She knew that she would recover but her spirits were low and she wondered, lying in the narrow bed which had been hers until she had married, whether she wanted to do so. Edgar came to see her frequently, sometimes bringing Daniel, more often leaving the child with his mother. She did not tell him how she felt but he was aware that something was wrong.

'You must make an effort, love,' he said. 'For my sake and little Daniel's. We want you back'

'I'm being punished for my sins,' Opal said. 'I never wanted the baby and I didn't do enough for my mother. Now I'd give anything to have them back but it's too

51

late. God is just! He's not merciful, but he's just. He gives punishment where it's due.'

'I don't understand about that,' Edgar said helplessly. 'I'm sure you'll feel better when you're a bit stronger. I've been keeping the shop going,' he added, trying to turn the direction of her mind. 'People have been very kind asking after you. And I'm going to see Mr Ridley in a day or two. Perhaps you should think about what I ought to buy from him?'

In the end, though she did not come to it quickly, it was the thought of the shop which aroused Opal from her apathy. Yet even while she thought of it, sitting now in a chair outside the farmhouse in the July sunshine, looking up to the moors which were breaking into their covering of purple heather, she knew that it was not enough. She must do something, anything, to change her life, to change life for all three of them. And then she realized – it came to her quite clearly – where her hope lay.

When Mary came towards her with a cup of tea and piece of fresh curd tart to tempt her appetite she asked, 'Will Queenie be coming at the weekend?'

'I think so. Why?'

'Well, since they'll come over from Leasfield in her father's car, I thought she might take me back to Milton. It's about time I was going.'

'That's a bit sudden,' Mary said. 'Oh I know Doctor Lee said you could, and there's Edgar and little Daniel to think of, so I dare say you're right. But it's been a comfort to me to have you here to look after.'

When Queenie arrived on Saturday afternoon Opal took her at once into the parlour. Queenie's grief for Hannah Derwent had been deep, but simple, and without guilt, so that the tears she had shed had comforted her, as Opal's could not. Opal wished that she could be more like Queenie; uncomplicated, kind and good. But it was not in her.

'Do you remember at your wedding you mentioned a lady with a hat shop?' she asked quickly. 'You said she might be wanting an assistant and her sister liked my hats.'

'Why yes, I remember,' Queenie said.

'Did she engage anyone? Is the job still open?'

'I've no idea,' Queenie said with surprise. 'I don't even know whether it was serious. But Opal, you can't mean . . . You can't possibly do it! You're not yet strong enough. Besides, you've got Edgar and Daniel to look after.'

'Never mind that just now,' Opal said eagerly. 'Will you find out if there *is* a job? And if there is, will you put in a word for me?'

'But I don't . . .' Queenie sounded bewildered.

'Oh *please* Queenie! I beg you! I assure you it's what I need if I'm to stay sane! And the woman won't regret it if she takes me on.'

'I'm sure she won't,' Queenie said. 'But what will Edgar say? And what about Daniel?'

'I'll deal with that,' Opal said hurriedly. 'Don't mention it to Edgar, or to anyone else just yet.'

Edgar would hate it, that was certain. Even after all this time without work he saw himself as the bread-winner, the one responsible for supporting his family. She had no wish to deprive him of this role, but somehow he must be made to see her point of view.

Back in Acer Street, she paused inside the doorway. How small the room looked! How small and shabby; tidy enough but not clean. The fireplace was dull, and behind the lace curtains, which were badly in need of washing, the window was smoke-grimed. True to his promise, Edgar had set out the shop, though not with her order and precision. It looked tatty. She doubted whether she could ever settle here again. One way or another, however long it took, she must get out.

She waited until they had had their tea and she had put Daniel to bed before she broached the subject which was burning inside her. In the end she could think of no subtle way of leading up to it, no tactful manner of introducing it. Her blunt announcement, she thought, sounded like an attack.

'You may as well know, Edgar, I'm thinking of going out to work.'

He stared, not believing his ears.

'What did you say?'

'I'm going out to work,' she repeated. She wished she did not sound so defiant. It was not how she had meant it to be.

'But I don't understand!' He looked confused. 'You're a married woman with a young child. *You* shouldn't be going out to work.'

'I want to. Please Edgar, I really want to!'

She watched the shadow pass over his face.

'You mean you need to. Because I can't keep my wife and family like a man should. That's what you mean, isn't it?'

She could have borne it if he had been angry, shouted at her, shaken her by the shoulders. It would have hurt her less.

She shook her head. 'You're wrong. It's not like . . . But you must admit that it would help?'

'So what makes you think you can get a job?' he asked. 'What can you do? You've no sort of experience.'

'Well I can make hats for one thing. And I can serve in a shop. I've proved that. So I shall look for something which combines the two. Of course I might not find anything.' But she would, she knew she would.

'And what about me and Daniel while you're out working?'

She was irritated by the self-pity in his voice, but even so she tried to speak reassuringly.

'You and Daniel have shown how well you can manage without me. You've looked after him very well. He's the picture of health.' She intended to say nothing about the state of the house. 'And I'm sure his Grandma will be pleased to have him when you have to sign on.'

'I see you've got it all worked out,' Edgar said. 'There's not much left for me to say, is there? I suppose, then, you'll be giving up all this?' He motioned to the house shop, laid out on the table.

'Give it up?' Opal retorted, stung to an anger she could no longer control. 'No, Edgar, we'll not give it up! Why should we? *You* shall run the house shop, Edgar! There's no point at all in giving it up!'

Chapter Three

'So there it is,' Madame Dora said. 'Since he's taking me to lunch. I can't be out when Mr Hessle comes. It's his last visit before he retires and he's bringing his nephew who's taking over from him. I shall want to meet him. So there's nothing else for it, Opal, you'll have to deliver the hats to Miss Taylor!'

Miss Taylor, though goodness knew she could be a nuisance, was one of their best customers. She seldom set foot in the shop (Opal had never seen her) but about once every couple of months she telephoned Madame Dora and asked her to bring a selection of hats up to the house, and she almost always bought one.

'Sometimes I wonder if I was wise to have the telephone installed,' Madame Dora said. 'But with a high-class business like this it's expected. It's not as if we were a sweets and tobacco or a greengrocer's.'

'I'm sure you 're right, Madame Dora,' Opal agreed.

Her employer liked to be addressed as Madame Dora though everyone in the locality knew that she was really Dora Barraclough, widow of the late Asa Barraclough, pork butcher, who had died of the Spanish flu in 1919. Indeed, the very premises which now, carpeted in beige Wilton and tastefully decorated, housed Madame Dora, High Class Milliner, had once contained Mr Barraclough, surrounded by sides of pork, legs of ham, dishes of chitterlings, faggots and, on Fridays at twelve noon, a leg of succulent hot roast pork which could be purchased, thinly sliced, by the quarter pound.

Sometimes when she was hungry Madame Dora imagined she could smell that roast pork, taste the crackling. Out of the whole business it was the only thing she had been able to stand. That, and the money her husband made. When he was taken she had genuinely mourned him, but she was glad to be rid of the butcher's shop and to put her inheritance into something more refined.

'Moreover,' Madame Dora said, 'I know Miss Taylor likes to see me personally. But you're more than capable of delivering the hats and you can tell her I'll call myself later this afternoon, even though it's early closing, to help her make a choice.'

'Supposing she wants to try them on while I'm there?' Opal asked.

Madame Dora frowned. She was aware that her assistant was more than able to help Miss Taylor choose a hat, and to trim it for her. She was the best assistant she had ever had in the salon. (Madame Dora never thought of it as a shop.) In fact, what with her instinct for fashion, her skill with a needle and her interest in everything to do with the business, Madame Dora thought that Opal might be a greater talent than herself. But, she comforted herself, clients did prefer the attention of the proprietoress.

'Well, the customer is always right,' she conceded. 'If she does insist, try to sell her the velour. It's expensive – a guinea untrimmed – but she can afford it. Her father was Taylor's treacle toffee, you know.'

'I'll do my best,' Opal promised.

'And before you go, let down the sunblind. The September sun isn't as damaging as the spring sun, but we can't afford to have the hats fade. In fact, I think you'd better bring the velvet toque out of the window. And cover the mauve felt with a sheet of tissue. Mauve's the very devil for fading.'

They waged a constant battle between the need to display the finest hat – though never too many at a time since both ladies agreed that that was common – and the propensity of every material to fade in the light. Sometimes a single, sunny morning was enough to ruin a hat.

Opal took the toque out of the window and placed it on a stand in the shop.

'I don't suppose this shape will ever go out of fashion,' she remarked. 'Not as long as the Queen wears it.'

It was a beautiful hat and she alone had made it, though for herself to wear she preferred something more up-to-date.

'You did a good job on that,' Madame Dora said. She believed in giving praise where praise was due. When she had first set eyes on Opal – tiny, thin, her face white and pinched – she had not been impressed by her. Height was an asset in a shop assistant, as was a fashionable figure to show off clothes and a pretty face to enhance a hat. Opal's figure, since in spite of her slenderness she had well-rounded breasts, was unfashionable. She needed a good, tight bust band to flatten that area. Nor was she, in Madame Dora's eyes, strictly speaking pretty, though she had good cheek-bones and fine, dark eyes. Nevertheless, Madame Dora recognized style when she saw it. It transcended many faults.

'I wanted to talk to you, Madame Dora,' Opal said. 'Could you spare me a minute later in the morning?'

'Well, we'll see how busy we are, shall we?'

She knew what it would be about and she was not worried. The labourer was worthy of his hire and she had no objection to giving Opal an extra half-crown a week.

'Right now you'd better be off,' she said. 'Oak House, Nab End Rise. Halfway up the hill.'

It was good to be out in the air on such a fine morning. Though Opal had often delivered hats to back doors she had not up to now been entrusted with an errand which might possibly take her inside a rich customer's home. In her two years' service she had done most tasks, from sweeping the shop floor and cleaning the plate glass window to making and trimming hats for quite important weddings and funerals. She knew how to start with nothing more than a length of millinery wire and finish up with a hat fit for a queen.

The only chore which she had never been allowed to touch was that of totting up the contents of the till and entering them in the ledger. This Madame Dora kept to herself.

'But I know the cost of all the materials,' Opal told Edgar. She talked to him regularly about her job in spite of the fact that he showed little interest. She doubted that he had ever forgiven her for taking it and she felt compassion for him that she had found a job so easily while he was still without.

'I know the cost of the buckram shapes, the linings, ribbons, feathers, flowers,' she told him. 'And I've a fair idea of the rates of the shop with the living quarters over. With the prices Madame Dora charges for hats she must be making a pretty good living.' It seemed to Opal that she deserved a bigger share of it than the ten shillings a week she was paid.

Her wages, though, had been a godsend. With them, plus the few shillings the house shop still made, and Edgar's dole money, they just about managed. There was still no sign of work for Edgar, nor for hundreds of others who formed long queues outside the Labour Exchanges. He seemed now to have settled down to a workless condition as if he had known no other. It worried Opal that he seemed interested in nothing, except for Daniel. Even politics no longer had the power to move him. He had not so much settled down, she thought, as succumbed.

As for any physical expression of love between them, well that almost never happened. Sometimes, aching with her own desire, and wanting also to give him comfort, in bed she tried to draw him into her arms. Too often he turned away from her, leaving her ashamed of her longings.

Resolutely she put Edgar out of her mind as she turned the corner into Nab End Rise. It was a road where people of substance lived in handsome houses set in large, tree-bordered gardens. Opal hesitated outside the large iron gates of Oak House, wondering whether she dare present herself at the front door. But that might be going too far.

'I'm from Madame Dora,' she told the maid who answered the kitchen door. 'Miss Taylor's expecting me.'

'That's right. This way if you please!'

Opal followed the maid along the stone-flagged passage to the other side of a baize-lined door. It was a different world here: a world of deep-pile carpets, gilt-framed paintings, embossed wallpaper, exotic plants in jardinieres. The room into which the maid ushered her was grander still, with green silk curtains and a green and gold Chinese carpet. Miss Taylor, standing in front of the white marble fireplace, was tall, angular, and expensively dressed in a brown frock coat which did nothing for her sallow skin and grey hair.

'I'm sorry Madame Dora couldn't come,' she said. 'She knows what I like.'

'She's disappointed too,' Opal said. 'But such a severe stomach upset.'

It was the fiction they had decided on. It would never do to let Miss Taylor know that she had been passed over for a commercial traveller.

'I hope I may help you,' Opal ventured. 'Madame Dora thought that if you were to try on the hats while I was here I might be able to assist you in your choice.' She could always tell Madame that Miss Taylor had insisted.

'Well, we'll see,' Miss Taylor said doubtfully. Opal wondered why she bought hats so often since she had a face so rugged and individual that there could be few hats which could actually adorn it.

'I suppose you had better come up to my bedroom then,' Miss Taylor said. 'We can't try on hats without a mirror.'

Opal followed her up the wide, curving staircase and into a large room with a dressing table set into the deep bay of a window. Miss Taylor sat herself in front of the mirror and waited for Opal to unpack the hats. They were not what Opal would have selected for Miss Taylor now that she had seen her, but she was here to sell and she must do her best. She was confident that she could change the nature of some of them with judicious trimming and she was glad that she had persuaded Madame Dora to let her bring a few things along. But the artificial flowers were out. Miss Taylor

61

was definitely not the type to be flower trimmed.

She placed each hat in turn on top of Miss Taylor's sparse hair while the lady frowned at her reflection in the glass. Opal knew that the rust-coloured velour was far and away the most suitable, so she saved it until the last.

'You could wear any of them, Madame,' she said politely. 'But I think this is really *you*! I always think it's a pity' she added thoughtfully 'that we only see ourselves in mirrors, because that's not any of us at our best. Something to do with 'reversed image'.' I don't understand it, but it's a fact that we all look nicer than we think.'

She held her breath while Miss Taylor gazed into the glass, frowning. Had she said too much, even though it was true? She was relieved when she saw Miss Taylor's expression soften, watched her lift her head and view her reflection with something like approval.

'I think you should have quite a severe trimming on this one,' Opal advised. 'A stiffish bow, almost self-coloured – I have the very ribbon here – and well to the side to add a little width.' Deftly, she formed the ribbon into intricate folds and held it in position.

'Yes,' Miss Taylor said. 'I think you're right!'

'Would you like me to complete it while I'm here?' Opal asked. 'I could do it quite quickly.'

'Very well then,' Miss Taylor agreed. She seemed amiable enough now. Not at all a bit of a Tartar. 'I dare say you'd like a cup of tea?'

Opal knew by the maid's down-turned mouth as she brought in the tea-tray that she did not approve of this gesture. Certainly Madame Dora had never mentioned tea, and surely she would have done had it happened? The tea was pale gold in colour, delicate in flavour, served in rose-patterned china. It was quite unlike the brew she and Edgar drank every day.

When she had finished the hat Miss Taylor tried it on again. 'Yes,' she said. 'That will do nicely. You're a gifted young lady. But I supposed you'll give it up and marry some man and have hordes of children!'

'I *am* married,' Opal said hesitantly. There was a polite fiction that no young woman in a job was married. She was always addressed as 'Miss Carson'. 'I have a little boy. My husband is unemployed. He couldn't get a job, so I did.'

But it was not as simple as that. Something other than economic necessity had driven her to seek for work and now her job had become all-important to her. She enjoyed leaving the house each morning and going out into the world, even a world no farther away than Madame Dora's.

'What about your little boy?'

'His father looks after him very well. And of course I'm able to do better by him – give him better foods, clothes. Daniel doesn't lose out at all.' She sounded on the defensive and was cross with herself that she should. After all, where Daniel was concerned, she was the loser. She missed him so much, was painfully aware that she had shut herself out from a part of his life and tried to make up for it in the time they were together. She was unreasonably jealous of the close bond she recognized between Daniel and his father.

'Isn't it hard work, going out to a job and running a home?' Miss Taylor asked.

'Yes. I have to be at the salon at eight-thirty in the morning and I don't finish until seven at night.'

She could have added that to save the tramfare she

walked the two miles each way from Madame Dora's to Acer Street, that on her half-day she cleaned the house, looked after the house shop and sometimes, usually taking Daniel with her, went to Ridley's for new stock. Also that on Sundays she did the week's washing, ready for hanging out on the line first thing on Monday morning.

'I think I should have liked to have had a job,' Miss Taylor said. 'But naturally I looked after my parents until they were taken. I don't know what I could have done, though. I'm not cut out for teaching and I could never have worked in a hospital. And what else is there?'

For you, since you're a lady, not much, Opal thought. For me, anything I can get.

'Tell me, Miss Carson,' Miss Taylor said suddenly. 'What does someone like you think of votes for women?'

Opal flushed. 'I only know what *I* think,' she said pertly – and was then aware that she had spoken rudely to a valuable customer. But when Miss Taylor's sharp eyes met her own she saw, with relief, that there was amusement rather than anger in them.

'And what *do* you think?'

'That it's right and proper. That it's unfair that we should have to wait until we're thirty. We should be equal with the men.'

'What you mean is that we should have equal voting rights with the men,' Miss Taylor corrected her. 'I agree with that. But we can never be quite equal with the men. It's not in our nature.'

'I mean,' Opal began, but thought better of it. She knew what she meant; that women should have the same chances as men. She wondered if Miss Taylor would have liked to have been a man with – for those who were lucky – a man's opportunities? For herself she was glad to be a woman, but she wanted the opportunities too.

'Well, thank you. I mustn't detain you any longer.' Miss Taylor spoke briskly, as if conscious that she might have spoken too freely with the milliner's little assistant. Perhaps it was to restore matters to their proper footing that she gave Opal a shilling as she was leaving.

Opal hurried back, from time to time restraining herself from breaking into a run from her joy at being out on so fine a morning. The shilling tip was most generous. She would spend it all on Daniel, perhaps even on a nice toy. She was glad she had sold the velour. It was important that she should please Madame Dora today.

When she reached the salon Mr Hessle had not arrived.

'So tiresome!' Madame Dora grumbled. 'I could have gone to Miss Taylor's after all. Still, I must say you've done very well.'

'As there's no-one in the salon at the moment, could I speak to you now?' Opal asked.

'Very well, Miss Carson. But if it's what I think it is you can save yourself the trouble. You've worked hard this last year and I've already decided to give you an increase of half-a-crown a week from the end of the month. There! Does that suit you?'

Opal hesitated. 'Not quite,' she said slowly.

'Not quite? Well I can assure you, miss, I can't possibly give you more! I consider I'm being most generous!'

'Oh you are, you are!' Opal cried. 'I didn't mean

that. It's just that what I had in mind was something a little different.'

'Something different? In heaven's name what?'

Opal took a deep breath.

'Well . . . if you could agree to it . . . I wondered if I might have . . . what I'd like to have is a small percentage, oh a very small one, of the profits. Instead of a rise, I mean.' She was astonished at her own audacity. She could get the sack for less than this.

'*A percentage of profits?*' Madame Dora sounded as though Opal had spoken in a foreign tongue. 'A percentage of profits? Why, some weeks I hardly make a profit at all – and some weeks nothing!'

'Then on those weeks you would only pay me my ten shillings,' Opal said quickly. 'You would save half-a-crown.'

Her voice was steady, but inside she was trembling. Now that she had come out with the idea it sounded impossible. 'And I mean profits over a certain amount, naturally,' she continued. 'Perhaps over what they are now. That way you couldn't lose. You'd only pay me extra if I earned extra first – and then only a small part of it.'

'What makes you think,' Madame Dora said slowly (though Opal could hear the interest creeping into her voice). 'What makes you think you could increase the profits?'

'I have several ideas,' Opal said eagerly. 'I've given it a lot of thought.'

'What ideas?'

'Well, for instance, I thought that perhaps we . . . I mean you . . . might introduce a few more lines. Not just hats, but other accessories – scarves, gloves, hosiery. Lots of people are wearing the new art silk stockings and since they last no time at all they have to keep buying more. And ladies underwear, or in our case, lingerie, for I know you'd only sell the best. They're beginning to sell it in the big stores. People don't make their own underwear as much as they used to. And no-one around here sells these items – at least not yet.'

'Well,' Madame Dora exclaimed, 'you certainly *have* been thinking about it, haven't you? I'm not sure that I can take it in so quickly!'

'And I thought you might change the name to "Madame Dora's Modes".' Opal said.

'Madama Dora's Modes, eh? Yes. But there's the question of space – that is supposing I were to agree to any of it in the first place. Have you thought about space?'

'I have—' Opal began.

She was interrupted by the arrival of Mr Hessle. Unlike some of their commercial travellers who crept into the salon as if uncertain of their welcome, his entry was that of a leading actor on to the centre stage. He was a large man, but it was more his air of bonhomie than his size which seemed to fill the shop.

'My dear Madame Dora! Dear lady! I do apologize if I've inconvenienced you in the slightest degree. We were unavoidably detained. Yes, unavoidably detained!'

In the Red Lion, Opal thought, smelling his breath.

'I have to blame my imminent retirement,' he continued. 'I had no idea, no idea at all, that I had so many friends in the trade. And far too many of them, I'm afraid, wanted to toast my future. But I've saved the best to the last, dear lady, and my time from this moment on is all yours. Wednesday afternoon, early closing, all the time in the world for a long, leisurely lunch!'

'I'm looking forward to it, Mr Hessle,' Madame Dora said.

'Capital! And now let me introduce my nephew Mr David Hessle, who will take over from me. David, step forward to meet Madame Dora! And her young lady assistant, Miss Carson.'

David Hessle was tall, all of six feet. He was well dressed in a light grey suit with a striped silk tie. On removing his silver grey trilby he revealed a head of rich, auburn hair. When he shook hands with Opal, with a grip that was firm and pleasant, he smiled directly at her and the smile extended to his grey-green eyes. Opal thought he looked a cut above any commercial traveller she had ever seen.

'Now unless there's anything you're particularly wanting – though we have a nice line in velvet ribbon which I *would* like you to look at – we won't concentrate on business today,' Mr Hessle senior said. 'Mr David will be around again in the second week in October and I know he'll have some new lines to discuss with you. But not today, Madame Dora! Today luncheon awaits!'

Over the top of Madame Dora's head David Hessle caught Opal's eye, and smiled. She wished she was being included in the party.

Opal took the iron from the fire, blew the ash from it, and spat on it to test the heat. Then, to help the iron glide over the cloth, she rubbed the hot sole with a piece of candle fat wrapped in a bit of cotton cloth.

'I shall have to have some stuff for a new work

dress,' she remarked to Edgar. 'This one's getting very shabby.'

She would buy the new black material from the savings in the toffee tin and she would make up the dress to the same pattern – long sleeves, high round neck (with a white collar which had to be washed every day) – only this time it could be a little shorter. Skirts were knee-high in London though no doubt she'd have to be a little more circumspect. She reckoned that wearing a new dress had helped her to get the job with Madame Dora; that and the fact that she'd had her hair bobbed. It hung straight and heavy, with a thick fringe across her forehead and the sides curving on to her cheeks. Edgar hated it.

'You need a new shirt too,' she continued. 'I saw some in Tatham's window; cotton and flannelette, lined across the shoulder, for three-and-eleven three-farthings. You can get them cheaper but cheap clothes don't pay in the end.'

'I can manage,' Edgar said.

'No you can't,' she contradicted. 'It's important to be decently dressesd. How much money is there in the savings tin?'

'I don't know.'

'Then count it.'

She didn't need him to do so. She knew there was thirteen shillings and fourpence, but anything to make him move, take an interest.

Reluctantly, he took the tin from the dresser drawer, spilled the money on to the table, and began to count.

'Thirteen and twopence,' he said.

'That's wrong! There should be thirteen and four-pence.'

He pushed the money away angrily.

'If you know how much there is why do you ask me to count it? And if you must know, I took twopence for a packet of woodbines. I'd none left. A man needs a smoke.'

Opal flushed.

'I'd have bought you extra if you'd said.'

Like most women she bought her husband's cigarettes along with the groceries. In work, the men handed over their unopened wage packets, out of work their dole money. The women handed back the man's pocket money and bought his cigarettes. It was the way things were done and there was simply no reason for the sense of shame Edgar's words had roused in her.

'Anyway,' she said, 'it's enough to buy some dress material *and* a shirt, and some socks for Daniel.'

She had never made a secret of the savings in the tin. They were more or less common property. But what Edgar didn't know, and she was not sure why she had never told him, was that she now had her own bank account with the Yorkshire Penny Bank. There was not much in it but it was growing steadily. The Penny Bank boasted that it would gladly receive any sum, from one penny upwards, and she therefore felt no awkwardness in paying in her small amount each Friday as soon as she drew her wages. She enjoyed looking at the bankbook, watching the balance increase. She had made no withdrawals, nor would she unless for something so extra special that it had not so far even entered her mind.

She put the newly-pressed dress on a hanger and, striding over Daniel who was playing on the floor with a small wooden cart which Edgar had made him, she suspended it from the ceiling clothes dryer to air off. She smiled at Daniel. At four years old he was still a quiet child, undemanding, easygoing. Which was just as well, she thought, for much as she loved him she had little time to spend on him. There was always so much to do. It would be better for Daniel when he could go to school, be with other children of his own age.

'I took some hats to a customer in Nab End Rise this morning,' she told Edgar. 'It was a beautiful house. She gave me a lovely cup of tea and bought an expensive hat.'

'It's not right,' Edgar said.

'What isn't?'

'It's not right that some women can spend all that money on a hat.'

'I dare say it isn't,' Opal said mildly. 'All I know is that if she and her like couldn't, then I wouldn't have a job. It's no use *me* grumbling at the Miss Taylors of this world. I have to be thankful for them. Anyway, she was nice.'

She would like to be one of them. She would like to live in a big house with a garden and have a maid to answer the door. She would even like to be Madame Dora, with a nice little business and living quarters over. Or rather, not Miss Taylor, not Madame Dora, but her own self in a similar position. It was her circumstances she wished to change, not herself.

'Old Mr Hessle came in for the last time today,' she said. 'He brought his nephew, who's to take his place.'

But Edgar wasn't listening. He was staring into the fire. She wondered, fleetingly, if Edgar could ever get a job as a commercial traveller, just supposing she ever heard of one? He was good-looking, reasonably well-spoken, and in his navy blue suit which he now seldom wore, he looked as smart as the next man. On the rare occasions when they went out together she was always proud to be seen with him. What he lacked, what, try as she might, she seemed unable to give him, was confidence in himself. Now David Hessle, she felt sure, had that quality in abundance.

Chapter Four

'It seems to me,' Edgar said, 'that you're none too pleased I've got the job!'

'That's ridiculous,' Opal objected. 'How can you think such a thing?'

But she felt mean that she hadn't shown more pleasure at his news, guilty at the lack of enthusiasm inside herself. Perhaps it was simply that she was so very tired. The week before Whitsuntide was a busy one in the shop and she had been on her feet since early morning.

'Well you're not saying much. Hardly a word. I'd have thought you'd have been as pleased as Punch!'

'I am, I am!' Opal protested. 'It's the shock. It's hardly five minutes since you told me. An insurance agent! I can hardly get it into my head!'

'I was dead lucky to get it,' Edgar said. 'I don't know that I would have but for the Reverend Atkinson putting in a word for me. It so happens that the District Manager is his churchwarden, and Ma knew that, you see.'

'How did you know about the vacancy?' Opal asked. 'Had you written to the Company?'

She thought that unlikely. He had written for nothing in the last two years, saying it was a waste of time and stamps.

'No, it was Ma! She came dashing round here as if her coat tails were on fire! Told me Jonah Ramsden had had a seizure on his way to pay out the insurance on old Grandma Battersby. He fell down in the street with the money on him, Ma said, and as likely as not they'd be paying out on him before the week was out. 'So get into your Sunday suit, and around to Reverend Atkinson to ask him to put in a word for you,' she said. 'And then off into Leasfield with you.'

'But it's more than a week since Mr Ramsden was taken bad,' Opal said. 'He died yesterday. I can't understand why you didn't tell me you'd been after the job!'

He'd had good enough reason for that, Edgar thought. He'd gone off to the interview without any hope whatever. After more than four years hope had died in him. So what was the use of telling Opal? When he didn't get the job it would be simply another failure to chalk up against him. She would never say it, but sometimes he saw it in her eyes. He knew he was a failure.

'Shall you be able to do it?' Opal asked. 'I mean . . . well, you've not done anything like this before.'

'I don't know till I try, do I?'

'Of course not,' she agreed. 'Anyway, if Jonah Ramsden could go it, I'm sure you can.' It was so good to hear hope in his voice. 'I am truly pleased for you, Edgar,' she assured him.

And now – he could still hardly believe it – he was a failure no longer. The slow, terrible, gut-rotting years had ended. From now on everything was going to be all right. And yet, he thought, if he had not gone after the job so quickly, urged on by his mother, he would never have got it. He could not have stood up to the competition once they had seen several other candidates. For him, to be an insurance agent was a step up.

'I suppose you'll have to go after new business?'

'I dare say,' he said. 'But people always want a bit of insurance. The worse off they are, the more they need it. Nobody's going to risk being buried by the Parish if a penny a week will pay for the funeral. It stands to reason.'

'I expect it does,' Opal agreed. 'But don't you have to put down money for an insurance agency?'

'Twenty pounds,' Edgar said. 'Ma lent me her savings. I shall pay her back as soon as I get on my feet.'

He could have asked me, Opal thought. But he'd rather take his mother's last penny than ask me. Well, though it said nothing good about the state of their marriage, it had its compensations. Now that she had the arrangement with Madame Dora she had been able to put a bit more by, but she had no wish to dissipate her savings because she had at last decided what they were for. Her goal was now as firmly fixed as the pole-star, though no-one beside herself knew anything about it. Under the top surface of her mind it occupied her thoughts from waking to sleeping. Sometimes it pursued her in sleep, and she had vivid, pleasurable dreams of the future. But she would willingly have given Edgar whatever he needed, if he had come to her.

'So I start next Wednesday, after the Whitsun holiday,' Edgar said. 'They don't want the payments to fall into arrears. I thought you might give me a hand with the books. You're good at figures.'

Where does he think I'll get the time, Opal asked herself.

'I'll make a cup of tea and see to Daniel,' she said, turning to her son.

'And what did *you* do today, love?' she asked.

75

'I did a drawing,' Daniel said. 'I brought it home to show you. Look! Miss Potter said it was the best in the class.'

Opal studied the drawing with interest. It depicted a street scene, in coloured chalks. Though the houses, the children playing, the horse pulling the coal cart, were all crudely drawn, the picture had great life and vigour.

'Well I think it's nice too,' she said, smiling at him. 'We'll pin it on the wall, shall we, where we can all see it? And now into the scullery and start getting washed while I put the supper on. And don't skip the back of your neck, my lad!'

At five years old he was capable and independent beyond his years and (for which she was truly thankful) with the capacity for enjoying himself for hours on end. He was never as happy as when he had a box of wax crayons and some paper to draw on. That he had talent she was sure, though she didn't know where he got it from. Also, he could now read. He was no trouble and she loved him dearly. He was part of all her dreams for the future.

'We shall have to make some arrangement about Daniel,' she said to Edgar when the child had gone into the scullery.

'I'm sure his Grandma'll have him,' Edgar said. 'It'll only be for a week, until you've worked out your notice.'

Opal, in the act of laying the table, paused and stared at him.

'My notice?'

'You'll be able to give it in tomorrow. The job's certain, you know. From next week on, *I'll* be the breadwinner!'

'But—'

'Oh you can keep on the house shop if you want to. But no more working from morning until night, coming home too tired to lift a teaspoon. No, you'll be back in your rightful place. But don't think I'm not grateful for what you've done, love!'

Opal knew, now, the reason for the disquiet which had stirred her mind at the moment he had given her his great news.

'Edgar,' she said quietly. 'I can't give up my job.'

He leaned across the table and took her hand in what was an almost forgotten, loving manner.

'You're afraid I'll not succeed,' he said gently. 'Well I can't blame you. But I'm going to prove you wrong. I'm going to show you that all I needed was the chance.'

'It's not that!' Opal protested. In her heart she knew she had her doubts about him, but she would never show them. And what sort of a job was it? Where would it lead, compared to what she had in mind?

'It's not that,' she repeated. 'I'm sure you'll do well. It's that I *like* my job. I enjoy every minute of it, even though I do come home tired. I'm good at it, Edgar, and it's what I want to do.'

Edgar's forehead tightened in a frown. His eyes, meeting hers, were hard and puzzled. He doesn't really understand at all, Opal thought.

'We can't talk about it now,' he said. 'We'll discuss it when Daniel's gone to bed.'

'As you wish,' Opal said. 'But you may as well know that I haven't the slightest intention of giving in my notice.'

Edgar jumped up from the table. She saw his neck suffuse with red where it bulged against his collar. He bounded to the window, turning his back on her, his broad shoulders hunched in anger.

'You'll give in your notice,' he shouted. 'You have a working husband now and it's your place to run the home and look after your child!'

She left the table and went into the scullery, to Daniel. Her whole body was shaking but she tried to speak calmly to her son. He was the witness, recently, of far too many quarrels.

'Have you finished, love? Let me see.'

She bent down and kissed his shining face. He smelled deliciously of the Knight's Castile soap which was especially kept for his delicate child's skin.

'Supper and then bed,' she said. 'It's time you were asleep.'

During the meal she and Edgar did not speak, though she kept up a conversation with Daniel. She was thankful when supper was over and she could take the child upstairs. He had his own bedroom now, about the size of a cupboard. She tucked him in and heard him repeat the prayers his grandmother had taught him, then she kissed him goodnight and went downstairs again.

Edgar was standing with his back to the fireplace, his arms tightly folded against his chest, his head lowered as if he was about to charge.

'Now, madam, let's get things straight,' he said grimly.

'Certainly!' Opal flashed back. 'That's what I want, too! For a start, I do look after my child, I do run the home, working or not. How much housework do *you* do, though you're home all day? When do you cook a meal?'

'That's not the point,' Edgar said. 'A woman's place is in the home. Everybody knows that.'

'Well I can assure you, Edgar, I am *not* giving up my job, not for you, not for anyone.' She spoke calmly, but inside she trembled and felt sick.

'Not even for Daniel?' Edgar said. 'I know you've got precious little time for me, but don't you care about Daniel?'

His voice was quieter, too, but it pierced her more than his temper could ever have done. He knew her vulnerability all right. It was the vulnerability of all who carry a child in the womb, bring it helpless and dependent into life. It was a pain of the heart more deeply felt than any bodily pain and she was no more immune to it than any other woman.

Convention had nothing to do with it. She didn't mind what people said, and no-one was going to tell her where her place was. It was what she herself must give up, must be prepared to miss, in the hours of separation from Daniel. That, and the niggling question as to what such a separation might or might not do to her son. She knew the risks, but the fight was for her own identity, for the right to do as she pleased with her own life. In spite of the doubts which remained in her – and perhaps always would – it was a fight she intended to win.

'You're being unfair!' she cried. 'It's not true that I've no time for you, and you know it. But you don't own me. As for Daniel, you're talking as though I have to choose between loving Daniel and going out to work. Well, I don't! I can do both.'

'Not properly,' Edgar insisted. 'You can't do both things well and we all know who'll suffer.'

But for all the strength which had come to him with

the prospect of his new job, he was no match for this small, determined woman; this woman he loved but frequently did not understand. He had lost and he knew it.

'I promise you, Edgar, Daniel won't suffer,' Opal assured him. 'And now I'll go around and see your mother and we'll come to some arrangement. She'll understand.'

'I'm not sure I approve' Mrs Carson said doubtfully. 'Oh, your wages must have been a godsend over the last three years, but now that Edgar's got himself a job . . . Anyway, it's not my approval you're after, is it? Of course Daniel can come here to his dinner every day. And if Edgar's likely to be out on his rounds he can come to his tea as well.'

'He'll love that,' Opal said. 'You know how he enjoys coming here.'

'Aye, well, that's settled then,' Mrs Carson said.

She admired her daughter-in-law – so competent, so ambitious – but she did not always understand her and in this case she couldn't enter into her feelings. But she would do anything for little Daniel. The way things were going he looked like being the only grandchild she'd ever have.

'I'd best be getting back,' Opal said. 'There's some ironing to do.'

'You work too hard,' Mrs Carson said. 'I should have thought you'd have been glad of the chance . . . But there it is. Anyway, I've got a nice apple pasty for you to take back with you. Fresh baked today.'

She wrapped the pasty carefully, taking pleasure in the sight of it. There were few situations that a nice, well-baked apple pasty couldn't improve.

When Opal arrived home Daniel was sitting in the armchair, wrapped in a blanket.

'He's been sick,' Edgar informed her. 'I brought him down and gave him a drink of warm milk.'

His tone of voice said that if she had been in her rightful place this wouldn't have happened. Oh Daniel, she thought ruefully, did it have to be now?

She knelt down by the chair and put her arms around him. 'It must be something you ate, love. Did anyone give you anything at school?'

'Dick Foster gave me some pink sweets,' Daniel confessed.

'Then that's it! Are you better now?'

'Yes.'

There was colour in his cheeks and his eyes were bright enough, the whites clear and blue.

'Well then, back to bed or you'll be too tired for school in the morning.'

'Carry me upstairs,' Daniel demanded.

'A great big boy like you?'

'Well I *was* sick.'

'All right then' she said. 'Just this once. It'll have to be a piggy-back.'

She changed the sheet and tucked him into bed. He flung his arms around her and they hugged each other tightly. Who could possibly say that she did not love her son enough? Then he lay back on the pillow and closed his eyes. She traced the fine arch on his eyebrows with her finger, touched his cool cheek. He was asleep before she left the bedroom.

'Supposing this happens when we're both out at work?' Edgar demanded, 'What then?'

'We'll meet that when it comes,' Opal said. 'It's no

use, Edgar. You're not going to make me change my mind.'

By mid-morning it was really busy in the shop, but in this particular week that was to be expected. Everyone who could possibly afford it wanted something new for Whit Sunday, to wear to church or chapel, and perhaps afterwards to the brass band concert in the park. And if there was not enough money for a complete new outfit, then a new hat, and perhaps new white gloves, must do.

'We're selling a lot of white gloves,' Madame Dora said. 'I wonder if we should get another two dozen pairs when David Hessle comes in? Or is it too late? Will the rush be over? Thank goodness the General Strike's finished. If it had gone on even a day or two longer it could have ruined out Whitsuntide trade!'

'I think the rush is about over,' Opal said. 'But white gloves could sell right through the summer. What we *must* have, though, is more art silk stockings in that new beige shade. No-one wants lisle for best any more. Do you think he might make a special delivery?'

'He might,' Madame Dora said. 'Especially if *you* ask him.'

Opal bent her head over the deep drawer in which she was checking the hosiery stock. She had got on well with David Hessle from the start, but Madame Dora made too much of it. It was nothing more than a pleasant business relationship. How could it be otherwise, even if she were so inclined, which she was not. Though he was single, she was a married woman with a child. But she would not let Madame Dora see her irritation.

Her employer had been good to her, no doubt about

82

that. She had agreed to all her ideas for expansion and had even moved the office and stockroom upstairs into her flat to free more space. They now did a good trade in gloves, scarves, hosiery, artificial flowers and sundry other items to adorn the female form. Lingerie had done well though it was falling off a little at present, this being the season for outward show. Hats, though, continued to be their mainstay. They had many more customers now, and if they were not quite as exclusive as they had been, well, their money was good. And since Opal now had two-and-a-half per cent of the extra profits she wasn't complaining.

'Perhaps you'd better telephone him,' Madame Dora said. 'Order what you think best.'

Her confidence in Opal grew all the time. The takings had doubled in the past two years. And Opal, though she didn't know it, was to have her reward. Not an immediate tangible reward. Madame Dora hoped it would not be reaped for a long time to come. But something for Opal to look forward to, in a manner of speaking. It would also be one in the eye for her sister, Millicent, Madame Dora thought with satisfaction.

'Don't let me forget I'm to see Mr Ratcliffe at twelve noon,' she said. 'I mustn't be late. Solicitors charge you for the time you keep them waiting.'

'I'll remind you,' Opal promised.

'When I get back' Madame Dora said solemnly 'I'll tell you all about it.'

Opal scarcely heard her. She was making a list of items required from David Hessle. It was important to achieve the right balance between having too little stock to meet the demand and thereby missing sales, and having too much when the season was over. She must also try once more to persuade Madame Dora to have a July sale. Sales were the one thing on which she dug in her heels. A discreet discount on an item which had been slow to sell was one thing; sales, with price tickets in the window, were quite another. As for advertising . . . ! Opal wondered if David Hessle might get hold of any special sale items. She completed her list and was about to unhook the telephone receiver when he walked into the salon.

'I was coming this way,' he said. 'I thought I'd call on the off chance.'

'You're just the man we wanted,' Madame Dora said. 'But I'm leaving you to Miss Carson. I have to see my solicitor.'

'What's that about?' David Hessle asked when Madame Dora had left. 'Not trouble, I hope?'

'I don't think so. She's probably changing her will again. She does it to spite her sister. She hates her since their father died last year and left everything in the house to Millicent. Have you any white gloves, sizes six-and-a-half and seven? And art silk hose, beige dawn, sizes eight-and-a-half and nine?'

Their dealing was interrupted several times while Opal broke off to serve customers. Hessle stepped back out of the way and watched her. She was so competent. She had exactly the right balance of deference and friendliness towards the customers, and the skill to guide them, without ever seeming to hurry, to a reasonably quick decision. She was damnably attractive too, but a hard nut to crack.

By the time the last customer had left and he had completed his order book it was five minutes to one.

'Come and have a bite to eat with me,' he said. 'I'm always asking you and you never accept.'

'Well I can't today,' Opal said. 'It's kind of you but,

as you see, Madame Dora isn't back and we never close the salon over the dinner hour.'

'Always the ready answer,' he said with good humour.

She thought how attractive he looked. It would have been pleasant to have gone with him.

'Shall you be going to the band concert on Sunday?' he asked.

'It depends on my husband,' Opal said. 'It depends on what he wants to do.'

'Do you always defer to your husband?' David Hessle asked.

'Of course!' But her eyes, meeting David's, were not as demure as her words.

Then minutes after he had left, Madame Dora returned.

'Lock the shop door!' she said. 'Yes, I mean it! And come upstairs. I've got something to tell you.' She had an air of great importance, but her eyes were excited, like a child with a secret to impart. Opal followed her upstairs and took a chair in Madame Dora's private sitting room.

'Now!' Madame Dora said. 'Prepare yourself for a shock! A pleasant one – a *very* pleasant one – but a shock!'

'I'm prepared,' Opal said. What could it possibly be? Was Madame Dora perhaps going to get married again?

'Well I've seen Mr Ratcliffe, and the long and short of it is, Opal – and I'm far too excited to beat about the bush – I've changed my will and I'm leaving the business to you! There!'

'To *me*?' Opal gasped. 'You don't mean it! I can't believe it!' She felt dizzy with the news.

'I don't suppose you can,' Madame Dora said. 'It's not something that happens every day. But it's true. It'll all be yours one day; lock, stock and barrel. Or to be more precise, stock, fixtures, fittings and goodwill. You deserve it and it'll be one in the eye for that greedy pig of a sister of mine!'

The world stopped spinning. Opal was on firm ground again. It was a kind gesture of course, but in practical terms it could mean very little to her. Madame Dora was forty-two and in the best of health. She would live another thirty years or more, by which time Opal was quite certain she would have her own business, far bigger and more important than this one could ever be. It was her goal, it was why she was saving her money. Any inheritance from Madame Dora – who in any case might change her mind half-a-dozen times between now and then – would be of small account by the time she could claim it. Now if it were to happen *soon* . . . She stopped her thoughts in mid-flight, horrified by the direction they had taken.

'Thank you, Madame Dora,' she said. 'I appreciate it very much indeed. But of course I hope you're going to live a very long time yet, to enjoy Madame Dora's Modes to the full.'

'Shall we go to the band concert today?' Opal asked on Sunday. 'It's the Black Dyke Mills. You always like them.'

'I'd have thought you'd have been too tired for traipsing up and down in the park,' Edgar replied.

'A change is as good as a rest,' Opal said briskly. 'Besides, Daniel might enjoy it. If you don't want to go I suppose I could take him.'

'Well I dare say it would help to take my mind off things,' Edgar said.

As the time grew nearer he was increasingly nervy about starting his new job. Though little more had been said about it, Opal could sense that. She would have liked to have talked to him, tried to reassure him, but it was a sensitive area and she had no wish to provoke another quarrel. She had won her point and that was that.

'It would do that,' she agreed. 'But there's no need for you to worry, Edgar. You'll be all right. Especially as the Supervisor's going around with you for the first week. Anyway, do we go to the band concert?'

'I suppose we might as well,' he said.

'Then we must look our best. Wear your Sunday suit, and the tie I bought you.'

She changed into the cream gabardine which she had worn for Queenie's wedding three years ago. She had taken it in to suit her normal, slender figure, shortened the skirt, trimmed it with a new braid, changed the buttons. No-one would recognize it and the material was as good as ever. She had borrowed a hat from the salon, which was allowed since it was good for trade. Daniel had a new suit, as befitted the time of year. They made a smart trio, she thought with satisfaction as they set off.

They took a tram to the park, sitting outside on top at Daniel's request. At the park entrance Edgar tossed twopence into the canvas sheet at the entrance, which entitled them to a printed programme.

'It looks like a good selection,' he said. 'Poet and Peasant, Gondoliers, Il Travatore. And a nice cornet solo. Shall we treat ourselves to chairs and concentrate on the music?'

Though the band concerts, which started at Whitsun and took place every Sunday until the middle of September, were supposedly musical occasions, everyone knew that they were also the scene setters for fashion parades. Those who really wanted to concentrate on the music could pay twopence to sit in a deck chair in a roped-off enclosure around the bandstand. The rest strolled, preferably in groups of three or four, up and down the wide avenues of the park. For them the music was a pleasant background to the more important business of seeing and being seen, especially by the opposite sex.

For no reason at all Opal suddenly wondered just how interested David Hessle was in music? For instance, would he sit in the enclosure? Then she dismissed the thought. She had not come here to see David Hessle.

'I think Daniel might get bored, just sitting still,' she said. 'It would be best to walk. But why don't *you* take a seat by the bandstand while I walk around with Daniel. I know you appreciate the music more than I do. I like to see what people are wearing.'

'I'll come with you,' Edgar said. 'Anyway it's a bit chilly to sit still, in spite of the sun. I don't know how some of you women keep warm in such thin dresses.'

'Pride keeps women warm,' Opal informed him.

All the same she was glad she was not wearing the flimsy voile which was everywhere around, pretty though it looked. The crowded avenue with people sauntering up and down looked like a summer flower-bed moving in the breeze. The women's hats – by far the larger number of them of white straw trimmed with flowers – were interspersed by the men's fawn or grey trilbys or their cream-coloured boaters with striped hatbands.

'Your outfit's as smart as any, even though you did wear it to Queenie's wedding' Edgar observed.

A great deal had happened to Queenie since that June afternoon. She and Mark had two little daughters and were now hoping that the new arrival would be the son they both wanted. Mr Stone had died, leaving a fortune to his daughter. But nothing could spoil Queenie's nature. She continued as simple and affectionate as ever, and every day more in love with Mark. She was the only person in the world Opal envied, and not for her possessions.

Daniel tugged at Opal's skirt.

'Can we go to see the ducks?' he asked.

Opal frowned slightly. The pond was out of earshot of the band and, except for children, the area would be deserted. Everything of interest was here.

'Perhaps later,' she said. 'Not just now. Mother and Father want to listen to the music and look at all the people.'

'Perhaps we *should* take him,' Edgar said.

'He can wait a little while. He mustn't think he can have everything the minute he asks for it.'

Edgar looked at her in surprise. 'You've changed your tune,' he said.

And then Opal saw David Hessle. He was walking towards her, and clinging to his arms was a pretty, fair creature. The floating panels of her ninon dress lifted in the breeze, which also caused her to hold down her fine straw hat with a small hand elegantly gloved in white kid. Good quality, eight-and-eleven three farthings, Opal noted automatically. Hessle's gaze was concentrated on his companion and he did not see Opal until he was almost upon her. When he did, there was no doubting the pleasure of his recognition.

'Why, Mrs Carson!' he exclaimed. 'I didn't expect to see *you* here! How pleasant!'

'My husband is very fond of music,' Opal said. 'We come whenever we can, don't we Edgar?'

'Allow me to introduce my cousin, Miss Dolly Simpson,' Hessle said.

They chatted amiably for a minute or two. Opal was aware that David Hessle missed nothing of her appearance, also that he approved. She was pleased that, for once, he had seen her in something other than her black work dress, even though her gabardine was not nearly as glamorous as his companion's flowered ninon.

'We must go,' she said after a little while. 'Daniel wants to see the ducks and we've promised him he shall.'

'If she's his cousin' Edgar said as they walked in the direction of the pond 'I'm the Prince of Wales!'

It was while they were waiting for the tram, close by the park entrance, that the accident happened. The concert was over, everyone rushing home to tea, crowds pouring through the park gates. Opal, standing in the long queue with Edgar and Daniel, saw Madame Dora among them. She was unmistakable in her elegance. Her wide-brimmed, yellow hat had been trimmed by Opal only a few days ago.

'There's Madame Dora!' Opal cried. 'How strange we didn't meet her in the park!' She let go of Daniel and raised her hand, waving to attract her employer's attention.

Eventually Madame Dora saw her. She returned

Opal's wave and started to cross towards her. Afterwards, no-one in the crowd seemed to know where the motor car had come from. One minute it was not in sight and the next it had hit Madame Dora when she was no more than three yards from the pavement. For a split second she lay terribly alone, the yellow hat on the ground a few yards away where the breeze had carried it. Then suddenly people gathered around her still figure. Opal, already running from the opposite side of the road, pushed her way to the front of the crowd.

Madame Dora was alive, though unconscious, when the ambulance came. By the time it reached the hospital Opal, travelling with her, clutching the yellow hat as if it might work a miracle, did not need to be told by the ambulanceman that she was dead.

What horrified Opal for a long time to come was the speed with which the thought came into her mind. She pushed it away again, but it was already too late. The words into which it formed itself burned inside her.

'It's all mine! The business is all mine!'

Chapter Five

Opal looked up, frowning, as her new assistant rushed into the stockroom. The girl must learn to conduct herself in a more decorous manner. She was new, of course, and young – not yet twenty. But she would have to be trained.

'Oh Mrs Carson,' the girl began breathlessly.

'Calm down, Miss Browning,' Opal admonished.

'Well there's a great big car just drawn up at the kerb, with a chauffeur and everything, and I think the lady's coming in here! You'd better come, Mrs Carson!'

Opal smiled; not the polite, upcurving of her lips which she offered to customers, but a smile of real pleasure which lit up her face and shone in her eyes.

'That will be my sister-in-law, Mrs Mark Derwent,' she said. 'I'm expecting her.' She rose and hurried to greet Queenie as she entered the shop. Connie Browning was surprised at the warmth of the meeting between the two women. Mrs Carson was such a cool customer, she wouldn't have thought she'd have had it in her.

'You're looking wonderful, Opal dear,' Queenie said.

'You too!' Privately Opal thought, in the kindest possible way, that her sister-in-law's expensive outfit would have benefitted from being more up-to-date, but it was still true that she looked wonderful.

'Come along upstairs,' she said. 'Oh yes, this is my

new assistant, Miss Connie Browning. She's been with us just a fortnight. Miss Browning, do you think you could possibly keep an eye on the shop?' She no longer referred to it as the salon, as in Madame Dora's day. 'If there's the slightest problem, the very slightest, call me down at once.'

She went in front of Queenie along the corridor and up the narrow staircase which led to the living quarters above the shop. She heartily disliked this approach to the flat. It was so cramped and dark. When funds allowed she planned to have it decorated in light and bright colours, with a plain green carpet on the stairs; but for the last two years almost every spare penny had gone into the shop, expanding the range of goods, building up the business.

The living-room which they now entered was furnished almost exactly as it had been when Madame Dora was alive. Beige-covered sofa and armchairs, walnut table, brown curtains. Opal had inherited the contents of the flat along with the business and had lost no time at all in getting rid of almost everything which the Acer Street house had contained. Not that she liked Madame Dora's taste. She would have preferred more colour. But first things first and the shop was the most important. Except for Daniel, of course. He, she was pleased to think, now lacked for nothing.

'How is business?' Queenie asked.

'Very good. Very good indeed. As far as space permits I'm introducing new lines all the time. And the takings are well up on last year, let alone on what they were when Madame Dora had it.'

She had been surprised, and not pleasantly, to find how little money Madame Dora actually made. Her own small, regular share of the extra profits had seemed riches only because she was so used to having nothing. Studying the books after Madame Dora's death, she had at once seen several ways in which profits might be increased. The moment the lawyers had sorted everything out, dealing swiftly with Millicent's vigorous protests over her sister's will, she had started to put her ideas into effect.

'The trouble with Madame Dora was' she said to Queenie 'that she tried to make money by economizing on everything, cutting back everywhere. I believe you have to use money to make money. Invest it in goods and increase the turnover.'

Queenie smiled, shaking her head in wonderment. 'I don't know where you get it from, your business sense, I mean. You sound just like my father used to!'

And look where it got him, Opal thought. Look what his success gave you. A chauffeur-driven limousine, an ermine stole over your shoulders, diamonds and emeralds on your hands. But there was no animosity in her thoughts. Queenie wore her riches with such natural grace, with so little ostentation, as to disarm all criticism.

'I'd be glad to have half your father's business gifts,' Opal said. 'And I envy his training. It's what I lack.'

'Ah, but you have *flair*!' Queenie said. 'I'm sure that's worth even more. But where's Daniel? I expected to see him.'

'He's out with his father,' Opal said. 'Edgar thought he shouldn't be sitting inside on such a fine afternoon so he's taken him on his rounds. I don't really approve, but Daniel was dying to go.'

'It sounds a good idea to me,' Queenie said. 'What's wrong with it.'

'Only that . . .' She did not quite know how to tell

Queenie that she disliked the thought of her son being taken around the poor streets, entering the poverty-stricken homes – probably none too clean – which made up the larger part of Edgar's round. In little more than two short years she had left that behind for ever and as far as her son was concerned she would like him to forget that it had ever existed. She intended life to be very different for Daniel.

'You never know what's going around,' she said. 'Infections and so on. I wouldn't want him to catch something just as he's about to go to a new school.'

'Is he looking forward to going to Bishop Tanner's?' Queenie asked.

Opal was saved from replying by the sound of Daniel's footsteps on the stairs. He came running into the room, followed a moment later by his father. The boy's cheeks were flushed in his otherwise pale, bright-eyed face. Edgar's skin was tanned from being so much in the open air, but in spite of this, Queenie thought, he did not look healthy. It was difficult to say why. He had plenty of flesh on his bones and his decent navy suit sat well enough on his muscular body. It was perhaps something in his demeanour, in his stance. He entered the room quietly, his shoulders hunched, his head down, as if he was not sure that he belonged. And though he had been in work for two years now, it was the previous four years of unemployment which showed in the lines on his face and in the dullness of his eyes. She had seen little of him for some time and she was moved, shocked even, by his appearance. He was twenty-nine and looked at least ten years older. But when he raised his eyes to hers his expression brightened.

'It's such a long time since I saw you,' Queenie said. 'You must tell me about your job.'

'There's nothing to tell,' Edgar said abruptly.

'I can tell you,' Daniel offered. 'We went to a lot of houses today and some of them asked us in. There was an old man in a bed downstairs. He gave me a cough sweet from under his pillow.'

'I hope you didn't eat it,' Opal said sharply. 'It's not fit!'

'It was quite nice,' Daniel said. 'Sort of aniseedy.'

'I told you to watch him, Edgar,' Opal said. 'You know I didn't want him to go in the first place. You never know what he might pick up!'

'He only ate a sweet,' Edgar said. 'It won't kill him. And it gave old Mr Sykes a lot of pleasure. You remember old Sykes in Maud Street? He wouldn't hurt a fly.'

'A sweet from under his pillow! It could be riddled with germs!' Opal protested.

Edgar shrugged his shoulders. He poured himself a cup of tea from the pot on the table and took it to a chair by the window.

'I came to see if Daniel would like to come to stay with us for the last week of the school holidays,' Queenie said, changing the subject. 'But it seems he's going to Grandpa Derwent's at Highcliffe tomorrow. Well, you'll enjoy it on the farm, won't you Daniel? And Aunt Mary will be very pleased to have you for company, I'm sure.'

'Uncle David's taking us in his car,' Daniel said. 'He's got a Ford. It can go at forty miles an hour!'

'Uncle David?'

'He's a friend. A friend of the family,' Opal said. 'I can't think why you've never met him. He's a wholesaler and I buy a lot of my stock from him. He's always been very helpful to me.'

'So he's going to take you all to Highcliffe!' Queenie said. 'Well, that's very kind. It's not an easy place to get to.'

'Almost impossible in the evening,' Opal said. 'And I can't leave the shop during the day.'

'And Father can't go at all,' Daniel said. 'He has to work on Friday nights because that's when people have the money to pay him.'

Miss Browning's voice came from the bottom of the stairs. 'Mrs Derwent's car has come back for her, Mrs Carson.'

'I must be off,' Queenie said. 'Thank you for the tea. I'm glad I managed to see all three of you this time. Couldn't you all come over for the day one Sunday? I know how busy you are, Opal, but surely you could take a day off?'

'I usually do the books and see to the stocks on a Sunday. And a thousand other things. But yes, we'd like to come. And we will, just as soon as I can manage it.'

'And you must let me know how you get on at your new school, Daniel,' Queenie said. 'Are you looking forward to it?'

'No,' Daniel said flatly. 'My friends won't be going. And they'll make me do a lot of arithmetic and spelling and things. I only like to do drawing. I don't suppose they'll do much drawing.'

Opal put her arm around him. 'Of course they'll do drawing,' she said. 'And painting. I especially asked. They do it every Thursday. And, you know, you can't get through life without arithmetic and spelling.'

'Why not?' Daniel demanded.

'Well, you'll never be successful,' Opal said. 'You want to be successful, don't you?'

Queenie drew on her gloves and went downstairs, accompanied by Opal, and by Daniel who wanted to inspect her car. Edgar watched them go. If only all women were like Queenie! Gentle and yielding. There wasn't an ounce of hardness in her. Of course she wasn't half as clever as Opal, and no-one worked harder than his wife. She had earned her success. But what she couldn't understand was that not everyone was cut out to be successful. She thought that it was simply a matter of putting your mind to it. Well, even if he had a mind as clear and decisive as Opal's, and he knew he never would have, what was there in his job to put it to?

He had quickly come to hate his job. It was not that he disliked the homes into which he had to enter, though his patch was one of the poorest, but he hated collecting coppers from people who could scarcely scrape them together. And when they could no longer keep up the payments, which happened all too often, he was embarrassed by the meagre surrender value which the Company offered. It was always so much less than had been paid in and sometimes, if they hadn't made enough contributions, it was nothing at all. Oh, he knew all the Company's arguments, and they sounded reasonable enough. Nevertheless they grew richer and richer, and he saw where the money came from.

He was no good at the job. It didn't need Mr Hardaker, the Supervisor, to tell him that. The main idea was to get new customers to replace those who were so frequently lost, and at this he was hopeless. It was bad enough pushing in where new babies had been born, persuading the mother to do her best for the child by taking out insurance she could ill afford, but it was not as bad as intruding on the bereaved, advising them, even in the act of paying out on the deceased, to take proper precautions against their own demise by investing in more insurance. He had been reminded more than once that if he was to keep his job he must do better.

'The trouble with you' Mr Hardaker complained 'is that you're not Company minded! I'm not at all sure that you're cut out for insurance!' It was true enough. But what was he cut out for? Was there anything in the world he was good at? He doubted it.

'Mother says to tell you she'll be down in the shop until closing time,' Daniel said, coming back into the room. 'And she says I can have two custard cream biscuits.'

'Oh! And what does she say I can have?'

Daniel laughed. 'She didn't say. I expect you can have the same as me.'

Never, Edgar thought. I'm not in the same class. Everything for Daniel. He pulled himself up sharply. What was he coming to, to begrudge the boy? He cared for his son with a love at least as deep as Opal's. It hurt him that he couldn't do the things for him that she could. If he'd been capable at all of getting new business, as the Company wanted, he'd have done it for Daniel. But Opal took care of it all. Paints, drawing paper, toys, clothes – anything the child wanted. And now a fine new school, the fees for which, had he been required to contribute, would have taken every penny he earned.

Daniel sat at the table painting. There wouldn't be

another word out of him. Edgar stood and stared out of the window. In the street a September wind blew up the dust. He disliked the autumn because it led so quickly to the winter, and here the winters were long. Before he knew it he would be trudging from house to house in the snow and the sludge.

It was a quiet afternoon in the shop. Summer being only just over and the autumn a fine one, no-one was prepared to buy for the winter. Thankfully, most of the warm-weather stock had been shifted in the July sale. It had been a good sale, Opal thought. The items she had bought in specially – hosiery, gloves, lingerie – from a bankrupt stock in Leeds, had all sold out. The marked-down goods from her own stock had gone well too. Everything had been sold at a profit, if sometimes a small one, and more important for the future, she had many satisfied and appreciative customers. The sales at Madame Dora's – she had had half-a-dozen over the last two years – were now acknowledged to be something special.

'All we need now' Opal said to Connie Browning 'is for the weather to turn cold for a day or two so that people will come in and buy their thick stockings and winter nightdresses. In the meantime I think we should dress the millinery window with hats suitable for wearing to the Harvest Thanksgiving services. Browns, rusts, reds, I think. Autumn colours.'

'Yes, Mrs Carson,' Connie said. 'Shall I empty the window?'

'Good gracious no!' Opal replied. 'Never have the window empty while the shop is open. You can clear it just before you leave and I'll dress it again right away.'

She searched through the millinery drawers, looking for hats which would suit her theme.

'When I first started here,' she remarked, 'I used to make hats starting with nothing more than a length of millinery wire twisted into a ring – building everything up from there.'

That was ages ago, now. It was five years to the week since she had started here, but it seemed twice as long. She had soon known that one day she would have her own business, though she had never expected it to happen the way it had. Sometimes, against her will, she recalled the thought she had had when Madame Dora had told her about the inheritance. 'If it could happen *soon*'. But she had never wished her to die. She had had nothing to do with it, it was pure accident. And every year on Whitsunday she visited the cemetary to place fresh flowers on her late employer's grave.

But I've not come all the way yet, Opal thought. Not by a long chalk. This shop was far from the summit of her ambition, in fact she felt she had already outgrown it. She wanted something much bigger, preferably in Leasfield itself, and she knew she would get it in the end. As well as putting money into this business she was saving hard, still paying her weekly visit to the bank but no longer depositing coppers or the odd shillings as she once had. When the opportunity for expansion came she would reach out and grab it with both hands.

'Who taught you to make hats?'

Opal was aware by the loudness of her assistant's voice that she was repeating the question.

About to say 'Madame Dora taught me' she stopped and considered. In fact Madama Dora had taught her very little. She had provided the tools and a place in which to use them, but in their use Opal had out-stripped her employer in no time at all.

'I suppose you could say I taught myself,' she said. 'But you won't need to learn all that because I've moved away from bespoke hats, except for a few old customers like Miss Taylor. There isn't the profit in it. Ready-to-wear hats are the thing now. One can always change the trimming to put up the price. The special orders I *do* take I can cope with quite easily.'

'By the way, Miss Browning,' she continued, 'I want to get away in good time tomorrow evening. Mr Hessle is kindly taking Daniel and me to my father's. Daniel's going to stay on the farm for the rest of the school holiday.'

A smile spread over Miss Browning's face and her blue eyes sparkled. She really is quite pretty, Opal thought, in a conventional sort of way.

'Oh I do like Mr Hessle,' the girl said. 'He's a real Prince Charming! Ever so handsome. I'll bet he's a right one for the ladies! Why, he even made a pass at me and I've only met him twice, both times here in the shop. He's not backward at coming forward, I must say. Of course he's too old for me. He must be pushing thirty.'

He's twenty-eight, the same as me, Opal thought. But men did not have to worry about age. What did the girl mean by saying he'd made a pass at her?

'That will do, Miss Browning,' she said in a cool voice. 'Now get on and check the glove drawers. I want to know exactly what we have and in what sizes. And please remember for the future that I don't allow gossip. In any case, I'm sure you must have misunderstood Mr Hessle.'

Miss Browning jerked open the glove drawer and

began to count. Oh no I didn't misunderstand, she told herself. Do you ever go to the pictures was what he said to me and I don't need anyone to tell me what he meant. As sure as eggs is eggs, Madame is jealous. But better to tread carefully. Jobs were not all that easy to come by and she quite liked this one.

Later, after Miss Browning had departed on the dot and she had arranged what she thought would be an eye-catching display of hats in the window, Opal locked the shop door, emptied the till and went upstairs.

'Time for bed, love,' she said to Daniel. 'Clear your things away now and I'll poach you an egg for your supper. If I know your Auntie Mary you'll be having a week of late nights. She spoils you.'

Her sister spoiled Daniel by giving him unstintingly of her time. Opal was aware that Mary was never too busy to play with Daniel, or walk up on to the moors, or down to the village for sweets, however much work there was in the house. She does all the things I don't have time for, Opal thought. But it's all very well when you're not a parent. And I give him all the rest. He understands. He knows I love him and that I'm working for him, she consoled herself.

'A bit of spoiling never did anyone any harm,' Edgar said.

'I dare say I shall be back latish tomorrow night,' Opal said. 'Dad will be disappointed if we don't stay for a bit of supper and we can't rush away straight afterwards. But David will see me back safely.'

'I don't see why it couldn't have waited until Saturday morning,' Edgar protested. 'I could have taken Daniel then. We could have made a day of it, walked over the moors. We'd both have enjoyed that.'

'It's too far for Daniel to walk,' Opal answered. 'Besides, *I* want to see Dad and Mary.'

'Then the three of us could have gone on Sunday,' Edgar persisted.

'In any case,' Opal said finally, 'Daniel wants to go in David's new car. I'm going tomorrow evening to please Daniel.'

There was nothing more to be said. Edgar picked up the newspaper, though he had already read it. It was full of petty crime, social chit-chat, politics – which had once interested him and now no longer did. But there was nothing else to do. Opal had already opened her account books and was engrossed in adding up figures.

'I must go upstairs and finish Daniel's packing,' Opal said to Miss Browning towards the end of the busy Friday. 'We must be ready to leave the minute the shop closes. In fact if we don't have customers in I might just close a few minutes early. Mr Hessle should be here any minute. Ask him to come straight upstairs will you?'

She wondered, as the girl obviously had silly ideas in her head, whether she should wait in the shop until David came. But there was too much to do. Edgar was out working and Daniel could not be trusted to get himself ready entirely without supervision. But how silly she was being! David, she was sure, had scarcely noticed the girl. Notwithstanding, as she packed Daniel's case she kept an ear open for the sound of the shop bell. When she heard it, but David did not appear, she went downstairs again. Most likely it was a late customer. She might be needed, if only to sell her something quickly and get her off the premises.

There was no sign of a customer. Miss Browning was stretching up to a high shelf and David Hessle was standing close beside her.

'I heard the bell several minutes ago,' Opal said. 'I thought it must be a customer.'

'It was,' David said quickly. 'She was leaving as I came in just now.'

'Were you not able to help her, Miss Browning?' Opal asked.

The girl hesitated. 'No. That is . . .'

Of course there had been no customer. The girl's manner gave her away. But how silly of David!

'Very well, Miss Browning, you may go now,' Opal said. 'And by the way, when you can't reach the high shelves, remember there's a step ladder. That's what it's for.'

She knew at once by the swift smile which David could not conceal that she had said the wrong thing. If there was one thing more attractive than another about Miss Browning it was her long, shapely legs beneath her short skirt. What man would not be pleased to watch her climb a step ladder?

'Good night Miss Browning,' Opal said firmly. 'Be on time in the morning. We're hoping for a busy day.'

There was hardly any traffic on the moorland road. On either side, and as far as the eye could see, the heather was still in bloom, a blazing reddish-purple in the light of the setting sun. By the time they reached the farm the daylight had gone, leaving only a strip of dark blue in the western sky. As David drove into the farmyard Mary came out of the house to meet them. Daniel, who had fallen asleep despite all his efforts not to do so, wakened as the car stopped.

'We can't stay long,' Opal said, following her sister into the kitchen. 'It's going to be late as it is when we get back. I have to make an early start on Saturday mornings. It's good of you to have Daniel. I know he'll enjoy himself.'

'It will be a lovely change for me,' Mary said. 'Nothing ever happens here. You don't know how lucky you are, Opal. Anyway, you must have a bite of supper.'

'Where's Grandpa?' Daniel asked.

'In the stables, seeing to Victor.'

'Can I ride Victor tomorrow?'

'Of course you can. Providing you go straight to sleep tonight.'

If she had a son, Mary thought – if ever she did, which seemed unlikely since she was stuck here on the farm without the slightest prospect of marriage – she would like him to be just like Daniel. But even if the chance of marriage came, how could she ever leave her father? He depended upon her entirely. Yet all she had ever wanted was a husband and children, and time was passing. She was already twenty-three. Opal had married at eighteen.

Ben Derwent came in from the stables, washed his hands at the sink and sat to the table.

'You look well, Dad,' Opal said.

He looked much less tired than Mary, but it was she who bore the double burden, that of deputy wife and of daughter. In the five years since his wife's death her father's duties had not changed. Opal knew that she could never have been as unselfish as Mary, she would have had to get out long ago, found her father a housekeeper. But Mary was not like that.

They ate supper; lamb from the farm, salad from

Mary's garden, freshly-baked bread. After supper Opal wanted to leave at once but the two men were immersed in conversation.

'It's gone ten, David,' she reminded him.

She could not think what he could find to talk about with her father, though it was part of David's charm that he could get on well with anyone. Even with Edgar, if Edgar would only let him. But she knew that her husband – though he never said so – hated David Hessle.

She went upstairs to Daniel but he was fast asleep. She kissed him gently, hating to part with him even for a week. She loved him so very much, had such plans for him. At half-past ten David allowed himself to be dragged away. When they left the farm the night was clear and fine, with an early September nip in the air. The wide sky was navy blue, and star-filled. She looked forward to the drive back through the peaceful country-side.

Chapter Six

At first they drove in silence. The moorland road was narrow, not built for motor traffic. It stretched out before them like a silver ribbon, in the light of a moon so brilliant that, in patches here and there, it coaxed a pale lilac colour from the dark heather. Except for a rabbit or two, momentarily transfixed in the headlights, they had the road to themselves. It was as if they were in some magic country on the edge of the world. Would she like to be suspended there for ever? Opal asked herself. She thought not. In spite of having been brought up on a farm she was not at heart a country-woman. She preferred the hum and bustle of the town. She felt more a part of what went on there; the production of fine clothes in the mills, the buying and selling. In no time at all her mind was back in the shop. But with the thought of the shop came the niggling memory of Miss Browning.

'You seem to have made quite an impression on my new assistant,' she said, breaking the silence.

David laughed. 'She's an attractive kid. Lively too, I should think. You've made a good choice there.'

'She's pretty enough,' Opal agreed. 'But immature. She'll need a lot of training. By the way, she seems to have ideas about you! I wonder what put them into her head?'

David did not reply and his silence goaded her into a remark she regretted as soon as it was uttered.

'I would rather' she said 'that you kept off my assistant. She's young and silly. If you're going to turn her head she'll be no use to me.'

David, without answering, stopped the car by the side of the road and turned off the engine.

'What are you doing?' Opal demanded. 'You know we're in a hurry to get back. Edgar will be worried.'

He was looking straight ahead, his strong, beautiful profile etched in the moonlight. She wondered if he knew how attractive he was, and suspected that he did. But when he turned to face her his eyes were hard, his finely-curved lips unsmiling.

'Let's forget Edgar,' he said roughly. 'And Connie.' (She noted in spite of herself that he called her 'Connie') 'Let's forget everyone except you and me.'

'What do you mean?' She had never before seen him in this mood, so remote from his cheerful, well-mannered self. She felt a frisson of fear, tinged with elation.

'You know quite well what I mean. If you don't, you're not the intelligent woman I took you for – though sometimes I wonder if you're not all intelligence and no heart. But that's not true either. The fact that you're jealous – yes I said jealous – of Connie Browning shows that somewhere under that efficient exterior there is actually feeling.'

'What are you trying to say?' Opal asked.

'I'm trying to say – I *am* saying – that it's you I'm head over heels for. I think I have been ever since the first day I walked into Madame Dora's with my uncle. And now at long last I think you might just care a bit about me. So will you admit it?'

Was it true, what he said? she wondered suddenly. If not, why did his words not surprise her? She was fond of him, there was no doubt of that. She enjoyed his company, looked forward to his visits, missed him if he didn't come. There was a warmth in David, had been from the beginning, that was lacking in the rest of her life, especially in her marriage. There was none, any longer, in Edgar, nor did he want any from her. Whatever she offered, Edgar refused. She realized, then, that she would have liked to have been in love with David. And that even though she was not, she would like to throw discretion to the winds, to take whatever he offered and be thankful for it. But it was impossible.

'I'm married,' she said flatly. 'I'm a married woman with a child.' She was not sure whether she was speaking to David or reminding herself.

'I'm talking about your feelings, not your circumstances,' David said. 'Don't pretend to me that your marriage means a row of pins to you. I've seen you with Edgar, watched you together.'

She turned her head away from his searching look. Was it so plain to the world, the failure of her marriage? Did her hunger for physical satisfaction, which was by now almost entirely denied her, show in her face? Tears came into her eyes and she raised a hand to brush them away. David turned her face to his. His touch was gentle, his eyes compassionate.

'Don't worry,' he assured her. 'It doesn't show. Except to me because I care. Oh Opal, I want to give you so much!'

His arms went around her and his mouth sought hers. She did not resist; she had no desire to do so. In that awkward embrace, in the front of the little car, the longings of weeks and months, years even, rose up in her – though whether they were for David himself or for what Edgar would not, or could not, give her, she didn't know. Nor did it matter. His strong yet gentle fingers caressed her breasts. Wild delights and desires swept through her body. She knew that not far from here was the point of no return.

'Stop!' she cried. 'Stop! It's impossible!'

He held her more tightly, stopping her words with kisses, his hand now caressing her thigh. She felt the hard urgency in his body and the desire equally in her own. Then she jerked her head away from his and twisted and turned in his arms, fighting to free herself.

'We can't David! We can't'

He let her go, and for a moment looked at her as though he did not know where he was, who she was. His face was full of anger.

'We can,' he said. 'I love you. You love me. Don't deny it because I shan't believe you. I felt it in you just now. You can't go back on that. Your marriage doesn't mean anything, you know that. Leave Edgar and come to me. It's as simple as that.'

She looked at him in astonishment.

'You can't be serious, David.'

'I am serious.'

'And what about Daniel?'

'I'll care for Daniel. Edgar can see him whenever he wants to. He'd never be denied that. And I'll care for Daniel as I care for you. He won't suffer, I promise you.'

'And the shop?' Opal asked. 'Oh David, who will patronize a woman who has left her husband, gone to live with another man? Even if I was divorced, and we married, it would never do.'

She was surprised by the astonishment on his face. Surely be understood that?

'The shop?' he said. 'You don't have to bother about the shop. I can support you. I can give you a good life. The kind of life you deserve. Come to me, Opal!'

He took her hands in his, gently now, and in the silence which followed his words, in the pause while he waited for her answer, she could feel his body trembling.

'I can't,' she said at last.

'Why can't you? Why not?'

'I don't love you, David.'

'I don't believe you.'

'And if I did there would still be Daniel.'

It was the truth, she told herself, but in her heart she knew that it was not the whole truth. The truth included Daniel, it included her hopes and plans for the future; it included Edgar, though she was not sure why.

'You don't fool me,' David said slowly. The hardness of his voice stabbed her. 'You're using Daniel. I think you would use anyone to get what you wanted. It's the business, isn't it? You can't give it up. You can't relinquish the power.'

'It has nothing to do with power . . .'

'Oh yes it has. I know you better than you know yourself.'

Right now, she thought, that could be true. In the conflict inside her she hardly recognized herself.

'David, I swear to you . . .'

'Don't,' he said roughly. 'Don't, because you'd be lying. You can't stifle your ambition, can you? You have to be the one with power. Well, long may it serve you!'

'I recognize that I'm ambitious,' Opal said quietly. 'I can't help that. I can't change it.'

He turned on the engine, put the car into gear. 'It's the same old story,' he said bitterly. '*You* can't change, but others must – to fit in with you.'

'Being ambitious doesn't make for an easy life for a woman,' Opal defended herself. 'But right now I'm just desperately sorry and I wish I could comfort you.'

'Well, don't let that worry you,' David retorted. 'I promise you I won't lack for comfort!'

He pressed his foot hard on the accelerator and the car leapt forward, racing along the moorland road. The moon was covered by clouds now, and the roads and moor were a sheet of blackness pierced only by the headlights from the car. Opal put a hand on David's arm.

'Please slow down, David!'

He seemed not to hear her. She sat beside him in terrified silence until – and it seemed a lifetime later – he stopped the car at her door.

Then he said, 'I'm not sure that I can stop loving you, Opal. But the next move, if there's to be one, is yours. And don't expect me to wait for ever, or to behave like a saint while I'm waiting. It's not in me.'

When he had driven away she let herself in through the shop entrance, locked the door behind her and dragged herself wearily upstairs. She was so tired.

As she expected, Edgar was waiting up for her. He had, unusually for him, been drinking. There were several empty beer bottles around the room and the small bottle of brandy which she kept for emergencies was on the table, half empty.

'So you decided to come home?' He spoke with slow, deliberate articulation. 'You actually remembered you had a husband?'

'How could I forget?' Opal said wearily. She was

drained of emotion. All she wanted was to be on her own and to sleep.

'Easily enough I daresay. Do you know what time it is? Do you know it's after midnight?'

'We were late leaving,' Opal said shortly. 'Dad kept us talking.'

'I expect that wasn't all that kept you. I'm sure your fancy man wasn't averse to lingering!'

'You're drunk,' Opal said. 'Otherwise you wouldn't talk like that.'

'Yes I'm drunk' Edgar said. 'Why not? What else is there? A sod of a job. A bitch of a wife who doesn't give a damn!'

She felt his words like a slap on the face. They were undeserved. In the last half hour the thought of Edgar had been strong in her mind.

'For God's sake stop it,' she flared. She hated it when he was in a maudlin, self-pitying mood. 'If you don't like it here why don't you get out? Nothing I do suits you. You're no support to me at all. What do *you* ever give *me*?'

She felt weak now; in need of a man's strength, a man's arms about her, not in passion or sexual love but in comfort and security.

'I give you all I've got' Edgar said. 'It's not enough for you. You don't want me or what I can give. You haven't for years.'

'That's not true and you know it,' she said. 'You're the one who holds back. But I repeat, if you're so unhappy why don't you just go? Ours isn't a proper marriage any longer. Perhaps we'd be better apart. Go and live with your mother for a while.'

'You'd like that wouldn't you?' he shouted. 'Me leaving the field clear. Well, there's no way it's going to happen. There's no way I'm leaving Daniel – though God knows I'm not much use to him either!'

He knew too – it was more clear to him because he was slightly drunk – that as long as he lived he could not leave Opal. Though sometimes he almost hated her, he could not envisage life without her.

'I'm very tired,' Opal said. 'I'm going to bed.'

But upstairs she went into Daniel's room. There was no way she could bear to be near Edgar tonight. She was unutterably weary, tired of everything and everybody. Something must change soon. It must, it must.

At five minutes past one on the following Wednesday Opal locked the shop door after Miss Browning and went upstairs to put on her hat and coat. From time to time on a Wednesday afternoon she took the tram into the centre of Leasfield to look at the shops. Leasfield's early closing day was Thursday. It was not so much that she wanted to buy anything, more that she wanted to see what other people were buying. Leasfield was in advance of its neighbours in fashion and by carefully studying the shops there she could often judge what to buy for her own. Sometimes she would buy items in the Leasfield sales and sell them at full price at her own shop. And today, she thought, seeing her pale face in the mirror as she adjusted her hat, the expedition might cheer her up.

She had not seen David since he had left her at the door on Friday night. He was due tomorrow and she both dreaded and looked forward to his visit. By Saturday morning Edgar had seemed his usual self; quiet – but then he was always quiet so it was difficult to judge. They had carried on their normal, sparse conversations as though Friday night had not happened. But she had not returned to his bed and he had not commented on the fact. It was a state of affairs that, in the two-bedroomed flat, could only last until Daniel returned. After that she supposed they would resume their usual condition – miles apart in the same bed.

She took the tram to Leasfield, alighting in the centre of the town, from whence it was no more than a five-minute walk to Miller's fashion store, her venue for the afternoon. As always, she walked slowly and carefully around each department, noting everything of interest. An evening dress in lace, with insets of chiffon in the skirt, caught her eye. The saleswoman moved in on her as she studied it.

'It's the very latest from Paris, Madame,' she said. 'We had it copied. You see the new hemline, just dipping a little at the back?'

'I suppose it had to come,' Opal said. 'Skirts have gone about as high as they can. It's really quite pretty.'

She moved on. She had no room on her premises to stock dresses. It would mean fitting-rooms too. But what she had been wondering about was cosmetics. Most women now had abandoned the paper powder leaves in favour of real face powder, kept in a pretty box with a swansdown puff. Many used lipstick, discreetly applied. Rouge she was not sure about for her class of trade; but why not, if a woman wanted it?

There were several items on the toiletries counter she thought she might be able to sell: lavender water, eau-de-cologne, talcum powder – as well as make-up and the pretty containers to keep it in. Altogether, it need take up no more than a couple of drawers and a shelf or two. She must find out the best wholesaler for such goods.

She climbed the stairs to the balcony tearoom on the next floor, choosing a table with a good view of what went on below. The waitress came at once.

'I'd like a pot of china tea and some buttered toast,' Opal said.

While she waited to be served she watched a constant, if steady, stream of customers at the toiletries counter. They took their time about their purchases but seldom left without buying.

'I've been watching the toiletry counter,' Opal said when the waitress brought her tea. 'Is it always so busy?'

'I don't get much time to watch' the waitress said. 'I suppose it is. They sell what we all want, don't they? Something to make us feel a bit better.'

'That's true,' Opal agreed.

She wished she was near enough to see exactly what the customers chose. She was sure the enterprise would be a good one for her and she wondered why she had not thought of it sooner. She hoped she was not getting slack. She tipped the waitress, paid her bill at the cash desk, and left.

No daylight had penetrated into the store and she had forgotten how bright the day was outside. Perhaps, rather than taking the tram all the way, she would walk the first mile or two. She enjoyed walking and did it too seldom. She had walked about a mile when she saw the building. She could not imagine why she had never seen it before until she realized that the buildings around it had been pulled down, thus rendering the one which remained more conspicuous.

It was three storeys high, solidly fashioned in an ornate, Victorian style with a small, square tower rising from the roof above the main entrance. Along the front, at ground level, were eight, large plate glass windows. It must surely, once, have been a retail store? For what other purpose than to display goods would one need such large windows? Now, though, they were fitted with grimy venetian blinds, as if the building might have been more recently used as a warehouse. The paintwork was shabby and peeling but, as far as she could see, the woodwork and the stone were sound. Surely this building was not to be demolished with the rest?

She walked along the front, trying without success to peer in through the blinds. When she reached the centre door she found a notice fixed behind the glass. 'Enquiries to Davies and King, Estate Agents, Hart Lane, Leasfield.' She knew at once, without the slightest shadow of doubt, without considering anything for or against, that she must see them. She did not even wish to walk around to view the rest of the building from the outside. Only let her get to Davies and King and the rest could come later. Directed by a passer by, she found them easily enough.

'If you'll tell me what it's about,' the clerk in the front office said, 'I'll find out if our Mr King can see you.' He returned two minutes later. 'Luckily,' he said, 'Mr King is available. Please come this way.'

'Please tell me, Mr King,' Opal said without preliminaries 'Was it originally built as a retail store?'

'How observant of you,' Mr King said pleasantly. 'That is exactly what it was. But some years ago now. I understand – it was before I came to the neighbourhood – that it was a nice store, but a little old-fashioned. Didn't move with the times. And then it's just a little too far out of town for a retail business. Almost a mile, you see. They couldn't make it pay.'

'And what is it now?' Opal asked. 'Or what was it before it was empty? It is empty, isn't it?'

'Oh quite. Except of course that most of the shop counters and suchlike are left. No-one ever bothered to move them. It's been such as a warehouse, on and off, for a few years now. All clean stuff, of course. Garments mostly. The last tenants moved out to smaller, more modern premises, when their lease ran out.'

'I notice that some of the buildings around have been pulled down,' Opal said. 'Is that likely to happen to this one?'

'Oh no,' Mr King said. 'I don't think there's any question of that. It was small, back-to-back houses which were pulled down. No loss to anyone. The tenants have been moved into Council houses with baths and gardens and that sort of thing.'

'And what would be the rent of the place?' Opal asked.

'Well now, that depends on how much space you would require,' Mr King said. 'If you would ask your husband to call in and discuss what he has in mind, we could perhaps put a figure on it.'

'My husband isn't the interested party,' Opal said coldly. 'I am. I'd like a price for the whole building, though it's possible that at first I'd only be able to rent one or two floors. Even so, I wouldn't take any of it without an option on the whole.'

She heard the words, like an echo, as she spoke them, but it seemed impossible that they were issuing from her mouth. Had she taken leave of her senses?

Mr King leaned back in his chair, surveying this small, neat woman, with clear bright eyes which met his without blinking.

'I see,' he said doubtfully.

Poor man, he doesn't see at all, Opal thought.

'I can't imagine the rent would be high,' she said. 'The place looks very run down. And naturally I'd like to see the inside. In fact, now, if that would be convenient. I have business committments which prevent me coming to Leasfield often.'

'Perhaps you would tell me what you propose to use the premises *for*?' Mr King said. 'My clients would naturally want to know that.'

'Of course,' Opal said. 'I propose to open a retail store.'

'A *store*? But as I've just told you, my dear lady . . .'

'A fashion store. Ladies' and children's clothing. Millinery, materials, gloves, haberdashery, cosmetics, hosiery and footwear. To start with, that is. I would hope to diversify later.'

'But how . . . ?'

'Leave the how to me, Mr King,' Opal said with more conviction than she felt. 'All I want from you right now is to see over the premises and have a figure for the rent. Of course any structural defects – worn stairs, plumbing and the like – would have to be made good by the owners before I could consider it. But I'm sure that would apply to any tenant. Shall we go?'

Mr King, as if mesmerized, called to his assistant for the keys.

'Could we open a few blinds?' Opal asked. 'It's all rather dark.'

Mr King, who without quite knowing how it had come about realized that he had surrendered his will to this commanding young lady, did as he was asked. Light flooded in.

'That's better,' Opal said. 'Oh dear, it *is* a dirty mess, isn't it? And everything such dark paint. I'd have a great deal to do on this floor before I could even attempt to use it.'

But she had noted that the paint, though grimy, was not flaking, and that the counters which had been left behind would be quite adequate when well polished. There were also plenty of drawers. Opening one or two, she found that they ran smoothly. No damp, she thought.

The staircase which ran through the centre of the building to the two remaining floors was as solid as a rock, though the carpet which covered it was worn, and would have to be thrown out. But no matter. Good oak treads, which these were, were quite adequate. On the first floor the windows were smaller, but more in number, and without blinds, so that everything seemed brighter. As on the ground floor, there were counters and other fittings, and a certain amount of carpet, which she thought might clean up well. This would be the floor for gowns, coats, millinery. One day, perhaps she would sell furs.

'Now Mr King, what about the second floor?'

'That has never been fully developed,' Mr King said, leading the way. 'A certain number of offices and, of course, stock rooms.'

'I see,' Opal said. 'Yes, it is rather makeshift, isn't it?' But she saw no sense of giving overmuch space to offices. Offices were non-productive. If one was to make a business pay, then every foot of space must be calculated to show a profit, and those which could not must be kept to a minimum.

'What's this small staircase here?' she asked.

'That leads to the tower room. A folly, I think you

could call it. Typically Victorian. It leads nowhere and has no especial use.'

It could be my private office, Opal thought.

When they had seen over every inch of the building she demanded that they start again at the beginning, and only when everything had been seen twice did she declare herself satisfied.

'But when I say "satisfied",' she amended, 'I mean that I would be provided that the owner would make the repairs which you have noted down, and that the rent is reasonable. The figure you suggested is undoubtedly too high. Not many people would be interested in such a property, would they? Especially surrounded by derelict land.'

She hoped he would not call her bluff on that one, for the spare land she saw as a real asset. When the time came she would buy it, build on it, expand even further.

'Well, my dear Mrs Carson, *you* are interested for one,' Mr King said smoothly.

'And how many others?' Opal asked. 'Anyway, let me know within the week. You have my telephone number. And in the meantime, thank you for showing me over.'

She left him, and walked to the tram stop. To take a tram was to return to the real world after the fairy-tale world she had inhabited for the last hour. But the real world, the world of rents and rates, of goods and wages – in short, of money – was what she now had to contend with.

She needed David's help. Not only his practical help, though she had marked out in her mind what he could do for her in that area, but his interest as a friend, his opinion as a businessman, his reassurance that she was doing the right thing. How much had she forfeited his friendship since the events of Friday night? She could only put it to the test. At seven o'clock in the evening she telephoned him.

'He's out,' his sister said. 'He came in and went out again. Ther's no telling when he'll be back.'

'I see. Well, when he does come in, will you ask him to telephone me? No matter how late.'

Edgar was also out, which suited her. She had no intention of telling him anything until her plans were more settled. She was certain of his disapproval. When he came in and saw her, sitting at the table, head bent over columns of figures, it was nothing new to him.

'I suppose you had a profitable afternoon in Leasfield?' he said.

'I believe so,' Opal said. 'I think it will turn out to be quite profitable.'

At midnight she decided that David was not going to telephone. She went to bed but, lying in Daniel's narrow bed, found no sleep until it was almost time to get up again. At half-past seven in the morning she went down into the shop to telephone.

'David! I expected to hear from you last night,' she said. 'Can you come over this morning? It's important.'

'It must be for you to ring me at this hour,' he replied. 'What's it about? Is anything wrong?'

'Nothing. I can't tell you about it on the telephone.'

'Very well,' he promised. 'I'll make you my first call.'

Miss Browning arrived at half-past eight, pale and yawning.

'You look half asleep, Miss Browning,' Opal remarked.

'I am,' Connie Browning said. 'Had a late night. Went to the pictures and out to supper afterwards. My Ma didn't half create a fuss when I got home after midnight!'

Her smile, as her wide blue eyes met the direct look from Opal's dark ones, was one of triumph. It was a pity it would be unwise to tell Madam just who had kept her out so late. She'd have liked to have had the pleasure. Bosses were all the same; thought they could rule your life twenty-four hours a day. Well, she was definitely one up now! Come to think of it, Madam looked a bit odd this morning. Sort of excited. Surely *she* couldn't have been living it up?

'Well it's too bad you don't feel at your best,' Opal said briskly. 'I've decided to start stocktaking today. So will you please begin by measuring all the ribbons, then count the hosiery and gloves. Write down the quantities and sizes and put the price per yard or per pair at the side. I will do the extensions.'

The bold look her assistant had given her had not gone unnoticed. It taunted her, as it was meant to; but no matter how strong her suspicions were, and she felt quite sure that the girl had been out with David, there was little she could do about it. She did not care to risk jeopardizing her own friendship with David any further. She was still unsure how matters stood between them. When he arrived, however, an hour later, his manner towards her seemed the same as always. He gave Miss Browning no more than his usual polite greeting, but this did not prevent her from looking like a cat which had found a rich source of cream.

Little fool, Opal thought. She's quite transparent. He won't like that. But she had more on her mind this morning than David's flirtation.

'Will you come into the office?' she said to him.

The second she had closed the door she began to tell him about the empty store, and almost as quickly, he stopped her.

'Wait a minute! Opal, there's no way you can do this! Have you taken leave of your senses?'

'Don't!' she cried. 'Don't say that yet. I asked you to come this morning because I wanted to tell you about it before anyone else. You are, I hope, still my friend? In spite of everything?'

'Yes,' he replied. 'In spite of everything. Perhaps against my better judgement. Do you want to talk about that?'

'No,' she admitted. 'Not now. I just wanted to know. David, will you do something for me? And not form any opinions until you've done it? Keep an open mind?'

'What is it you want?'

'It's not difficult. All I want is for you to go into Leasfield and look at the place. Not with me. In fact, you're not to let on that you know me. This is what I want you to do. Now listen.'

'I still think you're mad,' he said when she had finished.

'But you'll do it for me? And you'll go today?'

'Very well.'

'And you'll come back right away and tell me what happened?'

It was late afternoon when he returned.

'What did you think?' she asked eagerly. 'Tell me at once!'

'Well, there's one thing sure,' he said. 'I didn't have to put on an act for the benefit of the estate agent. It's hopeless! Oh, I agree the place is basically sound. But it's far too big, even if you only opened a floor at a time. How would you stock it? How would you manage for staff? You can't possibly consider it, Opal!'

'That's not a decision you have to make,' Opal said quietly. She did not feel the slightest bit discouraged by his words. 'But thank you, David, for doing as I asked. With you turning it down so flatly they might think seriously about my offer. What a pity I can't get half-a-dozen people to do the same thing!'

'I was pretty forthright,' David said. 'I told them I wouldn't touch it with a bargepole – which is the truth – and that I couldn't imagine anyone who would!'

'So I have every hope that they'll accept my offer,' Opal said. 'And if they do, then I shall go ahead and try to raise the money.'

'But *how*?' David asked. 'How can you *possibly*?'

'Well not through you for a start, since you don't have faith in me!'

'Of course I have faith in you! If you'd suggested taking a bigger shop – even twice the size of the one you have – I'd have said go ahead and good luck to you. But a department store! In any case, I haven't any money. All my money is in my warehouse stock.'

'I know,' Opal said. 'But if you do want to help me there is one way you can. Would you let me have long credit on your lines? I've always paid you promptly. Would you trust me a bit further if I managed to raise the money for rent and wages and so on? And could you give me introductions to other wholesalers who might do the same? Or vouch for me if I give your name as reference?'

'I'll do whatever's in my power to help,' David said. 'You know that.'

He felt quite safe in his promise. It would never come to fulfilment. There was no possible way that Opal could raise the money.

Chapter Seven

It was the first time, Opal reflected, that she had ever set eyes on a bank manager. They were creatures beyond her ken and until now her affairs had been so simple as never to need one. Mr Harper was not how she had pictured him on her way to the bank this Friday morning – tall, well-made, venerably greying, avuncular. He was a thin, hungry-looking man, the top of whose head, as Opal noted while he bent over the accounts she had given him, was bald except for a few wispy, black hairs.

'There's no doubt that you've got a good little business here,' he said, looking up. 'And you've built it up in a surprisingly short time. I commend you on your business acumen!'

'Then you'll back me?' Opal said.

He leaned back in his chair, clasping his hands together as if about to lead in prayer, and smiled a slow, gentle smile.

'Alas, my dear Mrs Carson, it's not quite so simple!'

'Why not?' Opal asked. 'You've seen my accounts, verified by the accountant. You've heard my proposals, to which I've given a great deal of thought. It's not a new idea to me, Mr Harper; not something thought up on the spur of the moment. It's something I've dreamed of for a long time. But not only dreamed. I've planned, too.'

'And most interesting your plans *are*,' Mr Harper

conceded. 'Though some of them, I must say, are a little . . .' He struggled for a word. '. . . Well, shall we say *innovative*? Yes, innovative.' Having found the word, he rolled it off his tongue with enjoyment.

'They're all feasible,' Opal assured him.

'But of course there's more to it than that . . .'

'Such as?'

'Well, in the first place I think what you propose would be an unwise move on your part. You're doing very nicely now, Mrs Carson. Why not build on what you've got? It doesn't do to be over-ambitious, you know. A young lady like yourself. A prosperous little business such as you have, easy to handle, not many staff, is much more suitable for the fair sex.'

'Would my ambition be more agreeable if I were a young man?' Opal asked swiftly.

'Now you're putting words into my mouth?' Mr Harper said pleasantly. 'But, naturally, ambition is more to be expected, and indeed more necessary, in a man. Though even a man might hesitate to take on what you have in mind. I suspect your husband would agree with me there.'

'Oh I'm sure he would,' Opal answered. 'But as I've already told you, my husband wouldn't be involved. I would be running the business myself.' And that remark will *not* have helped me, she thought. 'But do you mean you have a different policy towards a *man* who wants a loan?'

'Well . . .'

'Why?'

'It stands to reason, dear lady. Here you are, a young married woman.' He gave her a look which told her she was also attractive in his eyes. 'You have one child. Who is to say – and I hope you will forgive me for

129

being so plain spoken – that you will not be blessed with more children? And what would happen to your business then?'

He spoke with calm confidence, almost with benevolence, as one who has made an unassailable point. Opal's reply was equally confident.

'It would carry on. Being a mother, though I admit there are certain practical matters I would have to sort out, would not stop me any more than being a father would stop a man.'

'More easily said than done,' Mr Harper said. 'Now if you were a widow . . .'

I would be a widow first and a woman second, Opal thought. And I would suddenly be capable of running a business. But she did not say it out loud. Nor did she consider herself as unlikely as any widow to have another child. It was clear, in spite of the polite smile which had not for one moment deserted him, that she had antagonized this man. Well, he antagonized her. He was a patronizing idiot.

'And there is another matter, equally if not more important,' he continued. 'You see, you have no collateral to offer me. The Bank must have security, you know. We owe it to our shareholders.'

'But I've shown you my trading figures,' Opal protested. 'You've seen what I 've done in the time I've had Madame Dora's. Doesn't that count?'

'But surely, Mrs Carson, if you were to move into something bigger, Madame Dora's would have to go? If you failed in your new venture the bank would have nothing at all to realize on!'

Opal rose to her feet. Anger flooded through her so that she could have beaten her fists against this man, wiped the everlasting smile from his face. She was furious with herself, too, that she could not hold back the tears which filled her eyes. It was exactly what he would expect of her. But she managed to keep her voice steady.

'So that's your last word?'

'I'm afraid so, Mrs Carson. Though of course if by some means you *were* to be successful . . .' The tone of his voice said that the possibility was as remote as the farthest star from the earth. 'If at any time you wanted to expand a little, don't hesitate to consult us. We're always ready to listen!'

He held the door open for her, watching her as she marched out of the bank into the street. A pretty little thing. Lively. Quite clever too. He must ask his wife if she ever patronized Madame Dora's.

Opal walked quickly, looking neither to right nor left. She admitted to herself that, angry though he had made her, she was not entirely surprised by the bank manager's attitude. Banking was a man's world. Well, no matter. She was not beaten yet, not by a long chalk.

The shop was empty of customers when she returned, but evidence that there had been some lay strewn around in the form of gloves, hosiery, scarves. She bit back the sharp reprimand which rose to her lips as she saw Miss Browning standing idle amid the disorder. It would be necessary to absent herself from the shop, to leave it in Miss Browning's hands, on more than one occasion in the near future. In the last few days Opal had become curiously unsure of her assistant's temperament. That she was capable of taking charge of the shop for short periods Opal didn't doubt. But there was a boldness about the girl which suggested that she would not be driven.

'You've been busy I see,' Opal said, keeping her tone level.

'Nothing I couldn't handle,' Miss Browning said.

'I'm glad about that. It so happens that over the next few days I might have to leave you in charge for the odd hour or two now and then. I have some business to attend to. Shall you be able to manage?'

'I dare say' Miss Browning answered.

She really must find out what these mysterious absences were about. But if she was persuasive, and she knew exactly how to be persuasive, David Hessle would tell her. He was sure to know because he and Madam were as thick as thieves. Well, perhaps no longer as thick as thieves since she was sure Madam hadn't an idea what he was up to. You'd be out on your ear otherwise, Connie Browning, she told herself. As a matter of fact she quite liked being left on her own. She got to serve the customers, which she enjoyed, and didn't do so often when her employer was around. Also, she could use the telephone when she felt like it, even though David had told her not to 'phone him.

'That's good,' Opal said. 'And now perhaps we should tidy things away while we have the chance.'

By which she means *I* should do it, Miss Browning thought. Correctly.

'It all sounded so mysterious on the telephone,' Queenie said, seating herself, drawing off her gloves. 'And so unlike you to summon one! An important matter to discuss, you said. Oh, Opal, I hope there's nothing wrong! It couldn't be anything to do with Edgar, could it? I mean . . .' She hesitated. 'I mean . . . you and Edgar?'

132

'Why of course not,' Opal said. Her sister-in-law was more perceptive than she seemed. 'It's got nothing to do with Edgar. Not in the way I think you mean. There's nothing wrong. It's just that I have something of importance to tell you . . .'

'Opal, you're not – you're not *expecting*. Oh, Opal!'

'Of course not, Queenie dear! I've told you before, I've got my little Daniel and I love him dearly – but I've never wanted a large family. I leave that to natural-born mothers like you.'

'Then whatever can it be?' Queenie asked.

If only you would give me the chance to tell you, Opal thought. But one could not rush Queenie. In any case she was far too fond of her to be really impatient.

'I'm about to tell you,' Opal said. 'And if what I have in mind comes off, then it will be the best thing that's happened to me, and to Edgar and Daniel too. But I don't think I can do it at all without your help.'

She sat down beside Queenie and told her what she had in mind. She told it, not in outline as she had done to Mr Harper, but in detail; in colourful scenes which she could so easily picture. And as she talked and Queenie listened, Opal felt the store come alive, as vividly as if she were standing in it, surrounded by her merchandise, thronged by customers. And she thought that if she could not have it she would die of disappointment.

'So you see why I need the money,' she concluded. 'Quite a lot, I'm afraid. Needless to say, however generous you are – and I know you *are* generous – I couldn't do it all on a loan from you. It's my intention to approach, also, an old and very rich customer. She's already agreed to see me.'

'Do I know her?' Queenie asked.

'I don't think so. And I'd rather not tell you who she is without her permission. I thought that if she would act as guarantor for the rent, lighting and so on, and you would lend me the money to start the alterations – which I shall keep to a minimum – and to help with stock – then I could manage the wages out of the profit I made and with what I get for this place. To start with, that is.'

'I must admit, you seem to have it all worked out,' Queenie said. But from the tone of her voice it was impossible, Opal thought anxiously, to tell what she really thought about it.

'Oh I have,' she said. 'I really have. And I'm sure I can do it, only given the chance. You'd get your money back, every penny and with interest. How quickly will depend on how quickly the business takes off. I have to be frank with you and say that I would need to give priority to paying wages and buying stock. It might be five years before you were paid. But you would be paid, I promise you! Oh, Queenie, what do you think? Please put me out of my misery and tell me what you think!'

'Opal dear, you mustn't rush me,' Queenie said gently. 'It's all so new to me. I have to take it in. Could we possibly have a cup of tea, do you think?'

Opal jumped to her feet.

'Of course! How remiss of me, Queenie. I'll put the kettle on at once.'

In the kitchen she set about making the tea. Her hands trembled as she laid the tray, so that she thought she would drop a cup or spill the sugar. When she carried the tray into the living-room her hands shook so much that it was difficult to pour.

'Just look at me!' she said. 'I'm so nervous. But then I'm not used to asking for loans, not even of family!'

She remembered, suddenly, the winter Saturday, all that time ago it seemed now, when she had asked her mother for the loan of five pounds and had been given ten. Was that a good omen?

'Well,' Queenie said thoughtfully, sipping her tea, 'it's no secret that my father left me a lot of money. Anyone who reads the Leasfield Argus knows that. And Mark is doing well in the business, so we never touch my money. Of course, even though the money is my own to do with as I wish, and Mark never questions what I spend, I shall have to consult him. I shall show him your figures and I daresay he'll have some questions to ask. But apart from that . . .' She put down her teacup and stretched out her hand to take Opal's.

'Yes, Opal dear, I'm agreeable to lending you the money!'

For a moment Opal stared at her. She couldn't believe it! It was her dream, and it was beginning to come true! Then she fell to her knees and buried her face in Queenie's lap, not trying on this occasion to keep back the tears.

'Oh Queenie,' she said at last, 'there's just no way I can thank you!'

'I'm your family' Queenie said. 'Why shouldn't I be the first to help? And I remember how much my father thought of you. He said you were a very clever woman. I'm sure he'd have approved of my decision, just as I'm sure Mark will.' She laughed. 'Anyway, if half you say comes true you'll be an enormous success and I'll have done myself a good turn!'

'Please don't go on about it,' Opal begged. Edgar had arrived home shortly after Queenie's departure and she had decided it was now time to tell him what was afoot.

'Mary will he here with Daniel any minute and I don't want it mentioned then. It's Daniel I'm thinking about. He starts his new school on Tuesday and I don't want him to have anything on his mind other than that. Anyway, nothing is settled. Time enough to let everyone know when, and if, it is.'

'I suppose I'm lucky you bothered to tell me,' Edgar complained. 'Perhaps you wouldn't have if you'd not been afraid Queenie or Mark might spill the beans!'

'Don't be silly,' Opal said. 'You're my husband. I'd want to tell you. In any case how could I do anything without your knowing?'

'Easily! You managed to find the property, didn't you? See the bank manager, fix a loan with Queenie and get it approved by Mark, all without me knowing a thing!'

'It all happened so quickly,' Opal protested. 'Anyway, I knew you wouldn't approve. I wanted to take one or two steps first. If they'd all come to nothing, well, that would have been that. Please let's not quarrel. Edgar. Daniel will soon be back and you know how it upsets him when we quarrel.'

'He's going to get a good deal more upset when he learns about this. Have you actually given a single thought to me and Daniel? Do you care in the slightest what it's going to do to us? When you have your precious store, where do I fit in?'

'I'm glad you say "when" and not "if",' Opal said dryly. 'It shows you have faith in my getting it.'

'Oh I'll back you to do that,' Edgar said. 'I'll back you to get anything you set your mind on, no matter what it does to anyone else.'

'That's unfair,' Opal flared. 'I think about Daniel a very great deal, and you know it! Who is sending him to a good school, who is making sure he'll get the best possible education? And what I'm proposing now will ensure a good future for him. One day, when he's ready, it will all be there, waiting for him. As for you, it can do you nothing but good. When I get the business off the ground you can give up that job you hate so much and come in with me. I'd like that, Edgar, I really would. There's bound to be something to suit you.'

'Thank you,' Edgar said. 'I suppose it doesn't occur to you that I might not want that? I hate my job all right but it's my last bit of independence. Everything else is yours.'

Opal sighed. When he was in this kind of mood, and it happened more and more often, there was no pleasing him. All she wanted for herself and Edgar was for them to live in some degree of harmony. She had given up the high hopes of marriage she had started out with. She supposed she might even, in the end, lose her desire for physical love, though her encounter with David had shown her that it was still there in strength, just below the surface. But she would settle now for tranquillity, and just a little warmth. Everyone needed that. She tried hard, but Edgar never responded.

'Perhaps you'll find that Daniel doesn't want the future you've so carefully mapped out for him,' Edgar said bitterly. 'Perhaps he'll have ideas of his own. You won't like that, will you? You like to be the one with the ideas. And another thing, when you've sold Madame Dora's and we have to leave here, where are we going to live? Have you thought of that?'

'Of course I have. I've thought of everything. We'll find somewhere, you'll see!'

It was true that she had thought of it but it had not

loomed large in her mind. There had been – still were – so many other things to consider. If Miss Taylor didn't turn up trumps, then where else could she turn? But if Miss Taylor *did* agree to give her backing then there were a thousand new problems, large and small, to be settled. A place to live was just one of them. If she had only herself to think of a camp bed anywhere in the store would do for her. But Daniel, and, she supposed, Edgar, were dependent on her.

The downstairs door banged and Daniel bounded up the stairs as fast as his short legs would carry him. Mary followed close behind. He flung himself at Opal and she knelt on the floor and held him close.

'Oh, it's so good to have you back!' she cried. 'I'm not sure that I shall ever let you go away from me again, even to Aunt Mary!'

At last she let him go and he turned to his father. Edgar scooped him up in his arms and lifted him high in the air, high enough to touch the ceiling.

'You've put on weight,' he said happily. 'You weigh a ton, lad!'

'He's eaten well,' Mary admitted. 'Everything that was put before him. I can't think why you said he was finicky about his food, Opal.'

'I expect he plays me up,' Opal said indulgently. 'I must say, he does look well.'

'Grandpa taught me to milk Daisy,' Daniel said. 'And I helped to pick the apples. I've made you a picture of the apple picking, Mother. And one for you, Dad, about the sheep. Grandpa says I can go again in the Easter holidays when they've got the new lambs. Can I go, Mother?'

'Hey! You've only just got home,' Opal said. 'It's a

long time to next Easter. There's Christmas to come first.'

'So you'd like to be a farmer, would you?' Edgar asked.

Daniel looked at his father in surprise.

'Oh no! I'm going to be an artist. But I might be an artist and live on a farm. That would be a good idea!'

Edgar, catching Opal's eye, raised his eyebrow. With Daniel's return home he seemed to have recovered his temper. He was usually better when Daniel was around. They both were.

'He's painted scores of pictures,' Mary said. 'I've pinned them up all over the kitchen to remind me of him when he's not there. Oh, Opal, I do envy you being married and having Daniel. If I had your lot in life I'd have nothing left to wish for!'

How unobserving Mary was! She lived in cloud-cuckoo land. But Opal doubted whether she would wish to be the one to wipe that starry-eyed look from her sister's face.

'I enjoyed meeting that nice Mr Hessle,' Mary said. 'Dad liked him too. Shall you bring him again?'

Opal gave her sister a sharp look. Surely Mary couldn't be getting ideas about David? No two people could be less suited to each other. Except – the thought stabbed her – that they were both free. But Mary, so quiet and domesticated, so naïve in her approach to life, could never satisfy a man like David. He was smart, sophisticated, up-to-the-minute. Why, even a chit like Miss Browning would fit him better than Mary. The thought came, uncomfortably, that in some ways Miss Browning and David were two of a pair. Both sharp. But he would never take Miss Browning seriously because she was too common.

When Mary had left it was Daniel's bedtime. It was with great pleasure that Opal bathed him. Mostly, now that he was seven, he did it himself, but occasionally Opal indulged herself and soaped his soft child's body. When he was in bed she sat on the edge of the bed and read to him, though he was capable of doing that for himself too. 'You can have as many stories as you like tonight' she said. 'I'll read until you fall asleep.'

He fell asleep quickly. The week on the farm and the moorland air had done him good, she thought, gazing down at him. He had a healthy colour in his usually pale cheeks. She kissed him gently and left him. Back in the living-room she took a sheet of paper and, sitting at the table, headed it in bold capitals 'THINGS TO BE DONE'.

In the three years since her visit Opal had called upon Miss Taylor many times. Miss Taylor had continued one of her best customers, buying not only hats, but expensive lingerie, gloves, lace-edged handkerchiefs and the like. She had shown an interest in all Opal's ideas for getting the most out of the small business and nowadays would often call in at the shop to see what was new. But today was different. Opal was going to see Miss Taylor; and instead of a box of hats, which she would have borne with confidence, she carried her account books in an attache case.

Should she on this occasion, she wondered, nearing 'The Oaks', present herself at the front door or the back? It was a matter for fine judgement which she was mercifully freed from making since Miss Taylor was in the garden and called out to her.

'Good morning Mrs Carson! I'm just taking a turn around my garden while there are still flowers to see.

A sad, though beautiful time of the year, the autumn. Don't you think so?'

'I suppose that's true,' Opal said. 'Though I've never had a garden to bring it home to me.' She thought of it more as the beginning of a new season for various items of apparel.

'Well, let's go into the house,' Miss Taylor said.

Opal followed her through the front door and into the drawing-room.

'Now,' Miss Taylor said briskly. 'What is it you have to tell me? It all sounded quite mysterious on the telephone.'

She sat upright in her chair while Opal, nervous at first but gaining confidence as Miss Taylor from time to time nodded her understanding, put her case.

'And I've brought my accounts for you to look at,' she said.

Miss Taylor waved them aside.

'I'll look at those later. I haven't any doubt they're all you say or you wouldn't have brought them. There are, however, one or two fundamentally important questions to be asked. For instance, you admit that the building is at the wrong end of the town. Now I'm no businesswoman but it would seem to me that in a case of this sort, position was everything. What do you say to that?'

'I would say that you've put one of the most important points of all,' Opal replied. 'I don't quite agree that position is everything, but it is tremendously important and I've given a great deal of thought to overcoming this particular disadvantage.'

'So what would you do?'

'Well,' Opal said, 'in the first place I would have to make it worthwhile for the customer to come a mile out from the centre of town – which means that my quality must be good, my range wide and my prices keener. I'd need to offer more in every way than the shops in the centre of Leasfield. I would also need to make myself known – customers aren't likely to find me by chance – so I'd need to advertise. I would count money spent on advertising *well* spent. And I have several ideas for bringing customers in. Would you like to hear some of them?'

'I would.'

Opal, for the first time, put into words the notions which had been whirling around in her head since last Wednesday afternoon. It was wonderful to hear them spoken out loud and she was encouraged by the deep, sometimes amused, attention which Miss Taylor gave her.

'Most ingenious,' Miss Taylor said. 'And now another important question for you. Why come to me? Why me particularly? You can be quite frank – indeed you must be.'

Opal hesitated.

'Perhaps' she said 'because the first time I ever came here you treated me like a real person. It wasn't just that you gave me tea, but you asked my opinion on something not to do with trimming a hat.'

'I remember,' Miss Taylor broke in. 'Women's suffrage. Well, we've got the vote now. Let's hope we know how to use it.'

'You've continued to treat me in that way,' Opal said. 'But I'm also asking you because that what I want to do is the kind of thing you might have done yourself, had you been encouraged. Don't think me presumptuous, Miss Taylor, for I don't mean to be – but I think that in some ways you and I are two of a kind.'

The girl was right, Miss Taylor reflected. She had spent her life doing nothing more useful than a few charitable works. She would have liked to have done so much more, and she was sure she had the talent for it. But her parents, perhaps because they had risen so quickly and successfully from trade themselves, had not wanted to see their only child soil her hands with it. How wrong they had been! Why, she might have been running her father's factory now!

'And then' Opal continued 'I came to you because you are a woman. I think a woman is better able to see my point of view.'

'Are those all your reasons?' Miss Taylor asked.

'Not quite. I asked you because I thought you could afford to help me. Because you are rich, and have the money I need.'

Miss Taylor nodded her approval.

'I'm glad you admit that reason. It shows a hard, practical streak, which goodness knows you'll need. And now I have something to ask you. If I were to help you, would you consider taking me as a partner?' Miss Taylor felt herself suddenly fired with enthusiasm. Perhaps it was not too late, after all, to make her mark?

Opal's spirits plummeted. It was not what she had in mind at all. 'Would that be a condition?' she asked.

'Why? Do you dislike the idea?'

'Not for any personal reasons,' Opal said. 'I wouldn't want you to think that. If I had to have a partner I think you would be a good choice. But this is something I want to do on my own. It's important to me.'

'I understand,' Miss Taylor said. She could, she supposed, hold out the partnership as a condition. But would she want to do that?

'But I would consider having you as a sleeping

partner,' Opal said. 'You could be *au fait* with all I did. But . . . I have to say it . . . I would want to keep control. And I would like the option to buy you out in, say, ten years time.'

'Well,' Miss Taylor said. 'I must have a day or two to think things over. It's a big decision. And I would like to see over the premises, though that, I think, I would prefer to do on my own.'

'I would prefer that also,' Opal agreed. 'It would be better still if you didn't mention that you knew me.' She told Miss Taylor about David Hessle's visit on the previous Thursday. 'A similar one from you might work in my favour,' she said.

'Perhaps you might like me to suggest to them that they'd be wise to snap up any offer they receive?' Miss Taylor said with a gleam in her eye. 'And now before you go I think you might like a glass of sherry. I seldom drink it myself but on this occasion I think I shall join you.'

She poured sherry into thin, crystal glasses.

'Where would you live when you'd sold Madame Dora's?' she asked.

'I don't know,' Opal admitted. 'I would have to look for a small house in a suitable position. My son starts school in Leasfield tomorrow.'

'And your husband's work?'

'Is in Milton,' Opal said. 'I dare say he'd manage with the tram. And it's possible that, eventually, he might give up his job and come into the business.'

'Well,' Miss Taylor said, 'I'll be in touch with you quite soon.'

'Mr Hessle called while you were out,' Miss Browning said. 'He said he didn't have time to wait. And of course I couldn't tell him where you were because I didn't know.'

And you would dearly love to, Opal thought, but I'm not going to tell you.

Wouldn't Madame be furious if she knew who he really came to see, Miss Browning thought. Well it might be that she would have to get used to it. The way things were going it couldn't be kept hidden for ever.

Two days later Miss Taylor came into the shop.

'Can we talk privately?' she asked.

'We'll go upstairs,' Opal said. 'Miss Browning, will you take over for a little while, please?'

'I won't waste time,' Miss Taylor said. 'I've thought over everything we discussed and I've been to see the premises, and you'll be pleased to hear that I've decided to help you. I will guarantee the rent, rates, heating and lighting for the first three years. At that point we'll look at the situation again. Mind you, I almost changed my mind when I actually saw the place! There's so much to be done to it. But there again I might be able to give you a little help. You see I have faith in you, Mrs Carson.'

I'm going to faint, Opal thought desperately. I know I'm going to faint! She gripped the arms of her chair and took a deep breath. She was sure that Miss Taylor must hear the loud beating of her heart.

'Oh Miss Taylor! I don't know . . . I can't find words!'

Miss Taylor put out a hand as if she would have touched Opal, but did not quite do so.

'I would like to take you up on your offer to have me as a sleeping partner,' she continued. 'I'm not making it a condition, however. I realize, after thinking about it, that I'm not young enough to be a full partner, even if you had been agreeable. But in the background I could perhaps be helpful, and it would be of great interest to me.'

'Oh Miss Taylor I'll be delighted to have you!' Opal cried. 'I really will. And now all I have to wait for is the agent's reply!'

It came the same afternoon, after the shop was closed. David Hessle had called just before closing time and, to Miss Browning's visible chagrin, had elected to stay with Opal after her assistant had left. A minute later the telephone rang.

Opal unhooked the receiver, held it to her ear and listened. 'Thank you,' she said quietly after a time, and then hung up. Then, turning to David, she rushed into his arms, burying her face in his jacket, sobbing wildly. He held her tightly until the spasm of tears had passed.

'Never mind,' he said 'Something else will turn up.'

Opal stared at him.

'Something else? But don't you understand? I've got it! They've accepted my offer. Oh David, I'm so happy!'

'Then I'm happy for you,' David said quietly. 'It's what you've always wanted, isn't it?'

'Yes,' Opal said. 'I think it is. And do you know what I shall call the store? I shall call it "Opal's". Nothing more. And I shall have my name plastered everywhere so that everyone will know it belongs to me!'

Chapter Eight

Opal gave a last look around the flat. How poky it appeared now that the furniture was out of it! Though she was not happy about the location of their new house – it was in an area of Leasfield which had been acceptable at the turn of the century but was now run down – at least they would have more room. This place, though, was quite suitable for the new owner of Madame Dora's, a woman on her own.

Opal did not think for a moment that Mrs Fletcher, an attractive woman in her thirties, would spend too much time alone. She had concluded in the first few minutes of the lady's visit that she was the mistress of the elderly man who accompanied her. Also that it was doubtful that she had the ability to run so much as a bran tub, let alone a busy shop. But that's not my business, Opal had told herself firmly. The lady wanted it, the gentleman – Opal never knew his name – was pleased to buy it for her, once he had inspected the accounts. Opal had never dreamed it could be so easy.

Connie Browning came into the room.

'I've made some tea. I thought you'd like a cup before you left. I didn't bring it up because there's nowhere to put it. Doesn't it look strange in here without so much as a table or a chair?'

Opal followed the girl downstairs. It had been good of Miss Browning to stay and help her on her half-day. She had wondered, at first, whether she should offer her a position in the new store; but she knew that, good worker though Miss Browning was when the spirit moved her, she did not really want her. Opal was never quite comfortable in Miss Browning's presence – which was absurd considering their respective positions – so it had been a relief when Mrs Fletcher had asked Miss Browning to stay on and the girl had accepted.

'Another cup?' Miss Browning asked presently. 'There's plenty in the pot.'

'I won't, thank you,' Opal said. 'There'll be a lot to do at the other end and I must get there as soon as I can.' She held out her hand. 'Well, goodbye Miss Browning. Thank you for your help over these last months. I hope you get on well with your new employer.'

She gave a last, swift look around and left. You think you've seen the last of me, Madame High-and-Mighty, Connie Browning thought, watching Opal walk with never a backward glance towards the tram-stop. But you haven't, not by a long chalk. You won't be so lah-di-dah when you hear *my* bit of news!

The furniture van was at the door when Opal arrived at number seven, Alma Place. She entered the house behind one of the removal men who was carrying an inverted armchair on his head. Their possessions, seen thus, seemed meagre and shabby. She supposed the neighbours were assessing them. Edgar, standing in the narrow entrance passage, leapt out of the way as the removal man tried to pass him.

'A good thing you've arrived,' he grumbled. '*You* can try telling them where everything goes!'

'But Edgar, I wrote it all down! I made a plan of each room and indicated the positions of the furniture.'

'Oh I know you did. You gave me my instructions

all right, but *they* don't want to bother with them. All they want is to get shot of the stuff. It's mostly dumped in the front-room, except the bedroom stuff. That's piled in our bedroom.'

'That reminds me,' Opal said, following him into what would be the sitting-room when she had had time to sort it out. 'I forgot to tell you. I've ordered a single bed from Cobley's. Has it arrived?'

'A bed?' Edgar queried. 'What's wrong with Daniel's present one? He's had it no more than four years. A bed should last a lifetime.'

'It isn't for Daniel.' Her voice came muffled from inside a tea-chest packed with curtains. 'It's for the spare room.'

'Spare room? What do we want with a spare room? No-one comes to stay.'

She straightened up, moved a step-ladder to the tall window and ascended, curtain in hand.

'Well, they might, now that we have three bedrooms. Mary might come, or Aunt Garnet. Also I'll be working late a lot of time over the next few months. It might be useful if I were to sleep there at such times so as not to disturb you.'

She slid the brass rings on to the pole and let the curtain drop. 'They're still going to be too short,' she said. 'I shall have to do something to lengthen them. Edgar, hand me the other one.'

There was no reply. He was not in the room. Looking out of the window she saw him walking away down the street. She sighed. She had tried to be tactful, but trust Edgar to turn awkward. How could he pretend that a shared bed meant anything any longer? And whose fault was that? Not hers, certainly. He was always the one to turn away. And it was not as if she had suggested that she should occupy the spare room permanently, though in her heart she wondered if it would come to that. Somewhere there was a limit to her feelings.

She climbed down the ladder, fetched the other curtain and hung it unaided. He had most likely gone off to find the nearest public house. Now that he had a little more money to call his own he spent more time in such places. To be fair, he seldom drank too much, and he did not usually go out until Daniel was in bed. He spent a lot of time with Daniel; taking him for walks, playing card games, talking with him. Opal wished that she could do the same.

Daniel was spending the week with Queenie. On first seeing the new house he had disliked it intensely and for this reason she wanted to have everything shipshape, his own room with his familiar possessions ready and waiting, when he came into it.

'That'll be it then, Missus,' the removal man said, coming into the room.

She paid him and he departed, leaving her in sole possession of her new home. She went from room to room, standing in the middle of each one, trying to decide what she would do with it. She had given herself no more than forty-eight hours to get everything into place. After that she must concentrate entirely on the store.

She had planned the store's opening for Saturday the twenty-third of March. The first Saturday of spring would be an auspicious date. It was less than four months away and almost everything was still to be done. There could be no question of postponing the date since from now, until the first sale took place in the store, she would be earning no money at all. They would have to rely on Edgar's meagre earnings and – but only if it became absolutely necessary – her savings. They must economize in every possible way.

When David Hessle arrived, entering without waiting for his ring at the front door to be answered, he found her in the kitchen, putting away china in a high cupboard. Looking down at him from the top of the step-ladder on which she was precariously balanced, she knew that something was wrong. His face was drawn, his eyes troubled. When he greeted her there was none of the usual pleasure in his voice. She was about to ask him what was wrong but something in her warned her not to. She must let him tell her in his own time.

'I'm sorry I couldn't get here any sooner,' he said. 'I called in at the shop but you'd already left. Connie was expecting Mrs Fletcher any minute. So what can I do to help?'

'You can hand me up all the stuff from the table,' Opal said. 'These cupboards are far too high.'

He would continue to see Connie Browning. There was no getting away from that since Mrs Fletcher intended keeping on the same wholesalers. Oh well, it wasn't important. But in that case, Opal thought uncomfortably, why did the thought niggle her?

'I was so lucky to get this house,' she said. 'I was just about at the end of my tether, with Mrs Fletcher waiting to move in on me. If Miss Taylor's tenants hadn't moved to Huddersfield and she hadn't offered me the house at next to no rent, I don't know what I'd have done.'

He was not listening. And when he dropped a willow-pattern jug he was handing to her, let it fall to the floor where it smashed into a hundred pieces, she forgot her resolve not to question him.

'What is it, David? What's wrong? I know there's something.'

'Come down here,' he said quietly. 'I have something to tell you.'

They sat on kitchen chairs, facing each other.

'Where's Edgar?' David asked.

She shrugged. 'Your guess is as good as mine. Out somewhere. So what is it?'

He sat with his head bent, shoulders drooped. He looked at his hands, examining the long fingers, the well-tended, filbert-shaped nails, as if he was seeing them for the first time. The silence seemed without end. Then he raised his head and looked at her.

'I'm going to be married,' he said.

She stared at him. She must have misheard. Who could he possibly . . . ? But before she could frame the question, she knew.

'I'm going to marry Connie.'

'No! No you can't!' She was already shouting in protest 'Not Connie Browning! You can't!'

'It's fixed,' he said quietly. 'We're to be married in a fortnight's time.'

'But how can you? How can you, David?' The words rose in a scream. She did not understand the wild panic in her. 'She's not right for you. You know that. You'll be miserable for the rest of your life.'

But she knew inside herself that it was not David's future she was thinking of. It was her own. How could she give him up to Connie Browning?

'Come on Opal' he said 'She's not as bad as all that! She's a nice kid really.' He spoke without conviction. 'I know – and so do you – that she'll never be to me what you could have been. But you prefer to continue with your sham of a marriage . . .'

'I've got to,' she said quickly. 'You know that.'

'So why begrudge me someone else?'

'I don't.'

She wondered whether she spoke the truth, whether she wouldn't feel the same whoever he was marrying; her sister Mary, for example.

'It's just that . . . Connie Browning . . . David, it's not reasonable!'

'On the contrary,' he said. 'There's every reason. She's pregnant.'

Slowly, holding on to the chair-back because all the strength had gone from her limbs, she rose. She wanted to say something but the words would not come. Her lips were icy cold, and stiff. Was it possible that even at the time . . . ? She choked back sick memories of his arms around her, his hands on her body. She took a deep breath, squared her shoulders, turned and began to run.

She ran along the passage and out of the house, down the flagged path. David came after her and as she reached the pavement he caught her wrist, swung her round and dragged her back into the house.

'Opal, please! Please don't turn away from me! We can't lose each other. Not you and me. We mean too much to one another.'

'I thought we did,' she said. 'I was mistaken. Let go of me!'

'You were not mistaken,' he said, 'and you know it.'

He pulled her roughly towards him and held her. His kisses, on her lips, on her closed eyes, on her throat, were fierce with longing. At first she was leaden in his embrace, her arms stiff by her side. And then the yearnings, the frustrations, the body's needs, rose up in her again and she responded to him, her hands caressing him, her mouth seeking his, willing to succumb to every demand that his body made of hers.

Then her head cleared. She shivered violently, summoned all her strength, pushed him away from her. These were the demands he had made of Connie Browning. What she herself had a moment ago been so willing to give, her former shop assistant had already given. And carried the proof within her, soon to be seen by all the world.

'No!' she cried. 'No!'

Then she heard the squeak of the gate, recognized Edgar's step on the path, and went swiftly into the kitchen, David following.

'We're here, Edgar!' she called out.

She could hardly believe that the calm voice was hers since, as she mounted the step-ladder, hid her face in the china cupboard, her body was still shaking. She wondered if she might be sick. With an effort that was almost beyond her she spoke again.

'Edgar, somewhere there's a bottle of port and some glasses. Can you find them? We have to drink a toast. David is to be married – to Miss Connie Browning!'

The words were bitter in her mouth. She tasted them like poison on her tongue. But no-one would ever know her feelings.

Standing in the window, Opal saw Miss Taylor's chauffeur-driven car pull up at the gate, and went out at once. It had been Miss Taylor's idea to call for her since they were to go to the store together. Miss Taylor was interested in every detail of the alterations and could hardly wait to inspect them. In the car Opal leaned back in the thickly upholstered, leather-covered seat and wondered if, one day, she might have such a car, with a chauffeur. It was an idle dream and not something for which she longed. It's value would be as an outward sign that she had succeeded in what she'd set out to do.

'I like the date you've set for the opening,' Miss Taylor said enthusiastically. 'There's something symbolic, something hopeful about the first week-end of spring. But shall you have everything ready in time?'

'I hope so,' Opal said. 'But I shall open in any case. I shall make certain that the whole of the ground floor is completed, and as much as possible of the first floor. If everything there is not absolutely ready I'm sure people won't mind. They might even enjoy seeing it take place over a period of time. Who knows? I intend, you see, right from the start to establish a *rapport* with my customers.'

It was a short drive only to the store. Miss Taylor instructed her chauffeur to collect her in an hour. 'But I shall stay on,' Opal said. 'I have a lot to do.'

'You see how it's taking shape,' Opal said as they entered. 'See the floor! Under all that dirt the parquet is in really good condition, and bit by bit we're getting it clean.'

Miss Taylor frowned.

'I see that,' she admitted. 'What is finished looks fine. But there's so much still to do! Acres of walls and ceiling – and this is only one floor. You need an army of people in here, not two women on the floor and a couple of men painting.'

'That's all I can afford,' Opal said, 'I've budgeted most carefully. But don't worry, Miss Taylor. It *will* be done. I myself am going to clean and polish all the old counters and shelves.'

'I'm not at all sure . . .' Miss Taylor began doubtfully.

'Come and see if you approve of my choice of colours,' Opal interrupted. 'I thought this red for the walls would make the whole place look warm and cheerful; and then the ceiling, which is rather beautiful, is to be picked out in red and white. Don't you think it will look very welcoming?'

'Perhaps so,' Miss Taylor said. 'They're not *fashionable* colours, are they? Beige, cream, green . . . they're more usual.'

'I shall *make* them fashionable,' Opal said firmly. The light fittings I shall have painted gold. There's no way for a long time that I can have them gilded, but gold paint will look pretty. A quick effect is what I have to aim for.'

'Well, you seem to have it all worked out' Miss Taylor said. 'Shall we go up to the next floor? What departments do you intend to have there?'

'To begin with, very few,' Opal admitted. 'Most of what I sell will go on the ground floor, until I can expand both the stock and the sales staff. There I'll have dress materials and paper patterns, haberdashery, hosiery, gloves, cosmetics, a sort of general gifts counter, stationery. Children's clothes as soon as I can. Toys also.'

'On this floor,' Opal said as they reached the top of the staircase, 'I shall have my millinery. There'll be a great deal of space for it – too much – but that means that women can sit down and buy a hat in comfort and at leisure. I shall also have underwear here and, as soon as possible, ladies' dresses and coats.'

'Very well then,' Miss Taylor said. 'There is one thing I insist on. This floor must be better carpeted. A nice, grey haircord. I have friends in the carpet trade in Halifax and I shall persuade them to do the whole floor and give you a year's credit!'

'That would be wonderful!' Opal said. 'Especially since here I also want to create an area, however small at first, where customers can have a cup of tea and some light refreshment – or even just a rest in a comfortable chair. If they've taken the trouble to come the extra distance to my store, then they must be rewarded. Of course I'll see to it that they have to walk through several departments to reach such an area! Hopefully they'll spend on the way.' Miss Taylor laughed. 'How many hours have you spent, working this out, I wonder?'

'It hasn't been difficult,' Opal said. 'It all seems to be there in my head, ready and waiting. If it hadn't been for you and my sister-in-law, of course, it would have had to remain in my head. I shall always be grateful to you.'

'Well, you've given me a new interest,' Miss Taylor acknowledged. 'Money of itself isn't interesting. It's what one can do with it. You've shown me that. And how is Mr Hessle getting along with helping you to acquire your stock?'

She can't know the effect that even the sound of his name has on me, Opal thought. How could she. I dare say she's never experienced love, and in that case perhaps she's fortunate. Yet she remained clear-sighted enough to doubt that it was love she felt for David. Passion, yes. Jealousy, with some shame, she admitted to, could not deny. But not love as she had known it for Edgar.

'Well enough so far,' she answered levelly. 'But I'm not sure that he'll be as much help to me as I had hoped. He's getting married next week.'

'Getting married? You surprise me.' Miss Taylor looked keenly at Opal.

'He is marrying Miss Connie Browning, my assistant in Madame Dora's. You remember her?'

'Indeed I do. I always thought she was demure, yet bold. An unlikely and powerful combination. Well, we must hope that they'll be very happy together.'

'Come and see my office,' Opal said brightly. 'It's at the very top of the building, in the little square tower you can see from outside. Of course I shan't be spending much time there when the store is open. I shall be amongst the customers. That is where my place will be.'

Christmas came and went. On Christmas Day Opal took time off to be with Daniel, share in his presents, but on Boxing Day she knew she must be back in the store. There was not a day, not an hour, to be wasted from now on. They had been invited to visit David and Connie Hessle but Opal had pleaded pressure of work. She had, out of duty, attended the wedding with Edgar and Daniel, and the reception afterwards in a small hotel in Leasfield. Gnawed by her own feelings she had no compassion in her heart at the unhappiness in David's eyes as he stood with his bride. Connie was radiantly pretty, inordinately pleased. She showed, as yet, no sign of her pregnancy. I shall not be able to bear it when she does, Opal thought. I shall not be able to look at her.

'You could come to the store with me,' she said

to Daniel on Boxing Day. 'Perhaps you would like to come, too, Edgar?'

But Edgar had a chesty cold, a legacy of his time in the army. It was the same every winter.

'No thanks,' he said. 'I have to get right again for tomorrow.'

'Can I take my new paints?' Daniel asked.

Opal laughed. 'It's all you ever think about,' she said indulgently. 'But yes, of course you can.'

In the store she walked around with him, showing him all that had been done. 'You should be interested,' she said. 'One day it will all be yours! Think of that!'

'Can I start painting?' he asked.

'Very well,' she said. 'You can sit at this counter and I shall work nearby. Let's see if you can paint a picture of what the store will be like when it's finished!'

Perhaps, since I shall have more space than I can fill on the first floor, she thought, I could mount a children's art exhibition. Or set up a painting competition for the children of customers? It might bring people in.

Less than three months now and the people would be in this place. The counter she was now polishing with might and main would display – what? Gloves? Fine lace and ribbons? Silk or woollen materials? It was a detail she had not yet decided. What she *was* aware of, every waking moment of her life and often in her dreams, was that in such a short time, when the winter was over and the spring came, her dream would come true.

Chapter Nine

Opal drew back the curtains and looked out on to the street. In the small front gardens of Alma Place a few forsythia shrubs arched their flower-laden branches against the soot-blackened stone of the house, and daffodils poked their heads between the iron railings which divided each small plot from its neighbour. Nature had done well to choose yellow flowers for spring, she thought. If, in fashion, she were to follow Nature's guide in her choice of colours for each season of the year, she would not go far wrong.

'It's a perfect spring day,' she said. 'I knew it would be!'

'It wouldn't dare to be otherwise,' Edgar said from the bed. (She had not, after all, moved into the spare room). 'Not with you organizing everything.'

Opal could not tell whether his words were sarcastic of teasing. His face was expressionless and these days his moods were so variable that it was impossible to understand him. Yet not all that variable; more often black. His few lighter, gentler moods were saved for Daniel.

She did not take up the challenge, if challenge it was. Everything must go well today; nothing must be allowed to spoil the occasion. After all, Edgar *had* agreed to take the morning off work to be present at the opening, and she was grateful for that. In a place like Leasfield, to be seen to have the support of one's husband could do nothing but good. If she could have believed that she actually had it it would have meant a lot to her.

'I must be there really early,' she said. 'There are sure to be last-minute things to attend to.'

In fact, when she and David had left the store last night, well after midnight, everything had been in place; everything except the cash float in the Lamson room (to which, through a network of tubes still mysterious to her, money, hopefully, would speed from the counters) and her own personal flag which would be run up from the tower this morning. She had chosen a rich blue flag with her name emblazoned across it in large red letters. 'OPAL'S'. Nothing more. Nothing more was needed. From today her name would be synonymous with all that was best in department stores.

'Shouldn't you be up?' she asked Edgar. 'And I think I must go and waken Daniel. Be sure you're both there by half-past nine at the latest.'

'Stop fussing,' Edgar said. 'We'll be there on time.'

Inside the double doors of the main entrance to the store an area had been marked off by a yellow satin ribbon at waist height. The size of the area was so arranged that should a great many people attend the opening it could be enlarged by moving the ribbon, and should fewer people than hoped for turn up, the confined space was small enough to make them seem a crowd. At ten minutes to ten it was reported to Opal, in her office in the tower, that a respectable number of people had arrived and that more kept coming. It looked as though it might be necessary to adjust the ribbon.

'I'm desperate that I can't see them arriving from here,' Opal said.

Now that the moment had almost come she felt sick with apprehension, excitement, not a little fear. What if she had overestimated herself; her talents, her capacity, her potential? But she knew she had not. This was the day to which her life had been leading.

'It wouldn't do to show yourself,' Queenie said firmly. 'You're the star. You must appear at the precise moment. We shall all go down before you and set the stage for your appearance.' She put her arms around Opal and kissed her on the cheek. 'Good luck, my dear!'

'Thank you,' Opal said quietly. 'Thank you for everything, all of you here.'

'Well, I think we should go now,' Miss Taylor said briskly. 'Mr Carson, you are to escort me I believe. Then Mr and Mrs Derwent, Miss Mary Derwent, Mr Hessle and Daniel.'

Opal was still not sure whether Daniel should be there, in public. Mothers of young children who did jobs outside the home were frowned upon. But he had wanted to come and she could not deny him. She could never deny him anything.

'I'm sorry your wife couldn't be present, Mr Hessle,' Miss Taylor said. 'So unfortunate to have influenza on an occasion such as this!'

David smiled pleasantly. 'She was sorry too.'

They arranged themselves, and left by the narrow staircase from Opal's office and then went, in a little procession, down the wide staircase and towards the front entrance. Opal gave a last quick look in the mirror. Her face was pale against the grey wool dress. She would have looked better with a touch of rouge on her cheeks, but it was too late now. Her eyes, surprisingly, showed nothing of the hard work and fatigue of the last few months. They were clear and shining. She adjusted the small pink rose which David had given her to wear, and which she had accepted as a token that things were all right between them again, or as right as they ever could be. Then she smoothed down her already immaculate hair, and left.

A ripple of applause greeted her as she walked towards the respectably-sized crowd. Sensing that David was about to introduce her, she raised a hand to stop him.

'Ladies and gentleman,' she said. 'I am Opal. This is my store, and I hope from now on it will be yours. Let me introduce you to my family and friends, and to some of my staff – though I hope that before long *all* my staff will be familiar to you. This is my husband, Mr Edgar Carson . . . my son, Daniel.'

She introduced everyone in turn.

'Mr David Hessle is my Store Manager and my right hand,' she said. 'He will always be there to help you though that will not, I hope, prevent you from seeking me out whenever you wish to do so.'

Six weeks ago it had not seemed possible that David could be working for her. Up to that time she had seen little of him since his marriage, no more than business between them had made necessary. On one of his business calls he had been accompanied by Connie. 'I want to learn as much as I can about David's job,' she'd said, 'so that I can be a help to him.'

'How enterprising of you!' Opal said. 'But will you have time for that once the baby is born?'

She had forced the words out through cold lips. It was unbearable to think of this . . . this *chit* . . . with David's child. By this time – it was the only way – she had laid the blame for the whole affair at Connie Browning's door. She had been too wicked, too subtle for David. Demure and bold, as Miss Taylor had said. He had been well and truly caught.

Caught, as it turned out, was exactly what he had been. When the weeks went by with, on Connie's part, no sign of a swelling stomach, of breasts more than usually burgeoning, let alone morning sickness, fancies for strange foods or a preoccupation with baby clothes, Connie's mother began to have her doubts. When Connie admitted that she was not, and never had been, pregnant, it was her mother who insisted that he be told at once. 'If you leave it too late,' she counselled, 'if you make him a laughing stock in front of all his friends, it could be the end of your marriage! You don't want that do you?'

Connie did not, though her marriage had turned out to be much less exciting than she had expected. Boring even. So her no-longer-interesting condition was presented to David as a mistake on the part of the doctor, a wrong diagnosis for which she could not be blamed. But this time David was not deceived. His resulting anger was of a degree Connie had not thought possible, and since then it seemed that whatever she did was wrong.

Small wonder, Opal thought fleetingly, seeing David standing beside Miss Taylor, that Connie had feigned influenza. Unless obliged to do so the Hessles now went nowhere together. She believed it likely, though David had not spelt it out and it could be wishful thinking on her part, that already they no longer shared the marriage bed. 'Come and work with me,' had been her solution. 'Help me build my new store. It's something we can do together.'

Perhaps he had accepted to spite Connie? Whatever the reason, day by day they worked side by side; planning, discussing, arguing, agreeing. Life was undoubtedly enriched by David's presence, though no word passed between them which might not be heard by the whole world; and he never touched her. Their relationship was entirely platonic.

But David was not in her thoughts now as, smiling, she spoke to the people gathered around her in the store.

'I am here to serve you,' she said. 'It is as simple as that. To give you the best value for your hard-earned money. I know that we don't live in the easiest of times, so I shall always be on the lookout for bargains for you. But I also believe that when times are difficult a little variety, a little luxury, are more than ever needed. I shall run my store so that you will find these too. And if my store is not all that you want it to be, then please let me know. Never be afraid to stop me and speak to me when you see me in the store. Seek me out and tell me what you want.'

She realized, suddenly, that this was the first speech she had ever made in her life and that people were actually listening to her with interest.

'And now since you have been good enough to make the journey here,' she continued, 'there will be a cup of tea for everyone in Opal's café on the first floor – though when we reach our twenty-first year of trading I promise you champagne!

'The cafe is small – like the rest of the store it will grow according to *your* needs – so we shan't be able to serve you all at the same time. May I also remind you that if you *do* make a purchase – but please don't feel obliged to do so, feel free to look around – but if you do buy you will receive a small gift to remind you of your part in this special day in my life – and I hope in the life of Leasfield.'

When the applause had died down, David stepped forward.

'Before I ask Miss Phoebe Taylor, whose family is so well known to most of us, formally to declare Opal's store open, just let me remind you of the offer in our advertisement. If you have made the journey from the centre of Leasfield by tram, then simply hand in your tram ticket at the desk by the cosmetics counter on this floor, and your fare will be refunded. But not only for today, ladies and gentlemen. This refund will be made to you for at least the next three months. It is Opal's way of saying "Thank you for coming".'

He brought Miss Taylor forward to cut the ribbon, but she beckoned to Opal.

'*I'm* not going to make a speech,' she said. 'But in front of all of you I want to present Miss Opal with a memento of this occasion. Opals, some say, are for tears. I'm sure that this day will prove the opposite to be true!'

To Opal's surprise she slipped a pendant on a silver chain over her head. Then she cut the ribbon and the crowd surged through into the store. My store, Opal thought. My dream has come true. She watched the people fanning out this way and that into the various departments. This was her supreme moment. Nothing would ever surpass it.

She stayed near to the entrance for a few minutes, greeting new customers as they came in, introducing herself. The advertising over the last few weeks, culminating in the half-page spread in yesterday's

Leasfield Courier, had paid off, though David had been against such extravagance.

'There's no way you can afford a half page,' he said. 'The cost is prohibitive!'

'On the contrary, there's no way I can afford *not* to,' she had told him. 'Not only once, but for some time to come. Advertising must be a top priority.'

The Courier had not been her only form of advertising. Several boys and girls in and around Leasfield had acquired unexpected riches by the payment of half-a-crown for leaflets pushed through every letter-box in their neighbourhood and posters fastened to every available board. David thought it undignified. Miss Taylor had also looked doubtful.

'As yet I can't afford too much dignity,' Opal said. 'I need every ounce of publicity I can get. In fact I can tell you now that mine will never be one of those companies which goes under in dignified silence because it's too refined to seek publicity! When I need help I shall call for it.'

What she needed to know now was which way of advertising had brought people in. As she moved around the store she would ask them.

There was a short queue of women – no men amongst them – at the desk where the used tram-tickets were being redeemed. The fare from the centre of Leasfield was twopence. Though she felt sure that not everyone who was entitled to it would bother to claim it, she must keep an eye on what was paid out over the next three months and make sure that the amount was offset in some other way, though not necessarily, indeed preferably not, at the customers' expense.

'Good morning ladies!' she said. 'Welcome to Opal's! Now tell me, do the trams run often enough from the town centre, or did you have to wait?'

'They run fairly often,' a woman said. 'But they don't stop near enough. If it was a rainy day we'd get wet walking from the tram-stop, wouldn't we?'

'Then there's a clear case for having the tram-stop moved,' Opal said cheerfully. 'Perhaps you would sign my petition for that? Miss Conran has it right there on the desk. I'm sure all you ladies between you will be much more influential than I!'

That should do the trick, she thought. When she had approached the Tramways Department (she wished to put 'Trams stop at the door' in her advertisements) they had laughed at her. They wouldn't laugh at a hundred or two paying customers, and a petition sent in every week until they did something about it.

She noticed that the nearby cosmetics counter was busy. That had been a good idea. She was convinced that its success would increase, especially as she aimed, by every persuasion she could think of, to encourage women to make the best of themselves. She thought of organizing demonstrations in the store. There was plenty of space for such events. Indeed, filling the space while she did not really have enough departments, or sufficient stock to put in the existing ones, was a major preoccupation with her. It must all seem to be done naturally, as if space was part of her plan. Customers must never suspect that she could not yet afford to fill it.

She saw Queenie and Miss Taylor by the glove counter, and went to join them. Queenie, already with several parcels in Opal's distinctive blue-and-white striped wrapping paper, was completing the purchase of a pair of doeskin gloves while Miss Taylor was trying on beige kid with gauntlets. Opal spoke to the assistant.

'Please see that Miss Taylor and Mrs Derwent are always given House discount on their purchases, Miss Feather.'

'I've done that, Mrs Carson,' the woman said. 'Mr Hessle gave me a list of people for House discount.'

'Good! And please remember to call me Miss Opal, won't you? Have you had many customers? What is selling best so far?'

'The doeskin at four-and-eleven are going well,' the woman said. 'But the special line in white fabric at two-and-sixpence is selling like hot cakes. We might run out!'

'Opal, everything's really splendid,' Queenie said enthusiastically. 'Just as I knew it would be. Oh I *do* wish I could help!'

'By the look of your parcels I think you have,' Opal replied. She glanced towards Miss Feather who was rearranging her display, out of earshot, at the other end of the counter. 'Seriously, Queenie, if it hadn't been for you and Miss Taylor this day could never have happened. And Miss Taylor, my pendant is quite beautiful!'

She held the opal up to the light, admiring the ever-changing blues, the iridescent pinks, greens and purples which shot through the large, oval stone.

'There's no way I can ever thank either of you enough. I shall never forget what you've done.'

'But I mean *really* help – like selling something,' Queenie said. 'I always thought I should like to work in a shop.'

'*Store*, if you don't mind!'

'Store then. But first I was needed at home by my parents and now Mark won't let me go out to work. He says my place is with the children.'

'Opal' Miss Taylor interrupted 'I'm suddenly rather tired. Do you think you could possibly have me a pot of tea sent to your office, and tell Gregson to bring my car around to the entrance in about twenty minutes?'

'Oh I'm so sorry, Miss Taylor,' Opal said. 'I'll take you up to my office at once.'

She really did look unwell. Was it fatigue from the excitement of the morning, or had it been coming on for some time? Am I getting so absorbed in my own affairs, Opal wondered, that I can't see anyone else?

'There's no need to go with me,' Miss Taylor said firmly. 'You have plenty to occupy you here. I'll just drink a cup of tea and then go home. Telephone me this evening if you have time.'

'Of course I will!'

As Miss Taylor walked away a tall, stout woman in a fur coat approached Opal.

'I am Mrs James Carstairs,' she announced, 'and I'm taking you up on your word. About supplying what the customer wants.'

'Why certainly,' Opal said. 'What can I do for you?'

'I bought this material to make a blouse,' the woman said. 'Now I find your haberdashery department has neither ribbon nor sewing cotton to match it!'

'Dear me! May I look at the material?'

Opal took the parcel from the woman and opened it out on the counter. 'What an unusual shade of green, isn't it? But very pretty. I think green is going to be fashionable this coming summer.'

'Well, what are you going to do about it?' the woman demanded.

'Why, find you something to match, of course!' Opal said pleasantly. 'I shall try to get it today, but I might not be able to find it until Monday. However, if you'll allow me to take a small snip of the material, and give me your address, I'll see that it's delivered to you.'

'Very well,' Mrs Carstairs said. 'I want three yards of double-sided satin ribbon, three-quarters of an inch wide, and one reel of sewing silk. And I want a perfect match.'

'We'll do our very best, Mrs Carstairs,' Opal promised. 'Now if you haven't yet visited our millinery department on the first floor I think you might find the new season's straws in a shade which would go beautifully with your new blouse. If you have any difficulty, please ask the assistant to call me.'

'What an ungracious woman,' Queenie said. 'I've suddenly decided I'd never make a saleswoman. I'd have been quite rude to her.'

'*You* wouldn't be rude to anyone! But if you really want to help me, here's your chance.'

'What do you mean?'

'Would you be an absolute angel and take this pattern to try to match it with ribbon and thread. There's no-one I can ask right now. I rather think you'll get it at Miller's'

'Why Miller's?' Queenie asked.

'Because I dare say that's where she bought the material in the first place. She certainly didn't buy it here. We don't stock this one.'

'I can't believe it!' Queenie gasped. 'I can't believe anyone would have the cheek! Why didn't you say anything?'

'Because though I'll start by supplying her with cotton and ribbon at no profit at all, I reckon I'll eventually make her a customer. I should say she's well-to-do. It takes a lot of pennies to buy a dyed ermine coat like that.'

'Especially in her size! Oh, Opal, can you imagine how she'll look in green satin?'

Opal pulled a face. 'But are you going to be a darling and match it for me?'

'Of course! And I'll take great pleasure in having it delivered to her by my chauffeur.'

'I shall have to think seriously about deliveries before long,' Opal said. 'All I have at present is a boy with a bicycle. But please excuse me, Queenie, I must go and see Miss Taylor before she leaves, make sure she's all right.'

Miss Taylor had finished her tea and was about to depart by the time Opal, waylaid by another customer, reached her office. She looked pale and cold, in spite of her all-enveloping fur coat.

'You really don't look too well,' Opal said anxiously. 'I do hope you haven't caught a chill. Did you feel a draught, standing in the entrance so long?'

'I never feel draughts,' Miss Taylor answered. 'But I am quite exceptionally tired. I shall go straight to bed with a hot toddy. I'll be as right as rain in the morning, you'll see!'

'I must thank you again for this beautiful pendant,' Opal said. 'I shall treasure it.'

'Well, I thought that the day ought not to go by without some memento, something tangible you could see and touch. You'll always have memories, of course.'

'Always,' Opal said. 'As long as I live.'

There was a tap on the door.

'Ah, here is Gregson!' Miss Taylor seemed glad of the interruption. 'Goodbye for now, Opal. Don't forget to telephone me.'

Opal was about to go back into the store when

Edgar came in, accompanied by Daniel and Mary. She realized, guiltily, that she had seen none of them since the opening, nor had she given them a thought.

'Well then, what do you think, Edgar?' she asked.

'Very good,' he said. 'It's going to be a big success. You've done well.'

'Thank you, Edgar'. She felt genuinely pleased by his approbation. 'There's still a lot of ground to cover. But I'm on the way.'

'You certainly are,' he agreed.

'We came to tell you that we're leaving now,' Mary said. 'We thought we should get back.'

'I'm starving,' Daniel complained. 'I wish you had a proper café with meat and potato pie and jam pudding!'

'We shall have one day, I promise you,' Opal said. 'Do you know, I'd forgotten all about food. How awful of me!'

'Don't worry, Opal,' Mary said. 'I'll make a meal for Edgar and Daniel the moment we get back. Since I'm staying the night I have lots of time. And I think your store is wonderful! I bought myself some handkerchiefs and a new hairbrush.'

Mary thinks it's wonderful, Opal thought, watching them go, but she'd rather have a husband and children than all the stores in the world. Well, I shall show everyone that it's possible to be a good mother *and* a good businesswoman at the same time. I could have been a good wife to Edgar, but he wanted another sort of wife. She was not his kind any more, she thought, though she had been once.

She left the office and went downstairs, meeting David on the way.

'Satisfied?' he asked.

'More than! Very, very happy. Aren't you glad you came in with me, David?'

'I couldn't be otherwise. I still wish that you'd let me have a partnership.'

'We've discussed all that,' Opal said. 'It was never on the cards. I wanted, as I've always wanted, to go it alone.'

'I sold my business to join you,' David reminded her. 'I could have bought the partnership, put money into the store.'

'I appreciate that. But you've not done badly, have you David! Apart from my own, yours is the most important job in the store. It always will be.'

He had sold his business, she knew very well but did not choose to remind him, because having inherited it from his uncle, he had never really liked it. And when Connie started taking an interest he liked it less than ever. He had jumped at the chance of joining Opal's – so much so that she wondered if his own business had not been doing well. But she was glad to have him. She had wanted him all along.

'I must go and speak to more people,' she said. 'We both must. I'll see you at the Staff Meeting.'

The Staff Meeting took place in the café as soon as the store had closed at half-past six.

'I won't keep you long,' Opal said. 'It's Saturday and I'm sure you all have things to do. I chose to open on a Saturday because in Leasfield that's the big spending day and I wanted us to start with a bang. Well, we've done that, and I'm grateful for your part in it. I've learned several things today that will be of use to all of us, but I won't go into them now. I'll save them for the proper Staff Meeting on Tuesday. We shall meet every Tuesday at the close of business and I want you all to feel free to express yourselves, put forward your ideas on anything.

'The only thing I want to tell you right now is this. As you probably know, there's a bill before Parliament to enable shop assistants to have holidays with pay. We don't know that it will ever become law, but I've decided that whether it does or not, every member of my staff is to have a paid holiday, each year, of at least eight days. We shall be the first store in Leasfield to do this. Mr Hessle will start next week drawing up this summer's holiday lists for each department.

'That's all for today. Again, thank you all, very, very much!'

As they filed out she called back one man.

'Mr Burton, will you see to it that what I have just announced gets into the Leasfield Courier? I think it might even be of interest to the Yorkshire Post. See what you can do!'

'I'll give you a lift home,' David said.

'Thank you, but no. It's not far to walk and the fresh air will clear my mind.'

'Are you sure?'

'Quite sure, thank you,' Opal said.

Getting ready for bed, Opal told Edgar the amount of her first day's takings.

'Do you remember' she said 'my first day in the house shop in Acer Street? I had one penny float in an Oxo tin.'

'I remember,' Edgar said.

They climbed into bed and lay back to back.

'That was the beginning of my success,' Opal said drowsily.

And the beginning of the end for me, Edgar thought, wide awake in the darkness. Why does every stroke of Opal's success drive us farther apart? Why aren't I capable of sharing it? He had no doubt that he loved her, admired her, looked up to her. But he could not enter into her success any more than he could now, and for many months past, enter into her body. Why? He lay awake, pondering, until another spring day crept into the room.

Chapter Ten

'I don't want to go!' Daniel growled.

His voice, these days, alternated between a deep growl and a high squeak and was at times quite beyond his control. 'I shall hate it! You're cruel to send me!'

Opal faced him with all the patience she could muster. She did not want another scene, not now as they were about to set off. There had been enough of those over the last few weeks, ever since she had broken it to him that he was to go away to boarding school.

Daniel was changing fast; not only physically – he was already taller than she and would soon top his father – but in character also. As a small boy he had been so gentle, so acquiescent. She had felt him so close to her. Now, at thirteen, he was a creature of moods, one minute enthusiastic and responsive, the next dour and truculent, shutting himself up in his room, painting for hours on end. And such weird, incomprehensible paintings too.

'Don't talk nonsense, Daniel!' she said firmly. 'You were just the same when you first went to Bishop Tanner's and that turned out all right, didn't it?'

'Then if it's all right, why do I have to leave?' he demanded. 'I could have stayed on until I was sixteen. Why do I have to go away from home?'

She sighed. 'We've been through all this before. Because it's best for you. Because a public school education will help you in later life. One day you'll thank me for it.'

She turned to her husband.

'Edgar, can't you talk some sense into him?'

It was foolish of her to appeal to Edgar since he disapproved of Daniel going away. But then, if their son's education had depended upon Edgar the child would still have been at the local Council school. However, Edgar would no longer argue with her in front of the boy. For Daniel's sake they had made an agreement not to do so. Their quarrels, now, took place in private. When Daniel was present they were polite to each other. They avoided controversial topics – which meant, in practice, that they spoke little.

'Father doesn't agree with you,' Daniel said. '*He* doesn't believe I should go!'

He stood squarely in front of them, looking angrily from one to the other.

'Don't think I don't know that!' he cried. 'I know what you're both like. You can't hide it from me. You . . .' he shouted fiercely at Opal, his voice rising to a treble '. . . you think you know what's best for everybody and you always get your own way. You, Father, you know she gets away with everything and you let her; even when you don't agree, you let her. You never fight for anything, not even when it's important!'

Edgar met his son's eyes, dark and angry, and was shocked at the accusation in them. He despises me, he thought. He sees me as the failure I am. He felt sick at the discovery. It did not seem so long ago that he and Daniel had been the best of friends. Always in the school holidays, when Opal was all the time tied to the store, they went about together: to museums;

to the cinema; to art galleries, for which Daniel had an insatiable appetite, where he would stand enraptured before paintings which Edgar neither liked nor understood, however hard he tried to. And in the last three years, since Opal had bought the car and he had found an unexpected pleasure in driving, they had gone farther afield. Scarborough, Manchester, once to Liverpool to see the big liners which had fascinated them both. He had thought until now that he and Daniel were friends. Was it possible that even while they were being so companionable his son had been contemptuous of him?

Daniel saw the hurt, the puzzlement in his father's eyes, and wished he had not spoken. Nowadays his anger came upon him so quickly that he could not control it, and afterwards he did not know how to make amends.

'After all, York is only forty miles away,' Opal said soothingly. 'You'll be going to Grandpa Derwent's for half-term, and then before you know it you'll be home for the Christmas holidays!'

She was pricked by his accusations against her, but determined not to show it. He did not really mean a word of it. How could he? It was all part of adolescence and she was sure he would settle down at his new school in no time at all. He was extremely fortunate that she had got him into so good a school, but now was not the time for him to appreciate that.

'Come along or we shall be late,' she said. 'Daniel, you can travel in front of the car with your father.'

She, too, had learned to drive, but she seldom did so. Edgar was so much better at it. In fact, she had some figures she wished to study on the way to York. And then she must give serious thought to how many temporary staff they must take on for the Christmas season. It must be as few as possible, yet enough not to miss any sales. She planned to start the Christmas season early this year – by mid-November at the very latest.

The journey passed in near silence, Opal in the back of the car busy with her calculations, Edgar and Daniel side by side, yet with a distance between them which neither could bridge. Arriving at the school they spoke with the Matron, were shown Daniel's dormitory, had coffee with the Housemaster. Daniel, pale and mono-syllabic, trailed behind his parents. When they left, Opal with a hug and a kiss which said she had forgiven and forgotten her son's bad temper, Edgar with a formal handshake, and eyes which pleaded forgive-ness for his guilt, it was Edgar, even more than the abandoned Daniel, who felt that his heart must break.

'Don't run away with the idea that I don't feel anything,' Opal said on the way back. 'I shall miss Daniel every waking moment. It's because I love him so much that I want him to have what's best.'

It was Daniel, though they had different ideas of what was best for him, who united himself and Opal, Edgar thought. But after the boy's outburst today, the revelation of what he thought of his parents if only in a moment's anger, how long could that last? He wouldn't be a child much longer, dependent upon them, needing them. The thought that Daniel saw him as a failure had come even more as a shock to Edgar since in the last few years, though he knew himself to be not much good as a husband, he had done unexpectedly well in his job. He was successful there. He liked it no better, but by hard work and a stroke or two of luck he had had several promotions.

In fact he was now in a position where, given the chance, he could have kept his wife and son in reasonable comfort. Though not including expensive public schools, he thought grimly.

But he knew he could never reach Opal's heights. Her success had been phenomenal, the talk of Leasfield. And she had made it for herself, with her talents and her hard work. He was proud of her, but the gap between them was wider than ever and he could find no way of expressing his admiration. He did not know how to get near her. His sorely needed consolation was that this clever, beautiful woman – every year she grew more lovely – was his. That she was his in little more than name was something neither he nor she was likely to divulge. At least he was grateful for that.

'Drop me off at the stores,' Opal said. 'I have a busy day ahead. Shall you come in and have some lunch?'

'No thank you,' he replied. 'I have a busy day, too.'

Opal had not quite finished what she called her 'walk around' when she was asked by an assistant on lingerie to return to her office to take a telephone call. Each day she went around the whole store, not always at the same time or in the same sequence, but walking through every department. She did not pause everywhere – though she always stopped to have a word with a customer she recognized and by now there were many of those; or she would speak to someone who seemed to be in need of help. It was said by her admirers that she thought nothing of measuring out a yard of elastic, or choosing a hairnet, for a customer waiting to be served.

Usually she would make about half-a-dozen stops,

enquiring about the health of a member of staff or –
as at the moment when the message came – examining
a line of merchandise. But though she might walk as
swift as the wind through some departments, seeming
to look neither to right nor to left, it was a fact that
nothing escaped her. Soon after she had returned to
her office a series of notes, brief but polite, would go
forth. 'To Miss Butler, Blouses: Please have an assistant fasten *every* button on the white crepe-de-chine
blouse on the model.' 'To Mr Simpson, Leather
Goods: There is an address book upside down in your
showcase.'

Her secretary, indeed most of her staff, knew that
the walk-around must not be interrupted unless the
matter was unusually important, so when the message
came she immediately put down the camiknickers she
was examining.

'They're certainly very pretty, Miss Williams,' she
said to the buyer. 'Is this new coffee shade selling well?
Are we getting a good mark-up?'

'The mark-up is all right,' Miss Williams assured her.
'And at four-and-eleven for art silk with lace trimming,
so is the price. But they've not taken off yet. Customers
still go for white or peach shades.'

'Then if we're fairly heavily stocked perhaps we
should include them in the next advertisement. The
new fashion shade – something like that. I'll talk to you
later.'

She left lingerie, trod the grey carpet through gowns,
coats, millinery, sportswear, to the door which con-
cealed the staircase to her office. On the other side of
that door the luxury ended. The stairs were uncarpeted
and her office was sparsely furnished, the only excep-
tion being a long, comfortable, chintz-covered sofa.

But there was a practical reason for that. She did not sit on it during the day, nor did she encourage anyone else to do so. It was there because there were times – in the Christmas season, during the January and July sales, at the financial year-end – when she worked so late that there was no point in going home. On those occasions she slept on the sofa.

Her secretary handed her the telephone as she entered.

'It's Miss Taylor's maid. I'm afraid it's bad news.'

Opal took the receiver.

'Miss Opal here. What is it, Jenny? I see, When? What does the doctor . . . ? Yes, I'll come at once.'

'Miss Taylor has had another heart attack,' she said. 'It sounds most serious. Will you get my car around at once, please. Inform Mr Hessle. You can sign any letters which must go today. I might not be back before closing time.'

In the car her thoughts were all of Miss Taylor, dreading what she might find at Oak House. Jenny had sounded genuinely frightened, though it was by no means her mistress's only heart attack in the last few years. The first had occurred five-and-a-half-years ago, the very day after the store's opening, and she had had three or four since then. But since each one had been less severe than the last, and the doctor had declared that if she would take things quietly she would make old bones yet, they had been lulled into security. At least I have, Opal thought. Had Miss Taylor?

The friendship between the two women, though in many ways still formal, ran strong and deep. Opal could not envisage a world without the older woman. She sometimes felt that Miss Taylor understood everything about her, even those things which were left unsaid, and that in understanding, she accepted.

She turned up Nab End Rise and into the drive of Oak House. How green I was when I first came here, she thought. A little shop assistant, delivering hats. It was a lifetime ago – yet it was only nine years, almost to the day. Jenny, who now opened the door, was the same maid who had let her in at the tradesmen's entrance on that occasion, who had grudgingly brought tea and Barmouth biscuits. I'm not sure that she's ever approved of me, Opal thought, walking past her, going up to the bedroom.

She was shocked by Miss Taylor's appearance. It was less than a month since she had seen her last, yet from the change in her it could have been a year. Propped against the pillows she seemed small and shrunken, her skin grey, the area around her mouth darkened by pain. And on her face was the look Opal had seen long ago on that of her own mother at Queenie's wedding; the indefinable aura of death. She knelt beside the bed and took Miss Taylor's hands in her own. The bony fingers were icy cold, as if death had already taken them and waited impatiently for the rest. In spite of her resolve to remain calm, Opal cried out in anguish.

'Miss Taylor! Oh Miss Taylor! You must get better! For my sake you must get better!'

The sick woman's voice was weak. She had difficulty in summoning enough breath to speak. Opal strained to hear her whispered reply.

'Not this time . . . Everything for you, dear child. Made me so happy . . . Enjoy it all.'

As she closed her eyes for the last time the pain left her face. Opal saw her grow young again, younger than she had ever known her; her features clear, her skin unlined. When the last sigh had left her body Opal cried out and flung herself across the bed, and cried out again and again until the maid came running.

'There was no need for you to come back to the store,' David said. 'You should have gone home. It's well after closing time anyway.'

She was sitting on the sofa in her office. David put a glass of brandy into her hand.

'Drink this,' he ordered. 'You look awful. Is there anything I can do if I go to Miss Taylor's now?'

'No. I saw to everything.'

Once she had pulled herself together she had done everything that was necessary: drawn the sheet over her dead friend's face, darkened the room, summoned the doctor, the undertaker. Then she had driven herself back to the store. No other death, not her mother's, not Madame Dora's, so terrible in its suddenness, had left her like this. She felt herself in an unreal world, as if her own spirit had died in her.

'You shouldn't have come back here,' David repeated.

'Where else would I go? Where else?'

At his insistence she gulped down the brandy and handed back the glass. He came and sat beside her, putting his arm around her, drawing her head on to his shoulder for comfort. The touch of his hand as he stroked her hair was all she needed to free the tears which, until now unshed, had felt like a great weight inside her. He let her cry and then with gentle fingers wiped away the tears, kissed her wet cheeks.

At first they held each other with no thought except to give and receive comfort. And then the grief of the moment merged, for both of them, with the sexual longings and needs of barren months. Their love-making was urgent, strong, passionate. She exulted in his fierceness and met it with a ferocity of her own. How had she borne without him for so long? Was anything in life as important as to love and be loved?

When the act was over, when – murmuring endearments, kissing her body gently now – he had helped her to dress, she remembered Miss Taylor. But now, though the sorrow, the loss, the bereavement were still there, the bitter anguish, the feeling of death in herself, had gone. As if, she thought in some confusion, as if the act which could give life had exerted some sort of supremacy over death.

Miss Taylor's words as she lay dying, her announcement that she had left everything to Opal, did not at the time penetrate Opal's consciousness. She was too overwhelmed by her friend's death to take it in. Unlike Madame Dora's death, when to her shame her inheritance had been almost her first thought, it was not until next day that it came back to her. When it did she wept again, knowing that she would have renounced it all to have bought Miss Taylor even one more day of life.

The inheritance, however, turned out to be less than might have been supposed. Miss Taylor's investments (the lawyer said after the funeral) had not done well over the last few years.

'Then she must have made a real sacrifice in putting money into my store?' Opal said.

'I think she did. But it was what she wanted to do. Of course you will, in addition, have Oak House. You will have to decide whether you want to live in it or sell it, though I should warn you that the market for large houses is not good at the present time.'

It took Opal no time at all to decide what to do with the money. She had wanted for some time to expand her small café into a much larger restaurant. There was plenty of space for it. She envisaged a place where business men or families might come for a good lunch, whether or not they were customers of the store. Since they would have to walk through the store to reach the restaurant she felt confident they would soon become customers. It was a scheme she had discussed with Miss Taylor, one which had found her approval.

On the evening of her visit to the lawyer she drew up rough plans for the extension. She would call her architect in the morning.

'What shall I do about Oak House?' she asked Edgar. He shrugged his shoulders.

'Do whatever you please. I don't see the need of a house that size for the three of us, but it's up to you, isn't it?'

'Well we shan't want to stay in Alma Place for ever,' Opal said. 'We've already been here longer than I intended. Of course I could sell Oak House and buy something smaller, but in a better area than Alma Place.'

They had not moved, partly because all her profits went back into the store, partly because she was always too busy to think about it. Now she would have to make a choice.

'I'll decide later,' she said to Edgar. 'It's coming up to the Christmas season and I'm going to be very busy. Also I want to start work on the new restaurant as soon as possible.'

*   *   *

Opal had little doubt that she was pregnant. By the middle of November she had missed a second period, and though she told herself that there might be other causes, her body contradicted her. Already her breasts were filling out, and when, on two consecutive mornings the room spun around as she rose from the bed, and she had to rush to the bathroom to be sick, she knew she could lie to herself no longer.

It was David who had sought out the doctor, a stranger on the other side of Leasfield, in whose consulting room she now sat. On David's advice she had not given her own name. The doctor's examination had been brief, his questions few. She had dressed quickly, and awaited his verdict.

'I am pleased to inform you that you are indeed pregnant, Mrs Derwent,' he said pleasantly.

He was quite sure she was not Mrs Derwent and that he had, somewhere, seen her before. It would come back to him sooner or later. In the meantime he must be careful.

'You seem to be in good health,' he continued. 'Though perhaps you are a little too thin. From now on you must take care of yourself, eat well. Remember that you are eating for two.'

'That is not the problem,' Opal said nervously. How could she tell him? How could she ask what she must? David had assured her that this man would immediately understand, but he gave no sign of doing so.

The doctor noted the way she twisted the gloves in her hands, saw the anxiety in her eyes. He knew well enough why she was here. She was not the first and would not be the last. He watched her struggling for words.

'I . . . you see, Doctor I . . . I can't have this baby! There are reasons why it's impossible.'

There always were. They were depressingly similar. He seemed to remember now that he had seen her photograph in the newspaper at some time. He was taking no chances.

'Please do something to help me!' Opal whispered.

He rose and walked towards the door.

'Mrs Derwent,' he said, 'neither the law, nor the ethics of my profession allow me to do what I think you are asking me. And if they did I would still not do it. Also, unless you are willing to take a grave risk, to submit yourself to pain and danger, I would strongly advise you not to seek out some less skilful means of achieving what you have in mind. And now I bid you good day. Since I can be of no possible use to you there is no fee for your visit.'

He held the door open and waited for her to leave.

In the street, coughing in the damp November fog, Opal's feelings swiftly changed. She was relieved, glad almost, that he had refused her. To rid herself of the child had been David's solution, and in her panic she had agreed. But in her heart she was against it. She was not sure that she could ever have gone through with it. And now it had been decided for her. She began to walk towards the town centre. It would be more sensible in this weather to take the tram, but walking would help her to think.

She was in an impossible situation. She knew for certain, now, that she would make no further attempt to rid herself of the baby, yet it seemed equally impossible that she should have it. Everything was against it.

Edgar must be told. It could not be long before

someone or other noticed the signs and she must not risk him finding out from some other source. But only he and she (and David who already knew) could have any idea that the child was not his. In Edgar lay her only hope. She had never before been afraid of him – what was there to fear? – but now she was. But it was not only fear which ate into her – of what he might do, of what he would say – but a deep aversion to the pain she must cause him.

They had given each other too much pain over the last few years, not by their actions so much as by the coldness which lay between them. She did not, as Edgar seemed to think, ever want to belittle him by her own success. She would have liked to have shared it all with him, but he was unwilling. Looking back, it seemed to her that except for the first two years they had seldom made each other happy. Yet it had not been deliberate on either side. They had never been cruel to each other and she believed she would have continued to love him had he not turned away from her.

The failure of their marriage had been the slow erosion of the bonds which bound them, and in the early days the strongest of those bonds had been sex. Now she must wound Edgar in the sharpest possible way, thrust in the knife where she knew him to be most vulnerable.

By the time she reached the store, almost an hour later, the wet fog had drenched her coat, her hat, her hair. She was not aware of it and wondered why Miss Morton looked at her strangely when she came into the office.

She broke it to Edgar that evening. She was glad that Daniel was away at school, thankful that no-one in the world could witness the pain, anger, disbelief in Edgar's face.

'It happened only once,' she said. 'It will never happen again. There were circumstances . . . Miss Taylor's death . . .'

'You think it makes it better that on the evening Miss Taylor died you went straight from her to him?'

She flinched before the disgust in his voice.

'It wasn't like that. You don't understand . . .'

'You're right! I don't!'

'Edgar, I beg of you! I swear to you that if you'll stand by me now I'll be faithful to you as long as I live. I never wanted to be anything else. I will be a better wife, Edgar. I will, I will! But you must help me.'

'Why must I?' he demanded. 'Do you know what you're asking? You are asking me to take this man's child and watch it grow up in my home – perhaps looking like him, reminding me every day of your betrayal! You're asking me to accept the child in your body – a body I haven't known for a long time – as my own.'

'Who else can I ask?' Opal cried. 'Who else can I turn to?'

He was silent for a while, his head buried in his hands. She could think of nothing more to say to him. At last he looked up.

'If we'd had a loving marriage,' he said slowly, 'if we'd shown each other any warmth and affection over the last few years – if it had happened in such circumstances – I think, though I don't know, that I could have accepted it, forgiven you. But it's not like that. I happen to be the only one who can solve your problem. There's no more to it than that.'

'That's not true!' Opal protested. 'I've offered you

love and affection. You've thrown it back at me. And I care deeply that I've hurt you so.'

'It's too late,' Edgar said flatly. 'And I won't do what you ask. This time I won't be your puppet on a string, dancing to your tune. I've had enough. I'm leaving!'

'You can't!' She was frantic. 'Edgar, you can't leave me!'

'Oh yes I can. Quite easily.'

'But Daniel? What about Daniel? Don't you care about him?'

Edgar lunged towards her, gripped her by the shoulders and began to shake her. She was frightened by the wild look in his eyes.

'I would like to kill you!' he shouted. 'I would really like to kill you!'

Then as suddenly as he had taken hold of her he flung her away from him and she fell to the floor.

'You know I love Daniel!' He was weeping now, deep, tearing sobs, which shocked her. 'I love him more than you've ever known how to. But I'm no use to him. You've seen to that. You're the one who can give him everything. He doesn't need me. When he finishes at his posh school he'll never need me again. But don't you ever dare to say I don't love him!'

It was Edgar who slept in the spare room that night. In the morning, by the time Opal rose, he had already gone. He had taken his clothes, and two photographs from the sideboard, one of herself and the other of Daniel. He had left behind the silver frames in which they normally stood.

Mechanically, as if she was sleep-walking, she dressed, did her hair, applied lipstick. Once she had to break off to be sick. When the time came for her to leave for the store she was ready.

'If I may say so,' Miss Morton said, 'you don't look at all well. Perhaps because you're the only one of us who hasn't had a holiday. Can I get you anything? A cup of coffee?'

Opal's inside heaved at the thought. 'No thank you,' she said.

She stood in front of the board, on her office wall, which showed a plan of the whole store and the deployment of staff.

'We must move two extra people into the Toy Department today,' she said. 'And I think we must steal a little more space from Sportswear to display the new Christmas stock of board games and jigsaw puzzles. Miss Deacon's not going to like it, but games and toys sell better than sportswear at this time of the year.'

Thank God for work. It could not solve her problem, which this morning seemed less than ever soluble (where had Edgar gone to? What could she do to get him back, to get him back she must) but while there were things to attend to in the store other questions could be pushed to the back of her mind for a few hours. At least she hoped they could.

'Is Mr Hessle in?' she asked her secretary.

'I think so. Shall I ask him to come up?'

'Yes.' She must tell him about Edgar. 'No, don't bother. I think I'll do my walk-around early today. After that I'll see Mr Hessle and then I'll go through the copy orders. Will you be getting them ready, please.'

She spent a long time walking around the store, visiting almost every department, asking questions, checking sales. Christmas cards were beginning to move, though the assistant told her that no-one seemed disposed to buy the new nineteen-thirty-five calendars. 'You get the feeling that they think it's bad luck to have them beforehand,' she said.

On Toys she met David. He was talking to an assistant she had not seen before, a pretty young woman with blonde hair to her shoulders, longer than the current fashion.

'I don't know you, do I?' Opal asked.

'This is Miss Nash,' David said. 'She's with us for the Christmas season.'

That explained it. She herself always saw permanent staff before they were engaged, but staff who were to be here for a few weeks only were engaged by David.

'I'm almost through,' she told him. 'Could you meet me in my office in fifteen minutes' time?'

She moved on to a disgruntled Miss Deacon in Sportswear and was pleased to have the lady's complaints interrupted by being called to the telephone.

'You have a visitor,' Miss Morton said. 'Mrs Carson. Your mother-in-law.'

Was it her imagination, or did Miss Morton's voice sound strained?

'How long has she been waiting?'

'Just a few minutes. But I think you'd better come, Miss Opal.'

She had not seen Mrs Carson for many months. There was somehow never enough time for visiting and her mother-in-law seldom came to the store. In any case she would scarcely have recognized the woman who awaited her in her office.

Her grey hair was wild and unkempt under the

old-fashioned hat; her coat unbuttoned as though she had rushed out of the house without bothering about anything. But worse than her clothes was her face – purple-red, blotched and swollen with tears, her eyes sparking anger.

'You may leave us, Miss Morton,' Opal said quickly.

'She needn't bother!' Mrs Carson shouted. 'She knows! Don't you think I won't tell everyone what you've done to my son, because I will! Don't you think you'll get away with it!'

Opal stepped forward, her hand outstretched to her mother-in-law, but the old woman pushed her away.

'My only one!' Her voice was a wail of anguish which cut into Opal. 'And now I'll never see him again! Never as long as I live! You've driven him away. Canada! Already he's on the train to Liverpool, and you drove him to it. I've seen it coming. I knew it would happen!'

She was screaming now, shaking her fist at Opal, when David entered.

'And you!' Mrs Carson yelled at him. 'You're the one! My Edgar didn't tell me that but I know. I've watched you. I've seen you look at her!'

'But it's you,' she shouted, turning back to Opal. 'It's you who've made him suffer. Don't think I haven't seen it all these years. Seen him grieving, eating his heart out because he couldn't keep up with you. May God punish you, Opal Derwent, and he will!'

She spat in Opal's face. The saliva caught her between the eyes, and ran down. The old woman collapsed in a sobbing, shaking heap on the sofa.

She's demented, Opal thought. She's gone mad. And

I'm going to be sick. She felt beads of cold perspiration on her forehead.

'Miss Morton, bring Miss Opal a glass of water,' David called out. 'Quickly, please!'

He took out his handkerchief and wiped Opal's face while Mrs Carson beat her fists against the sofa.

Chapter Eleven

Sleep evaded Opal that night. She who usually fell asleep instantly and knew nothing until the alarm sounded next morning, now stared into the darkness, waiting for the day to come, yet dreading it. If she closed her eyes she saw Mrs Carson's angry face, felt the spittle on her own face. Or she saw Edgar, white-faced and angry, his eyes bewildered by pain. She had not wanted to cause this hurt to anyone. But it was too late; all the repentance in the world could achieve nothing.

In her heart she knew that Edgar would never return. He was slow to move – how often she had been irritated by his inability to make a quick decision – but when he made up his mind he did not change it again. She flung her arms across the empty space where he should be. Why was it, when for so long his presence in their bed had meant little to her, that she could now miss him so?

Her thoughts swung around again to her mother-in-law. Mrs Carson had been so good to her when she needed help most. She had fed them, looked after Daniel to enable Opal to go to work. And now they were enemies. At least I am *her* enemy, Opal thought. I can never think of her as mine.

When she could bear the night no longer she got up and dressed, though it needed an hour or two yet to daylight. She would go to the store early. There was always work to be done and there would be other people. She, who had always valued solitude, longed for human company, could not bear the silence of this house.

She must speak with David today. He *must* help her, though she had no clear idea how. Would he leave Connie and come to her? And did she want that? Perhaps Edgar meant to divorce her, and if he did then perhaps she and David might make a fresh start, if only for the sake of the baby. And then, worst of all, there was Daniel to be told. How could she possibly tell Daniel that his father had gone, let alone that she was pregnant? But he must be told.

In the store she did two hours paperwork, carefully studied the latest issue of Vogue to see what high fashion ideas might be translatable to Opal's, and then began her round of the store. It amazed her that with her private life shattered into pieces she could give such close attention to her work. Thank heaven she could, and thank heaven that at least everything in the store seemed to be going well. She lingered in the fashion departments – always her favourite places – trying to find solace.

'It's a lovely time for fashion, Miss Baxter,' she said to her buyer on Gowns. 'Everything's so much more feminine and graceful than it was in the 'twenties. Don't you agree?'

'Oh I do Miss Opal,' the buyer said. 'Thank heaven those short skirts and that awful close-cropped hair have gone – never to return, I should hope!'

'I like your new stock of evening gowns,' Opal said, sorting through them on the rails. 'High front, back cut lower. Backs, by the way, are going to be lower still. Nice simple lines, cut on the bias. Yes, you've bought well, Miss Baxter. But I think one or two of these might be better with, say, the addition of a flower on the shoulder, or a chiffon handkerchief to tuck into a bracelet. Have a word with Miss Tyler and see what she has on Trimmings, and try something with the models on the stands. I'll be down later to have a look.'

It was the season for evening dresses and now everyone, of every class, wore them, since everyone went to dances. Opal was quite sure that not one of her girls, however junior, would be without a floor-length evening dress. It might lack the elegance of those on sale in the store – the girl would probably have run it up herself – but to go to a dance wearing a short dress would be unthinkable.

'If I may say so, Miss Opal,' Miss Baxter remarked, 'you don't look at all well this morning. I hope you haven't got influenza or anything. It's tricky weather.'

Would to God influenza was all I had, Opal thought. She felt wretched. The sickness now seemed to stay with her until the middle of the day and she felt a deep fatigue, far beyond anything caused by her sleepless night.

'I feel a bit queasy,' she admitted. 'Something I ate, I dare say.'

Work had begun on the new resturant, though there was no way it could be opened before the New Year since there was the matter of enlarging and re-equipping the kitchens. After the January sale has ended was the time she planned, so that the two events would not detract from each other. She tried to have new happenings in the store as often as possible; a fashion parade, a dressmaking expert, an artist to draw children's portraits, free make-up sessions. Always something new, something of interest to women.

Though the store was still a place to find a bargain – she made a practice of buying good bankrupt stock and selling it in special sales at rock bottom prices – the general trend was towards more expensive goods of finer quality. She now had a comfortable, and growing, number of well-to-do account customers.

On the ground floor she met David. He looked tired and drawn, as though he, too, had not slept. He eyed her with concern.

'You don't look too good!'

'So I've just been told. Don't you think, with all these women around, it can only be a short time before one or other of them guesses? I'll see you later. We've got to talk.'

Perhaps everything would seem better when she had talked with David, she thought, clutching at straws.

When she had toured the ground floor departments she walked outside to inspect the window displays. It was raining hard; ice-cold drops, dirt-laden from the smoky air. No-one but she would be mad enough to gaze into shop windows on a day like this. She went back to her office and was going through the copy orders with Miss Morton when the door crashed open and Daniel burst in. She jumped up from her chair, her stomach lurching, fear chilling the flesh on her shoulders and back.

'Why Daniel, what in the world are you doing here? Why aren't you at school? And you're absolutely soaking. Take your coat off at once!'

She turned to her secretary. 'We'll finish the orders later, Miss Morton.'

He stood there in the doorway, rain dripping from his hair, running in rivulets down his face. He made no move to take off his wet coat and she moved towards him to help him.

'Don't touch me!' he said harshly.

She stepped back. It was as though he had struck her on the face. What could he possibly know, and so soon? Mrs Carson could not . . .'

'You drove him away!' he accused her. 'It's your fault! Why couldn't you be an ordinary person? Why can't you be like Auntie Queenie, or Auntie Mary?'

He looked so young, so bitterly unhappy. She wanted to take him in her arms, and could not, because he would not let her. He was no longer the small boy she could comfort. There was suddenly a wide gulf between them. He was looking at her with eyes full of misery and hate.

'How did you know?' she asked. 'Who told you?' And how much, she wanted to add.

'I had a letter from Father this morning. I ran away from school and got the train from York. I expect they'll telephone you. But I'm not going back! He wouldn't have gone if I'd been at home. It's my fault as well because I was angry with him that last time. He doesn't know I love him and now we'll never see him again!'

The words poured out of him as if he had no way of stopping them.

'Daniel, don't! I'm sure he'll come back!'

Her words sounded futile. She had no idea what to say to this child whom she loved so much. And she was afraid to speak, too, not knowing the extent of his knowledge.

'Of course he won't come back!' he cried. 'Here, read this!'

He thrust the letter into her hands. It was damp, and

in places the ink ran down the page, as if he had read it and re-read it while walking in the rain.

'I'm off to Canada,' she read. 'By the time you get this I shall be on one of the liners we saw in Liverpool. There are fine chances for men in Canada. Forgive me, son, and don't ever think I don't love you. Take care of your mother.'

She handed back the letter. So he did not know about the baby. She would not tell him yet. The burden he already carried was too heavy for him to bear. She could not add to it now – though soon she must.

'Blame me if you like,' she said quietly, 'I dare say it is largely my fault, though perhaps not entirely. Things are never as black and white as they seem. But you must not blame yourself in any way. Your father loves you dearly, you know that.'

'You don't understand, do you?' he cried. 'You never understand!' The anguish in his voice, the fact that he could not command his voice so that it wavered uncontrollably, hurt her more, even, than the words themselves.

'I *know* he loves me,' Daniel said. 'I've always known it. It's that I didn't show him how much I loved him. You have to show people or they don't know!'

He dropped down on to the sofa, as if his legs would not hold him any longer, and began to sob. Opal put out a hand and touched him and this time he did not shake her off. Let him cry, she thought. It's healing for the young to cry.

'Did you have any breakfast before you left school?' she asked presently.

'No.'

'Then you must be hungry. I'll send for some sandwiches and some hot coffee. And you *must* take off your wet coat. I don't want you to catch cold.'

'I'm not hungry,' he said. But when the food came he ate it, and immediately looked the better for it.

'Now you must go back to school,' Opal said. 'I'll drive you back myself. I'll telephone Mr Cottrell before we go and make it all right.'

It was a silent drive. Daniel had calmed down, but he was still pale, and clearly deeply troubled. She knew he did not want to return to school. It was as if however angry he was with her, he needed her presence. Well, she needed him too, but it could not be allowed.

'You could come home for half-term next week, instead of going to Highcliffe,' she suggested. 'I'll be busy in the store and you might be a help to me. What do you think?'

He made no reply.

'I'll go round by Highcliffe on my way back from York,' she said. 'I shall have to tell them about your father and these things are better said face to face. I'm glad you came to see me, Daniel, even if you did run away from school. Anyway, I'm sure—'

'Look out!' he yelled suddenly. 'Mother, what are you doing? Didn't you see the man? Don't you know you have to give way to pedestrians at Belisha beacons?'

She sighed. 'I'm sorry, love. I know I'm not a good driver. I don't like driving and that's the truth.'

'You're a terrible driver,' Daniel said. 'You never seem to have your mind on it.'

Opal, as she had promised, called at Highcliffe on the way back to Leasfield. Without preamble she told Mary and her father that Edgar had gone, told them about the letter he had sent to Daniel.

'I can't believe it!' Mary said, horrified. 'Not Edgar!'

203

She clearly blames me, Opal thought. I can hear it in her voice, see it in her face. But she was getting used to that. Even without knowing about the baby it seemed that everyone blamed her.

'It's a bad do, our Opal,' her father said. 'Nothing like this has happened in our family afore.'

What will they say when they know I'm pregnant, she wondered. She could not bring herself to tell them, not yet.

Her father was not well. He sat in front of the fire, coughing and wheezing, an old shawl of her mother's draped around his shoulders.

'He should be in bed but he won't stay there,' Mary complained. 'Which means he'll have bronchitis on and off all winter.'

When Opal left, Mary walked out to the car with her.

'He's not said anything to you yet,' she said. 'But Father's thinking of selling up. It's getting too much for him. The weather up here on the moor is no good to anyone with a bad chest, not in winter.'

'What shall you do?' Opal asked.

'I don't know. Move to something smaller where it's a bit warmer. I shall have to take a job, though goodness knows what I'm fitted for!'

You're fitted for marriage and children, Opal thought, moved by the sadness in her sister's face. Why did it come to me and not to you? You wouldn't have failed at it. You would never find yourself in the mess *I'm* in.

David was waiting in her office when she got back. 'I thought you might have gone,' Opal said. 'I'm glad you haven't.'

'Miss Morton gave me your message. How was Daniel?'

'Better, by the time I left him. Of course he blames me and I suppose he's right about that.'

'Did you tell him . . . ?'

'That I was pregnant?' she said harshly. 'No I did not. He has enough on his plate right now. I'll break that to him in the Christmas holidays, as I will to Mary and Dad. David, what are we going to do?'

'That's what I have to talk to you about,' he said hesitantly. 'Opal, there's something I must tell you and I don't know how to begin.'

Why was he afraid? Anxious – yes – but there was something more. It came to her with absolute certainty that something was terribly wrong.

'Whatever it is,' she said, 'why don't you come straight to the point?' Yet she didn't want to hear it. She knew it must be bad.

'The fact is,' David said, 'Connie is pregnant!'

The silence seemed to go on and on, as if there was nothing left for either of them to say. And what *was* there to say?

'*Really* pregnant this time?' Opal said at last. 'Really and truly pregnant?' Her voice sounded like a stranger's. Hard, sarcastic.

'The baby is due next April. I've been meaning to tell you.'

'So she was pregnant when you and I . . . ?'

'Yes.'

'Well, you have been a busy bee, haven't you?'

Why do I speak so lightly, she thought. He is killing me. He is surely killing me.

'I take it that the baby is yours? Her baby, I mean. We know mine is.'

'Of course it is!' His voice was sharp.

'Why of course?' she asked wildly. 'Not every woman

in the world is bearing her own husband's baby. But perhaps Connie is finer material than I? Perhaps I'm a different kind of woman? Is that it?'

'Opal, you're being ridiculous . . . !'

'. . . Perhaps I'm what my mother-in-law said I was? A whore. Is that what you think too?'

'Opal, I'm bitterly sorry . . .' he began.

'I'm sure you're sorry . . .' she interrupted. 'But I'd like to reserve the word "bitter" for my own feelings. And now I have something to say to you, David. Please listen carefully because I don't think I shall be able to say it twice. Only you and I – and Edgar who has gone to the other side of the world because of it – know that the baby I am carrying is yours. When she hears about it Mrs Carson might suspect, but she can't know. So from this moment on the baby is *mine*. Mine entirely; mine alone! Do you understand? You have no part of it, now and for ever. If you have any feeling for this child, which I doubt, then turn it to your own child and leave me to mine. Is that clear?'

It was not her imagination that he looked relieved.

'If that's the way you want it.'

'It is. And I don't doubt that it suits you!'

She longed to punish him, yet what she was doing was setting him free. It could only be that way. She had to free herself, for once and for all, and with what little dignity was left to her.

'Do you want me to leave the store, look for another job?' David asked.

'I would certainly like that, but what good would it be to either of us? As you know perfectly well, I shall need you to take my place when I take time off to have the baby. No-one else can be trained in so short a time. And you would not find it easy to get another job as good as this, though that doesn't worry me. At the moment we're dependant on each other. I wish to God we weren't, but we are. And now will you please get out of my sight!'

When he had left the room she sat for a long time, staring at the pile of papers in front of her, not seeing them. It was impossible even to think any more. She did not hear the knock on the door and was startled when it opened and the night-watchman stood in the doorway.

'Just checking around, Miss Opal,' he said. 'Will you be working much later? It's gone eight o'clock.'

'I'm just going,' she said. 'Thank you, Mr Chambers.'

What was the point of going home, back to a house which was not just empty, but deserted? To another long night in which she would not be able to sleep? She realized, wearily, just how much she had been relying on David's support, counted, somehow, on having him by her side. There was no-one left now from whom she could take strength; Edgar gone, Daniel needing strength from her, Mary against her. And then, putting on her coat, she thought of Queenie. Queenie, who knew nothing of this and must soon learn it. Queenie, who would not sit in judgement, because she judged no-one. Opal went back to her desk and picked up the telephone.

'Why, Opal, how lovely to hear you! I was coming into the store tomorrow, as a matter of fact.' Queenie's voice was like the woman herself; clear, unaffected, warm.

'Queenie, can I come and see you? I mean now? I need to talk to you.'

'Why of course! Is something wrong?'

'Yes. But I can't talk on the telephone. You don't have guests?'

'No. And Mark's in London at the Wool Sales.'

'I'll drive over now,' Opal said. 'Bless you, Queenie!'

She could not, she thought, driving through the dark streets towards Barton, tell even Queenie about David's part in this. For the sake of everyone concerned that was a secret she knew she must bear alone, and bear as long as she lived. There was no-one in the world, save Edgar, with whom she could share that burden – and he would have nothing to do with her.

Queenie must have been watching out for her. She was at the door the moment Opal rang the bell.

'Opal dear, are you frozen?' she said. 'Come in by the fire. Let me take your coat. I've poured you a glass of sherry and you can be drinking it while I say goodnight to the children. I shan't be long.'

What a happy home this is, Opal thought, sitting close to the fire, sipping her drink. Why can't you be like Auntie Queenie, Daniel had said, and no wonder. But she could never be like Queenie. They were cast in different moulds. Queenie knew nothing of the ambition which drove some people so hard, and often so painfully. I didn't ask to be ambitious, Opal thought. It was born in me. And because I'm a woman, and ambition and femininity are ill-assorted, it's told against me. I shall never be what a man looks for in a woman. Yet she knew that even if it were possible she would not be without her ambition. It gave purpose to each day.

'There!' Queenie said, coming into the room. 'All tucked up for the night. Opal, can I get you something to eat? I suspect you've not had supper.'

'No thank you. I'm not hungry.'

Once begun, it was easy to talk to Queenie, so easy that the greatest effort was not to tell her everything. And Queenie was no fool. She had suspected for a long time that matters were not right between Opal and Edgar. But such was her unique gift that she could bring a positive sympathy, a deep feeling of support, to everyone. Her grief for Edgar in his lonely flight did not allow her to condemn Opal. If she wondered why a kind man who loved children, and his own son above all, should leave his newly-pregnant wife, she did not ask out loud, nor would she ever. She did not apportion blame in any direction, though this was not because she stood aside.

She accepts us, Opal thought. She accepts us all, exactly as we are. She doesn't ask us to be different or to measure up to some standard. For the first time since Miss Taylor's death Opal felt comforted. The tears which ran down her face now were tears of release.

'Opal, you must stay the night! It's a nasty wet one for you to drive home. In fact you must come here often in the next few months. I know Mark will want you to.'

Mark would want it, Opal knew, if only because his beloved Queenie did so. Whatever his wife did was good in his sight. The years which had driven herself and Edgar further and further apart had brought her brother and his wife ever closer to each other.

'And now I'm going to prepare some food,' Queenie said. 'I'm quite hungry myself. We'll have an omelette.'

Next morning Opal called Miss Morton into her office first thing. She would need her secretary's help over the next few months.

'I feel I owe you an explanation of the last day or

two,' Opal said. 'You must have wondered what it was all about. Well, it's true that I'm pregnant. It is also true that my husband has gone abroad. His Company wished him to spend a few months in their Toronto office, but we both hope that he will be back long before the baby is born.'

It was a fiction she had decided upon before she fell asleep last night. Leasfield, though it might like to think otherwise, was provincial and narrow. It liked its public figures – of whom she was now undoubtedly one – to lead regular, well-ordered lives, open to public scrutiny. And especially so if they were women. It had been a slight mark against her that she attended no place of worship, professed no religion. If they bought a yard of material from her shop they liked to know that the vendor was upright and honourable.

'Of course Daniel is upset. He's not yet settled into his new school. Adolescence is a difficult time. As for my mother-in-law – well, she is elderly so we must excuse her, but I'm afraid she doesn't quite see things as they are!'

She looked Miss Morton clearly in the eye.

'You can discount anything she may have said in her distress at parting with her son. There is naturally no truth in any of it. In fact I can tell you, though I do so in confidence . . .' She took a deep breath. She could hardly bear to say the words. 'Mr Hessle's wife is happily pregnant and they are both looking forward tremendously to their baby's birth. As I am to mine.

'Of course I don't wish anyone to know just yet that I'm pregnant. You know how people feel about pregnant women showing themselves in public – quite wrongly, I think. When I can no longer disguise my condition I shall take leave of absence until a few months after the baby is born. Mr Hessle will take over from me.'

The January sales had gone particularly well this year, Opal thought with satisfaction. Almost everything cleared, and at a good profit. And now the restaurant was open and beginning to do business. They could seat three hundred people for morning coffee, for a good, three-course lunch, or for afternoon or high tea. The prices were right – a shilling and tenpence for the set lunch, more if one ate *à la carte* – the menus were varied and, above all, the service was efficient and friendly under the new manager, Mr Soames.

Opal had been amazed at the number of women of all ages who were eager to work as waitresses for the low wages paid in the catering trade. She could not pay more than the usual rate, and keep her prices down, but she saw to it that her waitresses had a good nourishing meal each day, and two breaks in the staff rest room where they could put up their feet and look at a magazine.

She had felt better in health since Christmas, less inclined to sickness and with a return of her usual energy, though she tired easily.

'You have to remember you're in your mid-thirties,' the doctor told her. 'You're not a young girl. And you work far too hard. I do think that for the sake of both yourself and the baby you should give up work at Easter.'

The doctor, a woman, came into the store once a week. A room was set aside where she could be consulted by any member of the staff, at no cost to them. Opal believed that many an illness, with its consequent loss of work, was nipped in the bud by this system, and the girls related well to the sympathetic, female physician.

'I suppose I shall have to,' Opal said. 'I'm already beginning to show, and you know what people are like. By Easter I shall be six months pregnant.'

Christmas itself, which they had spent at Highcliffe, had not been easy, though in one surprising way it had been better than she had expected. Daniel had missed his father badly. He had been both consoled and upset by the arrival of a Christmas card, posted in Toronto; consoled because his father had thought of him, upset because he had sent no address. But about the baby he *had* been pleased, partly because he genuinely welcomed the addition to their small family but also, Opal discovered, for another reason.

'If Father could hear the news I just *know* he'd come back!' he said eagerly. 'If only we could contact him. Perhaps Grandma Carson might have had a bit more information than we have. My word, she'll be pleased about the baby! She's always on about having only one grandchild.'

His relationship with his grandmother had remained as unclouded as ever. Whatever she thinks about me, Opal realized, she hasn't passed it on to Daniel.

Her father's illness had been neither better nor worse over the Christmas holiday, but Mary had been worried about the winter still to come.

'He's had an offer for the farm,' she told Opal. 'I want him to accept it. It's really a question of where we would go, what we would do next.'

'I've been thinking about that,' Opal said. 'You know I still haven't made up my mind about Oak House?

What do you say if I keep it on and you and Father come to live there? You can have your own rooms if you wish. There's plenty of space.'

Mary flushed with pleasure.

'Oh, Opal, that would be marvellous! I'm so heartily sick of being stuck in Highcliffe. And Oak House would be so much better for Father. I would have to get a job, though. We couldn't live off you.'

'I've thought of that too,' Opal said. 'I shall need someone to look after the baby when I go back to the store, and Daniel in the school holidays. You're so good with children. Would you like to keep house for me and look after Daniel and the baby? I'd pay you a wage and you'd have a place to live. Besides, I'd like to have you. I know you don't always approve of me, but I'm not really difficult to live with. Anyway, most of the time I'm not there!'

Mary smiled.

'I've envied you, Opal. Perhaps I always will, a bit. But we get on well enough, so if Father agrees it's fine by me. Mind you, I'll bet Grandpa Derwent will be horrified at the thought of Father selling the farm. He thinks land is sacred. He'll hang on to it until he dies – if he ever does.'

'I think Grandpa Derwent is immortal,' Opal said. 'Eighty-four and still ruling his womenfolk with a rod of iron.'

Her father had been happy enough at the thought of moving into Oak House.

'I've had enough of this lot,' he said. 'I don't know that I was ever cut out to be a farmer. It was just something my father expected me to do.'

* * *

'When *do* you move house?' the doctor asked.

'Next week.'

She would not be sorry to leave Alma Place. It had not been a happy house.

'Don't you dare to get involved in the moving,' the doctor warned.

Opal left the medical room and went down to the first floor. She was always careful, these days, not to linger on Children's and Babywear, but there were courtesies to be observed and she stopped to speak to the buyer. She had not seen Mrs James Carstairs buying rompers for her grandchild. Mrs Carstairs pounced.

'Ah! I see you're interested in this merchandise!'

'Certainly,' Opal said smoothly. 'I'm interested in everything that's sold in my store.'

'But if what I hear is correct, and my eyes don't deceive me . . .' She stared frankly at Opal's figure. '. . . in this one especially! Come now, don't be coy!'

The buyer moved away. Opal saw her speak to two assistants who were whispering together.

Anger flamed in Opal's face. She clenched her hands around the notepad she was carrying.

'When *I* was in your condition,' Mrs Carstairs said, 'I never went out in public, except perhaps for a walk after dark, and then only when accompanied by my husband. We never flaunted ourselves. But then it's a different world, isn't it?'

'Not different enough,' Opal said. 'I look forward to the day when women don't have to hide what is a perfectly natural condition. When they can go anywhere they please, freely, right up to the last moment of pregnancy.'

'Now *that* is a word we *never* used!' Mrs Carstairs said.

As Opal left the department and continued on her way around the store she felt, uncomfortably, that she was being surreptitiously looked at. She was angry with the convention that caused this, angrier still that she must bow to it. But she must do so. The feelings of her customers – and she was sure that Mrs Carstair's reaction was the usual one – false though she thought them, were important. They were what she had built her business on.

When she returned to her office Miss Morton handed her a copy of the Leasfield Courier.

'I thought you should see this,' she said. 'Under "Gossip of the Day".'

Opal took it from her and read it.

A little bird tells us that a certain well-known business lady – a jewel of a lady it might be said – is in an interesting condition. We congratulate her, and commiserate with her that her husband is not by her side. Are we to assume that before long she will not be 'Open to the Public'?

'Get the editor of the Courier on the 'phone,' Opal said furiously. 'At once. Tell him that if he cares to send a reporter around, Miss Opal has a statement which might be of interest. And ask Mr Hessle if he can spare me a moment right away.'

She saw as little of David as possible these days, though of necessity they met to discuss business. When he came into her office she thought how fit and well he looked. His wife's pregnancy suited him. By this time next month he would be a father.

'Read this' she said 'And then read the statement I propose to give to the Courier.'

The paragraph appeared in the newspaper the next day.

Miss Opal (in private life Mrs Edgar Carson) has informed us that she and her husband are happily expecting a child in June. 'I shall take leave of absence from Easter until a few months after our baby is born,' she told our reporter.

'My store will carry on exactly as usual under the expert hand of my Store Manager, Mr David Hessle.'

Mr & Mrs Hessle are expecting their first child in April. A fruitful year for Opal's Store!

She left on Easter Saturday, at the end of a record day in almost all departments. On a day in June she sent another announcement to the Leasfield Courier.

To Mr and Mrs Edgar Carson (Miss Opal), the precious gift of a daughter, Emmeline.

A bare announcement, she thought, reading it as she lay in bed. It said nothing of the heartache, of her son's unavailing desire for his father's return, or the loneliness of her future. It said nothing, also, of the love which came with the new baby, which surrounded and enfolded it. My daughter shan't be like me, Opal vowed, watching the dark-haired child in her arms. I shall teach my daughter how to love, how to *be* loved.

Chapter Twelve

Afterwards, the summer of nineteen-thirty-five seemed like a dream; a pleasant dream, everyone moving lightly through it, until the moment when the nightmare took over.

Emmeline's birth had been straightforward and easy and from the moment she came into the world she was a good baby, sleeping and feeding well, seldom crying. Against her doctor's advice that she should go into a nursing home for the event, Opal had decided that her child should be born at Oak House. It had been the right decision. The child, though she seldom made her presence heard in the first few weeks, gave the house what it lacked; the feeling of a family home; three generations (Mary and her father were settled in) under the one roof. Not that they could ever be a complete family, Opal thought; children without father, wife without husband. But it was perhaps the nearest they would ever get.

In July, when Daniel came home for the summer holidays and the monthly nurse had departed, Opal rented a house at St Anne's for a month.

'Are you sure you're quite well enough?' Mary asked anxiously. 'It's early days. Emmeline's only six weeks old.'

Her sister had wanted the child to be named Mary. It was Jubilee summer, she pointed out, and it would be a compliment to the Queen as well as to herself.

But the name 'Emmeline' had come into Opal's mind – she had no idea from whence – and she liked it above all others.

'I'm as fit as a fiddle,' Opal said. 'And I've hired the largest car imaginable. We shall be chauffeur-driven, door to door. I can rest as much as I want to in St Anne's. Do you realize that Daniel is fourteen years old and he's never had a seaside holiday?'

'I'm thirty' Mary said 'and I haven't had one since I was six. Do you remember that week in Morecambe? You must have been about ten. George was Daniel's age. We went with Mother and Aunt Garnet because Father couldn't leave the farm.'

'I remember,' Opal said. It had been the long, hot summer of nineteen-eleven. They had stayed in a boarding house in a side street and her mother had shopped every morning for food which the landlady cooked for them. 'We went shrimping.'

'And saw the pierrots every day,' Mary reminded her.

The house in St Annes was on the sea front. Opal sat in the wide bay window, watching the passers-by. Or joined them, pushing Emmeline in the pram, her father by her side leading Floss, the sheep dog who because she was old, her working days over, he had refused to leave with the new owners of the farm. Mary and Daniel frequently took the tram into Blackpool, where Daniel was addicted to the newly-discovered delights of the South Shore Pleasure Beach.

'It's ridiculous,' Mary said. 'He comes off the Big Wheel looking as green as grass, and then insists on going on again the next day!'

'I might go with you one day,' Benjamin said. 'This holiday is doing me good. I feel a different man from when I was up at Highcliffe.'

'I'm glad,' Opal said. 'I feel pretty good myself.'

In fact she felt well enough to be back at work. She found herself thinking more and more about it. The July sales would be over, the autumn season not yet started. August was a quiet little *entre-acte*. Some of her customers would, like herself, be at the seaside. Prices, especially of food, were lower than they had been, so that for those who had jobs the standard of living was higher and a holiday could be afforded. It was more than likely that some of her customers, what she thought of (not meaning to be snobbish) as the lower end of her market, would be in nearby Blackpool. Her better class customers would be in Scarborough or Filey, or in St Annes itself. How much she looked forward to seeing them all again, even Mrs James Carstairs!

Though she had enjoyed it, she was not sorry when the month in St Annes was over and they were back once again in Oak House. She found herself frequently opening the diary in which the date of her return to the store was marked – Tuesday the first of October – and secretly wishing that the days would pass more quickly. But she enjoyed Emmeline, cherishing especially the moments when she held her to the breast and watched her suckle. If her milk would adjust itself she might still be able to keep on the night and early morning feeds. She enjoyed the baby's bathtime, too, though that was gradually being taken over by Mary.

It was good, also, to have Daniel at home for the long school holiday, to observe his tenderness and concern for his sister, whom he adored. But in spite of his new-found happiness Daniel seemed to fret after his father more than ever.

'Why can't we at least *try* to find him?' he asked, not

for the first time. 'We could advertise in a Toronto newspaper. He doesn't even know he's got a daughter. I'm sure if he knew that he'd want to come back!'

Once more Opal fended him off with excuses, but on the day she drove him back to school he took up the subject again. 'Why won't you?' he persisted. 'Why won't you give it a try?'

'If he wants to get in touch with us he knows where we are,' Opal pointed out. 'We must allow him to decide for himself. We mustn't try to force him.'

It hurt her that she must be less than honest with Daniel but honesty, in this case, was not the best policy.

'After all,' she said, 'we can't use little Emmeline as a sort of blackmail. And you must remember that it would be *me* he had to come back to, not just you. It was me he left.'

'And me,' Daniel said unhappily.

He was always at his most miserable when he was returning to school. He did well enough there but he did not enjoy it. He lived for the day when he would be sixteen, at which time, Opal had promised, he might leave York and start a course at the Bradford College of Art. She would have liked him to have come straight into the store with her but it was obvious that he would first have to get art out of his system.

'Not really you,' Opal assured him. 'If anyone could have kept your father it would have been you. Perhaps sometimes we're driven to a moment when our own needs are so demanding that we have to put them first. Your father's need was to get away from me. That had to take precedence even over you.'

But Daniel was not to be comforted. It was not only his father. Going back to school he was being separated from his mother, his aunt, his grandfather, and now from Emmeline, whom he loved more than he had ever thought possible. Sitting beside Opal in the car he was sunk in gloom, and though experience told him that the gloom would lift as the days went by, that was no comfort to him. He did not believe it.

By the last week in September Opal had weaned Emmeline from all except the night and early morning feeds and Mary had taken over the daytime bottle feeding.

'I really do believe, Mary, you'll be glad to see the back of me!' Opal teased. 'You'll be glad to have Emmeline to yourself.'

Mary looked up from the child on her lap. 'I don't mean it to be like that, Opal,' she said. 'It's just wonderful to me that you let me share the children.'

On the morning of the first of October Opal was up early. She had a new dress to wear today, to celebrate her return to the store, chosen from a selection she had had sent up to her. The new autumn colours were subdued, with a tendency to brown which, with her dark hair, did not suit her. But there had been one dress in Autumn Green, a lovely coppery green, dark, yet so much clearer and brighter than the old bottle green. It was perfect for her. She put on her opal pendant and took a last look at herself in the mirror. She had regained her figure quickly. She was absolutely flat.

'I shan't need a coat,' she said to Mary, walking down the stairs into the hall. 'It's quite warm.'

'I'll close the garage doors after you,' Mary said. 'Save you getting out of the car. Now remember Opal, don't work too late on your first day!'

The traffic was heavier than she had expected, as if the whole world was returning to work at the end of the summer. She was thrilled by the thought of the day ahead. She must see David first, get up to date – though she had had reports from him during her absence and all seemed to be going well. On a personal level she did not look forward to meeting him. There was a breach between them which would never be healed though, strangely, she no longer bore him malice for making her pregnant. How could she when she had Emmeline? But then she never thought of her baby as having anything whatever to do with David Hessle. Emmeline was hers and hers alone, as if she had been born of an immaculate conception.

She would do her walk-around early today, renew all her ties. And today was the day of the weekly staff meeting. She had forgotten to tell Mary that she would be a little late home because of that. When the store came in sight on her right, bright and uncommonly clean-looking in the smoky town, she tingled with excitement. She drove along the front of the store, quickly glancing in the windows, and at the far corner made a right turn towards the car park. She had no knowledge of, nor later did she ever remember, the car which came towards her on the opposite side of the road. All she knew, all she ever recalled, was the red film which came over her eyes, a redness in which she seemed to drown, in the second before she lost consciousness.

The surgeon backoned Mary over to the window, turning his back on the patient in the bed and speaking in a low voice.

'Can she hear us?' Mary asked anxiously.

'I can't be sure,' he admitted. 'We don't know how far a patient in a coma is aware of what's going on.

Sometimes we think not at all. At other times it seems as though some outside stimulus, perhaps something to which the patient would, when conscious, have a positive reaction, has a marked effect. But there's so much of which we're ignorant.'

'My sister will get better, won't she?' Mary asked. 'Please be frank with me. There are children . . .'

He looked with compassion at the white-faced woman who looked as though she had not slept for a week. He so often had to answer this question, yet experience never made it any easier.

'I will be frank,' he said. 'She's had an extremely bad accident. Her head injuries are most serious. We've done all we can in theatre. Now it's up to good nursing and Nature. But I should say she's a strong young woman, in good health. If she's a fighter . . .'

'She's a fighter!'

'Then she has a chance.'

'Thank God,' Mary said.

'I would like to keep her in this private wing,' the surgeon said. 'She will need constant supervision for a long time yet, and while we do our best in the general hospital, we're always short-staffed. But it's expensive. Perhaps you would like to think about it, Miss Derwent.'

'I will. My sister isn't without money, though of course I don't know the extent of her finances. But I'm sure she must stay here for the time being.'

'I'll look in on her again later,' he said. 'And of course I'm always on call if I should be needed. I think it might help the patient if members of her family – or close friends – people to whom she relates well in life – could be here as much as possible, at least during the day.'

'Day or night, Mr Talbot,' Mary said. 'I don't suppose my sister knows the difference right now.'

As he left the room, Queenie came in. She put her arms around Mary and kissed her.

'You look all in, Mary.'

'I am rather tired. Emmeline cried a good deal in the night. It's not like her. Perhaps it's because she had to be completely weaned all of a sudden.'

'Would you like me to take her for a few days?' Queenie asked. 'Let you get some rest?'

'No thank you, Queenie. She's used to me. Besides, in a strange way she's a consolation. The same with Daniel. Thank you for fetching him home from school.'

They stood by the bed and looked at Opal, lying so still beneath the heavy bandages, intently watched by a nurse for any sign of change.

'I don't know where we're going to put all the flowers and cards which keep arriving,' the nurse said. 'As you can see, we've no more room in here, and still they come.'

Queenie sat down and took Opal's hand in her own.

'Dear Opal! She's never understood how much people admire her! In spite of all her success she never thinks well of herself as a person. She's a woman surrounded by love which she doesn't know how to accept.'

Sister came back into the room as Queenie was speaking.

'That's a pity,' she said. 'I have the feeling that if she could know of all these good wishes, this tremendous goodwill, it might help her. I've been talking with Mr Talbot. We wonder if there's anything at all you can think of which might arouse Mrs Carson? Something which might pierce an abyss, the depth of which we don't understand. What does she care for most in the world?'

Mary and Queenie looked at each other.

'Opal's store, and her children, Daniel and Emmeline,' Queenie said.

'Well we can't bring the store to her,' Sister said. 'But the children . . . Her son, of course, has been here a great deal. But the baby . . . she's four months old, isn't she? If Mrs Carson were to hear her baby cry . . . ? Of I dare say it's fanciful, but what have we to lose? A baby's cry of need for its mother. Who knows how deep that goes?'

'Perhaps you're right,' Mary said hesitantly. 'Perhaps that's why Emmeline's cried so much these last few days. Being taken so suddenly off the breast . . . missing her mother's presence, not just food.'

'I'll contact Mr Talbot,' Sister said.

'In the meantime I shall stay here a little longer,' Queenie said, 'But, Mary, I insist you go home and get some rest.'

'Your sister-in-law is right, Miss Derwent,' Sister said gently. 'You're going to need all your strength in the next few weeks.' Whichever way it goes, she thought.

'My car's outside,' Queenie said. 'Ask Freeman to take you home. And if Mr Talbot should want you to bring Emmeline in later, I'll fetch you both.'

Later that evening Queenie returned to the hospital, accompanied by Mary, carrying Emmeline who was fast asleep. As they entered Opal's room a weary-faced Daniel walked behind them.

'Daniel wanted to come,' Mary told Sister. 'He thought he might be able to help.'

Sister looked at the boy; a lanky fourteen-year-old, badly in need of sleep and rest which he could not get;

stony-faced in his effort to be brave, but unable to hide the despair and helplessness in his eyes as he looked towards the still form on the bed.

'I'm sure he will,' she said kindly. 'Perhaps it would be a good idea if Daniel were to sit by the bed and hold the baby, instead of you doing so, Miss Derwent.'

It would make no difference to the patient, she thought, but the boy might feel he was doing something. She watched as the aunt handed the baby to Daniel, noted the careful, loving way he took his sister and held her in his arms. We must fight for this patient, she told herself. We must save her for these two children.

'It's Emmeline's feed time,' Mary said. 'She should waken any time now.'

As if she knew what was expected of her the baby wakened, screwed up her face and began to cry; the lusty cry of a healthy, four-month-old baby demanding attention.

'No, don't try to soothe her, Daniel!' Sister said. 'However cruel it seems for the moment, let her cry.'

The baby's cries, raucous, angry at being ignored, rent the air in the small room. On and on. The three women and the boy watched the bruised, lacerated face of the woman on the bed. Tears streamed down Daniel's face and at last he could bear it no more. He leaned over the bed and his loud cry rang out above the noise from the baby in his arms.

'Mother! Mother, you must come back! It's Daniel! I want you!'

He collapsed, sobbing, continuing to cry out. Mary took the baby from him. Queenie knelt down and took him in her arms. Only Sister saw Opal open her eyes.

*   *   *

226

It was a slow recovery. A little each day, and there were days when she seemed to slip back, called by some dark country of the mind, then somehow rallied again. It was a month before those so carefully watching knew that she would live. Christmas came and went and the winter of nineteen-thirty-six gave way to spring and then to early summer before Opal left hospital.

'But she has a long way to go yet,' Mr Talbot warned. 'She needs rest and quiet for many months to come. No worries. No business affairs. You must be very strict with her.'

'I will be,' Mary promised.

'Allow me one meeting with my Store Manager,' Opal pleaded. 'Just so that I can be assured that all is going well.'

Mr Talbot shook his head. 'It's against my better judgement,' he said. 'But one very short meeting to set your mind at rest, and then nothing more until I allow it.' He would have a word with Miss Derwent, get her to ensure that everything went smoothly.

On a morning in July David Hessle came to Oak House. It was a hot day. Opal was lying on a *chaise longue* in the garden, in the shade of the giant oak from which the house took its name, when Mary brought him to her. She admired his composure on seeing her. She knew how awful she looked, though Mr Talbot said the scars would fade with time. Her hair, though it was now growing well, was much too short to be fashionable. There was grey in it, too, though she was not yet thirty-six.

'I'm glad to hear you're recovering well,' David said.

'I hope to be back in the store for the Christmas season,' Opal told him.

'Well, I've been warned that we must keep our meeting short and that I mustn't overtire you.'

'As if hearing about my store could ever tire me!' Opal said scornfully. 'But if your time is to be limited please tell me everything as quickly as you can. How is the July sale going? Is the restaurant making a good profit?'

She had a hundred questions. He answered them all.

'I'm very grateful to you for taking care of things,' she said. 'I think you should get yourself an assistant, someone who'll really be of help to you over the next few months, until I return.'

'Actually,' David said, 'I did so a few months ago. As you rightly say, it's too much for one person. I took Miss Nash, from Toys. She's shaping well.'

'Miss Nash?'

'She was a temporary assistant on Toys two Christmases ago. I don't suppose you'll remember her.'

She didn't. Too much had happened.

'Here's Mary coming to see me off!' David sounded relieved, jumped to his feet.

Mary crossed the lawn hand in hand with Emmeline who, at thirteen months, was walking well. It was David's first sight of the child. If he feels any emotion, Opal thought, he is not showing it. The smile on his face remained fixed and his eyes revealed nothing. She herself felt nothing beyond the pleasure which the sight of her little daughter always gave her.

The child started to run, tottered, and overbalanced by Opal's chair.

'She is exactly like you, Opal,' David said. 'Exactly!'

Mary picked up Emmeline and set her on her feet again.

'Yes, isn't she,' she said. 'There seems to be nothing of Edgar in her.'

Opal had thought often about Edgar in the long days of her convalescense, but it was not the affair with David, but the years before, which ate at her conscience. 'If it had been a loving marriage,' Edgar had said. He was right. She knew now, she had learned painfully over the last months, that it was the warmth of love and affection, given and received, which made life worth while. She knew she would have died but for the love which had surrounded her, which had refused to let her go. Well, wherever he was, perhaps Edgar had found someone who would give him the affection he needed. But she would like him to know she had come to understand, and that she was sorry.

She had thought, too, about Mrs Carson, and longed to make her peace with the woman who had been so good to her. In the end she spoke to Mary about it.

'I want you to ask Mrs Carson if she will come to see me. Try to persuade her.'

'It will only upset you,' Mary objected. 'You know the doctor says you're not to be worried.'

'I shall worry far more lying here, thinking about it,' Opal said.

Mrs Carson came, and the meeting which Opal had wanted, yet dreaded, proved easier than she (and probably her mother-in-law, she thought) had expected.

'We've a lot to forgive each other for,' Mrs Carson said. 'Let bygones be bygones.'

'I have something to tell you,' Opal said. 'I intend to try to trace Edgar. I shall put advertisements in the Canadian Press – Toronto – and deposit a letter for

229

him at the newspaper office if they'll let me. Perhaps you could send a letter, too.'

'I can't write,' Mrs Carson said. 'Neither me nor Percy can write. Edgar knows that. But if I could just know where he was, even if I can't see him again, I'd be happy.'

Opal wrote that night – a short letter because she could not yet hold a pen well.

Dear Edgar, (she wrote) I have been thinking of you a great deal lately, realizing what I did to you. I am writing to ask you if you can find it in yourself to forgive me.

Daniel is well. He never forgets you. I would like it if we could be friends, for his sake. I saw your mother today. She longs to know where you are, as we all do. Please, if nothing else, let us know that.

She said nothing of Emmeline, or of her accident – which was why she signed and sealed the letter before telling Daniel what she had decided.

'Here it is,' she said. 'But you and Auntie Mary must see to the rest. I can't quite manage it.'

'I'll do *anything*!' Daniel said. 'Anything! Oh Mother, do you think he'll come back to us?'

'I doubt that,' Opal said. She was not sure that she wanted that. 'If we can establish contact with him, that's the most we should hope for.'

But as the months went by, as advertisement after advertisement appeared, with no word from Edgar, even that hope died in Opal. It never died in Daniel.

With each week that passed Opal grew stronger. But in spite of her pleas that she was as fit as a fiddle the doctor refused to let her go back to the store for the pre-Christmas season, or for the following January sales.

'If you progress as well as you are doing now, and if you behave yourself,' he promised her, 'you can start work at the beginning of February.'

With that she had to be content. Remembering a previous occasion when she had done so, she dare not mark off the days in her diary. But in her head she kept a count, and knew it would not be long now.

Chapter Thirteen

'What I want to do most of all, right away, is to walk around the store,' Opal said. 'See how everything's going, say hello to everyone. I've been looking forward to it so long.'

'Then I'll come with you,' David offered. 'Explain one or two changes and so on.'

'No. You know I've always liked to do this on my own.'

She was out of her office and hurrying down the stairs before he could reply. She made for the side door, intending to look at all the display windows before starting inside the store. She felt tremendously fit this morning, ready for anything. It was wonderful to be back.

But not ready for this, she thought, fifteen minutes later! What has happened? What has happened to my beautiful store?

At first she thought that it was just something wrong with the side windows, that they were still heaped with the sordid detritus of the January sales because the window dressers had been busy along the front. It was annoying, but she would quickly deal with it. But when she turned the corner to the windows which faced on to the main road it was exactly the same. The sale remnants – unsold skirts, jumpers, hats, tea-towels, gloves, materials, china – were still unattractively on show, though the sale was over. Not a single window had been cleared and the new season's display which custom said must begin just before the sale ended had not been started. In a fashion window two naked models had been left undraped, a vulgarity undreamt of in any decent store. Moreover, there was not a sign of a window dresser at work.

She marched swiftly into the store and made for the nearest telephone, on Haberdashery.

'Staff Office? Have someone find Mr Lambert and report to me at once! Ground floor, main entrance. Well if he's left send whoever's taken his place as Senior Window Dresser. *I* don't know where you'll find him. All I know is he's not where he should be!'

She turned from the telephone and saw a woman impatiently drumming her fingers on the counter. There was no assistant in sight.

'Could you find someone to serve me, Miss,' the woman said. 'I'll swear I've been waiting here ten minutes!'

'I'm sorry about that. I'm not quite sure what's happened but I'll be pleased to serve you myself. What can I get for you?' Opal was trying hard to control her feelings, to speak pleasantly.

'I want five yards of bias binding, navy, to match this.' She held out a piece of material.

'I'm sure we shall have that,' Opal said.

She opened the drawer marked 'bindings, bias'. True enough, there were some cards of binding in the drawer. There was also lace, tape, ribbons, and an odd card of grey darning wool. The ends of the bindings and laces had not been pinned after use and were coming adrift. She rummaged through the drawer.

'Ah! Here we are! But we seem to have only the one

shade of navy at the moment. Let's see if it matches.'
She placed it against the material.

'It doesn't really,' the customer said. 'It's too light.
More of a French navy.'

'You're quite right,' Opal agreed. 'It won't do! Were
you wanting to use it today?'

'Tomorrow at the latest. I'll try Miller's.'

'Oh, but I'm sure we can get it for you,' Opal said
quickly. 'If you like to leave you name and address we'll
do that today and we'll put it in the afternoon post to
you. We'll enclose a bill and you can pay next time you
come into the store. I dare say you come fairly often?'

'I used to,' the woman said. 'You wouldn't believe
what a good store this used to be.'

As the woman was leaving the haberdashery assistant
returned. She smiled happily at Opal.

'Ta! I had to go to powder my nose, so to speak.
Miss Titmarsh on ribbons said she'd keep an eye open,
but she seems to have disappeared.'

'You know the rules!' Opal snapped. 'No department
is ever to be left unattended. If Miss Titmarsh was not
free to relieve you, you should have remained at your
post until she was.'

'Here, I didn't know that was a rule!' the girl said.
'Come to that, I don't know who *you* are!'

'You soon will,' Opal said grimly. 'Where's your
buyer?'

'Miss Foster? Well she had a rotten cold on Saturday
so I reckon she must be tucked up in bed with a hot
water bottle.'

She looked again at Opal, saw, under the make-up,
the scar running down the left side of her face. 'Oh
Lord,' she wailed. 'You're not Miss Opal?'

But Opal had gone, walking swiftly away towards a

man in a brown overall who stood by the main entrance.

'Are you the Senior Window Dresser?' she asked sharply.

'Yes Miss. The thing is, Miss, no-one has given me the plans for the new displays. I can't dress windows until I know what's to go in them.'

'I want action, not excuses,' Opal interrupted. 'Go around to every buyer, tell them Miss Opal sent you and that they are to give you a selection of their new season's goods immediately. Tell them the theme is "Winter into Spring". We want plenty of yellow and green to brighten things up. And while you're doing that see to it that your assistants are cleaning the windows. They're filthy! I shall expect every window in the store to be cleaned and dressed today. If it means working overtime, then you must do that. Now get going!'

At first she told herself she had simply made a bad start, picked on two inefficient employees. But it was more than that. Everywhere was the same. As she progressed, her temper rising, her footsteps quickening as she marched from department to department, she saw all around her evidence of neglect such as she could never have dreamt of. Assistants chatting in corners, dirty showcases carelessly dressed, counters cluttered and, worst of all, customers unattended. She had been away less than two years. How could her wonderful store, which had run like clockwork, which had been a byword far beyond Leasfield for service and efficiency – how could it have come to this? This seemingly fourth-rate, run-down emporium?

She advanced into gowns, her high heels viciously

stabbing into the carpet. An assistant sat on a chair behind a counter.

'Are you ill? Or menstruating?' Opal demanded.

'No!' The girl looked startled.

'Then stand up!' Opal ordered. 'A chair is provided in each department for any assistant who is unwell, or unduly fatigued. You are not ill, and at ten-o-clock on a Monday morning, with not a customer in sight, you can hardly be fatigued. Where is Miss Baxter?'

'Gone to coffee.' the assistant said.

Opal walked around the department, examined the dresses on the rails, looked into the fitting rooms.

'Tell Miss Baxter that Miss Opal will see her later,' she said. 'In the meantime there are several gowns hanging in the fitting rooms. Get them back on the rails where they belong. They won't sell if they're out of sight! If there is a Junior, get her to clean the mirrors. If there isn't, then do it yourself.'

In the Fabric department she ordered that bolts of cloth be replaced on the shelves where they belonged. In Glass and China she demanded that the whole stock be dusted forthwith. She would have liked to have picked up the entire stock, piece by piece, and smashed it against the wall.

Last of all she went into the restaurant. By now she knew what to expect. Spotty tablecloths and messy cruets. My beautiful restuarant, she thought miserably. She sat at a table in the corner, which used to be reserved for her. She was trembling from head to foot with a mixture of rage and shock. She clenched her fists, took long, deep breaths to prevent herself breaking into angry tears.

'Why, Miss Opal! How nice to see you back! Shall I get you some coffee?'

She looked up into the bright, shining face of Kate Lewis, the waitress who always looked after her. Kate had worked in the store since opening day. At least *she* had not changed. She was as immaculate as ever in her black dress, snow-white apron, pleated cap threaded with velvet ribbon. And then, suddenly, Opal realized that nothing else around her had changed, either. The starched tablecloths were in pristine condition, there were posies of fresh flowers on each table, the cutlery and cruets gleamed. It was all exactly as it used to be, exactly as she had thought of it in the long time she had been away.

'I don't believe it,' she whispered, looking around her. 'I don't believe it. How can it be?'

The waitress looked at her with compassion.

'I can't pretend not to know what you're talking about, Miss Opal. I knew you had a shock coming to you, and as you walked into the restaurant I could see you'd had it. I just wish you'd come in here first. I'd have warned you.'

'Why *did* no-one warn me? Why did no-one say anything?'

Kate shrugged her shoulders. 'Ask me another! Of course we didn't know you were coming today, else it might not have been quite so bad.'

'No,' Opal said. 'No-one did. I'd arranged to start on Thursday but I changed my mind at the last minute, decided to come in earlier. I didn't tell anyone because I wanted it to be a surprise. Well, it was that all right!'

'It's a shame,' Kate said. 'Many's the time I've said to the girls "Miss Opal would be grieved to the heart if she could see what's happening." But you see *here* we have Mr Soames. That makes all the difference. *He* didn't change, even when the buyers' commission was cut, and his with it.'

'The buyers' commission cut?' Opal could not believe what she was hearing. It was like some bad dream.

'Well, everybody's commission, right through the store. But the buyers feel it most, don't they, because they've most to lose. But Mr Soames didn't let it make any difference to him and of course we still get our tips.'

Mr Soames. She had almost forgotten him, though she herself had engaged him to manage the new restaurant when it first opened.

'Mr Soames is a bit of a martinet,' Kate said. 'A bit like yourself if you'll excuse me saying so. It's what's needed. Oh he's always fair – like you were, Miss Opal. And he looks after us like you did. He's kindness itself when necessary. You might say he's the heart of this restaurant. But the heart went out of the store when you went, Miss Opal! I hear what customers say when they sit at my tables and I've heard them use those very words, more than once. Well, let's hope you've brought it back.'

'Oh I have,' Opal said slowly. 'I have!'

In the last hour she had felt that all the world's anger was contained in her; that it choked in her throat and soured in her stomach. Now, though the fury and the rage were still in her, they were combined with a fierce, grim determination.

'Let's say that you and Mr Soames have put new heart into me! Everything's going to be all right in the end, I promise you, Kate. Just you watch me!'

But to most of the people she had seen this morning it would seem, for some time to come, a heart of iron. She felt that she had a ball of iron where her heart should be and that iron ran in her veins. And David Hessle would be the first to suffer. She would gladly kill him.

'Give Mr Soames my compliments,' she said to Kate. 'Tell him I'll see him tomorrow. I'm going to be very busy the rest of today.'

Opal burst into David Hessle's office without knocking. He was comfortably seated behind his large desk. A young woman with corn-blonde hair bent over the desk beside him, their heads close together as they studied a sheet of paper. They looked up as Opal entered. David, half rising from his chair, was clearly apprehensive, disconcerted. Not so the girl. The look she gave Opal was defiant, self-satisfied. That something was going on Opal did not doubt, but it did not concern her now. All that mattered was her store, that here was the man to whom she had entrusted her most precious possession, here was the man who had wrecked it, perhaps beyond repair.

'You've not met Miss Nash,' David said nervously.

'Please leave us at once!' Opal did not look at the girl as she spoke to her.

'You'd better go,' David said.

The door closed noisily behind her. Opal had not taken her eyes off David.

'What have you done? How dare you do this to me? How dare you?' She hurled the words at him; cold, venomous, as if she would like to spit poison with them.

David sank back into his chair, raised his hands as if to fend her off.

'Opal, don't fly off the handle! Let me explain. Nothing has been easy these last two years. Business hasn't been easy!'

'Business is never easy! Do you think I found it so?

239

You undertook the job – for which, incidentally, you were paid a higher rate than most people in the retail world – and you didn't do it! You cheated me, David, as certainly as if you'd embezzled my money.' Her voice was hoarse, trembling.

'That's a harsh judgement, Opal,' he said defensively. 'You don't know all the facts. I can explain them to you.'

'I've seen enough of the facts in front of me this morning. Filth, apathy, carelessness. An almost total lack of discipline. But worst of all, you've damaged what I hold most dear – my relationship I had with my customers, the confidence they had in me!'

'How can you possibly know that?' David demanded.

'I do know it. And you can't deny it. You've been totally incompetent. As for your dishonesty, I've yet to find out how far that has gone! But it's what you've done to my customers that I care about most.'

David leaned back in his chair. His abject air had vanished and the look he gave Opal now was insolent.

'Well now,' he sneered. 'You could never expect me to come up to Miss Opal, could you? Who could ever do that? Miss Opal, Queen of Storekeepers!'

'And I will be again!' Opal shouted. How dare he mock her! 'But not with your help! I'm giving you a month's notice from this minute. It being February it will mercifully be a short month. During that time you will have nothing whatever to do with the running of the store.'

Somewhere, deep underneath her anger, her heart ached that she should be saying these words to David Hessle. How could such a thing be? She had realized more than two years ago that in personal relationships he was weak; that the strength for which she had admired him had never been his. It was a quality with which she had endowed him because she had longed for a strong man in her life. But she had always thought, until today, that in business he was reliable, talented, trustworthy.

'You can't do that!' he objected.

'Can't I? It's my store. I can do what I like! There'll be a staff meeting tomorrow evening. You can attend if you wish, or you can leave me to announce your departure.'

'I'm sure you'll do it very well,' he said dryly. 'For the sake of your store you won't say anything cheap. Actually, you might find there are some people who quite like me, won't want me to go.'

'After you've cut their commission? Don't be absurd. You've cheated them as you've cheated me. But if anyone wants to leave with you, they're welcome. And now I'd like the Minutes of the last two years' Staff Meetings. Have them sent up to my office at once.'

She turned to leave. She could not bear to be with him a moment longer. He called out after her as she went towards the door.

'We haven't been having staff meetings. People have better things to do after work – but you wouldn't understand that.'

Over lunch, which Kate brought on a tray to her office, Opal studied the accounts. It did not surprise her to see in the figures concrete evidence of falling sales and diminished profits, but what worried her more was the large amount of money owing to suppliers. The total was appalling. On starting the store she had been grateful for the lengthy credit many of her suppliers had allowed her, and as soon as she was established she had repaid that trust, and ensured their further good service, by paying her bills promptly. Desperately, she checked the figures again. These bills must be paid or her supplies would be cut off. Somewhere, she was dreadfully sure, she would find letters saying just that. There were going to have to be so many economies in the store; streamlining; perhaps merging of departments; cutting down of staff. It would not be popular.

She looked up as Miss Carver, who ran the Staff Department, entered.

'Ah, Miss Carver! I know Miss Morton left when she married her young man in Accounts. I can't manage without a secretary but I don't want us to take on any more staff at the moment. Is there anyone in your office, or perhaps in Accounts, who could be spared to help me? It would mean her present job being shared out among the rest of you, but for the moment that's how it is.'

'Well,' Miss Carver said thoughtfully, 'I suppose you could borrow Mrs Sylvester. She's an older woman . . . a widow . . .'

'Has she got lots of common sense,' Opal interrupted. 'Is she a hard worker?'

'Yes to both those questions.'

'Then send her along. At once if you can. I've got several things for her to do.'

She liked the look and sound of Mrs Sylvester; plump, neat, grey-haired, with a quiet voice and a matter-of-fact manner.

'The first thing I want you to do' Opal said 'is to get a notice right around the store, to be read and initialled by everyone on every department, from the buyer to the Junior, about tomorrow's staff meeting. Six o'clock in the restaurant. Make it clear that I want a full attendance.'

'And the agenda?'

'There isn't one. What I have to say won't fit into nice, neat headings. And just before you start that will you phone Mr Hessle and ask him to send Miss Nash up with the Customer Relations file? You can use this phone.'

Mrs Sylvester looked up a moment later.

'Mr Hessle says he can't lay hands on it at the minute.'

Opal took the telephone from her.

'You will lay hands on it and send Miss Nash to my office with it inside fifteen minutes!' she told him.

When Miss Nash came, carrying the file, she wore an expression which Opal, without knowing where, recognized as one she had seen before. Silently brazen, as if she had a secret which pleased her and would anger Opal. And then Opal remembered. It was the look she had seen on the face of Connie Browning a long time ago. So her impression of Miss Nash and David had been correct.

'I'd like to speak to you in private,' Miss Nash said.

'You can say anything you have to say in front of Mrs Sylvester,' Opal said. 'Make it short. I'm busy.'

'Very well then. I hear that Mr David is leaving. If that's the case I'm afraid I can't stay.'

'I quite agree,' Opal said.

'So I'm giving in my notice.'

'Wrong!' Opal said. 'I've already spoken to Staff Office. Your cards and your wages in lieu of notice are ready for you. You'll leave now and pick up what's due to you on your way out.'

'But you can't do that!' Miss Nash protested.

'As I recently told Mr Hessle,' Opal said, 'in this place I can do as I like. Good day to you!'

She stayed late that evening, working out what she would say at the staff meeting next day. By the time she arrived home Emmeline had been in bed and asleep for two hours.

'You look exhausted,' Mary said.

'I am. Why didn't you tell me about the store, Mary?'

Mary reddened. 'I wanted to warn you,' she said. 'I didn't know what to do. I don't go into the store much, as you know, so I wasn't quite sure about things. But what I thought most important was that you shouldn't be worried. Queenie thought so too. We discussed it between us and came to that decision.

'I think it was the wrong one.'

'Perhaps it's not as bad as you think,' Mary suggested. 'You know what a perfectionist you are.'

'On the contrary, I dare say it's worse than I think,' Opal said. 'I'm pretty sure I haven't seen everything yet.'

Opal was encouraged to see that most of the staff were at the meeting. Whether they had turned up from a sense of duty or merely from curiosity hardly mattered at this stage. She was also pleased to see that David Hessle was not present.

Standing on the small platform which had been arranged for her so that, tiny of stature though she was, she could be seen by everyone, she fingered her opal pendant and waited for silence. When it came she began to speak.

'I can't tell you how glad I am to be back! I'd like

you to know that I'm totally fit and in good health. I've never felt better in my life.'

There was a round of polite applause.

'I want to thank those of you who have served me loyally while I've been away. But now that I am back I think the time has come to make changes in the store. I'm sure you will agree with me.'

She looked at the rows of expressionless faces, trying to read the thoughts behind them.

'First of all,' she continued, 'I have to tell you that Mr Hessle will be leaving us at the end of the month. Mr Hessle has been of untold help to me in the past, but now he is moving on. He is sorry he could not be here this evening to tell you this himself.'

In the small movements of heads and hands, the slight shifting of bodies, she detected the signs of uneasiness.

'And now' she said 'I'm going to come straight to the point. This store is not what it was when I left to have my daughter two years ago. It has deteriorated sadly. In some ways it has deteriorated almost beyond belief. Those of you who were with me then – and looking around I can see many of you, though others I had hoped to see on my return are missing – you will know that what I say is true. It is now my intention, without wasting any time, to make this store what it once was! And that I can only do with the help and co-operation of each one of you, from the most Senior Buyer to the most Junior Assistant. I need to know that I can count on you. So, if there is even one amongst you who cannot give me that co-operation, then it is better that I should know. Please come and tell me tomorrow.'

A man on the back row jumped to his feet.

'*We* thought we could count on our commission,' he shouted. 'But we were let down! We're expected to work hard, give everything we've got to Opal's store, but where are the incentives?'

Heads swerved round to look at him, nodded in agreement.

It was a sign of the times, a sign that jobs were at last a little more plentiful, Opal thought, that he should dare to speak so. She did not blame him.

'If you had not mentioned that, Mr Bell, I would have. I feel bound to say that it was not with my knowledge that your commissions were cut . . .'

'Not cut – cut *out*!' someone called.

'I've gone into the question carefully,' Opal continued. 'I'm happy to tell you that it is my intention to restore your commission from the end of this month!'

She interrupted the roar of approval which went around the meeting.

'Wait! Please let me finish. I must tell you that the figures I have seen yesterday and today do not warrant me taking this step. The profit margins are far too low. But I am taking a gamble. I am gambling, as I first did when I opened this store eight years ago, on the loyalty and co-operation of my staff.

'There can be no commission without sales, no sales without customers. And it is you as well as I who must bring back the customers. People have more money to spend than when I first started in business but there is also more competition. Prospects of success are brightest when what we offer – be it goods or services – are better than those offered by anyone else in the area. That is the way it was with Opal's store – and will be again!'

She definitely had the meeting in her hand now. She

could feel the power returning to her and she knew that, however difficult the going was over the next few months, she would get there in the end. She held up her hand to quell the chatter which had broken out.

'I want you and our customers to feel secure, to have a sense of continuity in the very special world of a well-appointed, well-run store. Remember, where the customer is concerned, that you are not only selling the goods. Whether it is a yard of elastic or a fur stole you are handing across the counter, you are selling Opal's store.

'I told you there must be changes if we are to become strong again. What these will be, when they will take place, we shall work out together.'

She sat down. The applause now went far beyond politeness. When the meeting broke up she went and stood at the door of the restaurant, shaking hands, receiving good wishes. She hoped that the same mood would be upon everyone tomorrow when she started visiting the departments, began the work of pulling everything into shape.

She beckoned to Mrs Sylvester.

'Would you find Mr Soames and ask him if he could spare me a few minutes in my office before he goes home?'

She had it in mind, had had since yesterday's visit to the restaurant, to offer Mr Soames David Hessle's job. She hoped he would accept it.

The most worrying thing she had come across so far was not the accounts, not David Hessle, not the state of the store, even, but the contents of the Customer Relations file. After the staff meeting she had taken it home with her to study it more carefully, hoping that on a second reading it would seem less disastrous. It did not. It bulged with complaints: of sub-standard goods, delays in deliveries, mistakes in almost every area, but most of all with complaints of poor service; of indifference, indolence and, occasionally, insolence on the part of her staff.

It was the most serious discovery of all because her customers were the reason for her store's existence. And because she knew that for every customer who took the trouble to write and complain, there would be a dozen who silently went elsewhere. What made it all so much worse was that, as far as she could see, not one of the complaints had been dealt with. This, she resolved, was something she must attend to personally.

'In the meantime,' she said to Mrs Sylvester on the morning after the meeting, 'I want you to write to each of these customers – just a short letter. Explain that I have only now seen their complaint, that I'm looking into it and I'll be in touch with them later. Say that if they wish they can come in and see me. I'll sign all the letters.'

One of the many good things Opal had already discovered about Mrs Sylvester was that she could write a good letter without every phrase being dictated by her boss.

'Very well,' Mrs Sylvester said. 'And before you go down into the store, Mrs David Hessle is waiting to see you. I put her in my office.'

Connie? Why? If it was to plead for her husband's job back it was no go.

'Mr Hessle isn't in this morning,' Mrs Sylvester said.

'I see. Well show her in.'

It was not only Connie who came into the office. She was accompanied by her small daughter. Opal

248

gasped at the sight of her. The child was the image of David. The same red hair, clear skin, grey-green eyes, beautiful features. Though she never thought of Emmeline as having anything to do with David, she realized with a jolt that this was how her own daughter could have looked, instead of being a small replica of herself.

'Yes, little Dinah's the spit of her dad, isn't she? Connie said. 'Let's hope she doesn't take after him in character!'

'I won't beat about the bush,' she went on. 'David has hopped it. Packed up and went last night. Need I say who with?'

What have I *done*, Opal thought, what *have* I done?

'In case you're thinking of blaming yourself, don't bother,' Connie said. 'I've seen it coming. I knew he'd go sooner or later, if not with her then with someone else. I haven't come here to reproach you for sacking him. I've come to ask if there's any money due to him. I'm short.'

Opal hesitated. 'I'm not sure that I should . . .'

'Well you can't give it to him because you don't know where he is – though I happen to think he's gone to Manchester because that's where *she* comes from. So if you were to give me the cash to hand over to him – well, it's off your plate isn't it?'

'Very well,' Opal said. 'I'll give you a month's salary. 'Go into the restaurant and have some coffee while I have it made up for you. But how will you manage afterwards? I'd like to offer you a job here – you have some experience – but right now I'm not setting anyone on.'

'Oh don't you worry about me, love,' Connie said airily. 'What's sauce for the goose is sauce for the gander and I've got my friends, only too willing to step in when I say the word! Well, that's that then! Who would have thought it would come to this?'

As soon as Connie had left Opal rang Mr Soames and asked him to come to her office. When Kate Lewis had first mentioned George Soames yesterday morning Opal had hardly remembered what he looked like. Then, last evening, when he had come to her office she wondered how she could possibly have forgotten him. It was not that his appearance was in any way remarkable. He was a man of medium height, as dark as herself but, though a couple of years older than she, with no grey in his hair. The clear hazel eyes which looked directly into her own were kindly and honest. She felt an immediate trust in him. Kate had described him as a bit of a martinet, but it was not apparent in his manner. But then Kate had also described her as a martinet – which was absurd!

'Ah! Thank you for coming so soon,' she said. 'You already know how pleased I am that you've consented to be my Store Manager. Now I'm going to ask you if you could take over as quickly as possible. The very first minute your deputy in the restaurant can replace you. I hope it won't be long. There's so much to be done and I really do need you.'

Chapter Fourteen

'So you agree with me, now that Miss Tyler is leaving us, that Miss Foster should be asked to add Hosiery, Gloves and Trimmings to her present Haberdashery, Handkerchiefs and Scarves?' Opal said.

George Soames, sitting on the opposite side of the desk, nodded approval.

'Absolutely. As we've said before, the more we can amalgamate several departments under the one buyer, the better. It means lower expenses on buyers' trips to London, or Manchester. And of course it saves a salary.'

'Not quite,' Opal reminded him. 'A buyer who takes on extra departments must be paid more. Also, a buyer with several departments, even if they're small ones, must have an under-buyer – though that's a job which can be combined with First Sales. Most of our First Sales will be all the better for having the added responsibility. Like you, I'm a great believer in encouraging oeople to do more than they think they're capable of.'

'So will you see Miss Foster, or shall I?' he asked.

'I think jointly. I've always done it myself but I think now, when it's a question of senior posts, we should do it together.'

She picked up the telephone. 'Mrs Sylvester, will you ask Miss Foster if she can spare me a few minutes right away?'

Miss Foster was the first buyer to be asked to take on extra territory. After that Opal planned that Sports Equipment should be moved to the ground floor and placed under the wing of Mr Bell, of Menswear. Ladies Sportswear – swimsuits, hiking shorts and so on – would be amalgamated into skirts, jumpers and blouses in a department for which Opal still searched for the right name. These moves were part of a plan worked out by herself and George Soames soon after he had taken up his new post, but because of Opal's proviso that no buyer who wished to continue working for her, and was willing to work hard, should be either demoted or sacked, it was only now that the scheme could be started. When a buyer left, unless no other solution could be found, he or she was not to be replaced; at least not until better times.

Miss Foster knocked and entered. She was a large, regal-looking lady. Her black marocain dress strained over an impressive bosom. If appearance was anything to go by she should have been in charge of something very important, like fur coats or model millinery, rather than elastic and buttons. Opal put the proposition to her.

'We can't offer you any more staff,' she pointed out, 'but the departments are physically close together and I suggest that you train your staff to keep an eye on each other's counters as well as on their own. I would like them, as soon as you can manage it, to get to know the stock on each counter, so that they are really interchangeable. It's a policy we intend to follow right through the store. I'm sure you'll be an excellent person to show us the way.'

'Well I'll try,' Miss Foster said. 'But there's one thing I would like.'

'What's that?'

'I'd like to have Miss Singleton as my under-buyer.'

'Miss Singleton?' Opal said. 'Are you sure?' Miss Singleton was the young woman who had been missing from her counter on Opal's first morning back.

'Quite sure, Miss Opal. She made a somewhat frivolous start, but in the last few months she's improved enormously. She's a good saleswoman – she had experience before she came to us – she knows her stock thoroughly now, and she's particularly good with customers.'

'Well?' Opal looked at her Store Manager.

'If Miss Foster believes her to be the right person, then we should give her a chance,' he said. 'She knows the young lady better than you or I do.'

'Very well then,' Opal said.

'Do I sense, George,' Opal said when Miss Foster had left them, 'that you think our buyers should have more say in choosing their assistants – moving them around, promoting them and so on?'

'I do. I think they should have much more part in it, right from the first interview. As it is, we engage them and the first the buyer sees of the new assistant is on the Monday morning when she arrives on the department.'

'Well, you could be right. But you don't mean I shouldn't see the staff we engage?'

'No. But you could take less part in it. Your job is policy, not detail. And your overriding job is Customer Relations. No-one can do that as well as you can. Look how marvellously you dealt with all those complaints.'

'Well, however you flatter me,' Opal said, smiling, 'there's one job you'll never take from me. Nothing will stop me doing my walk-around. When I do that I just pick up the whole spirit of the place. I can feel at once how everything's going, both with staff *and* customers. And I must say, over the last few months the change is unbelievable. I have a lot to thank you for, George.'

He rose, ready to leave.

'You're the one who's done it, Opal. I've been privileged to help, but you're the one who's been the inspiration to just about everyone. Not really having seen you in action before, I wouldn't have believed it possible!'

'I reckoned from the beginning that my employees would be loyal to me,' Opal said thoughtfully. 'And with a few exceptions they were. I think it helped that I decided not to look back at what had happened, but just to push forward, make a fresh start. But I couldn't have put my ideas into practice without you.'

And now, she thought as he left, he's coming up with ideas of his own, which is good. He's showing me that there's another point of view, that I'm not right all the time. She blessed the day he had taken on the job. Not only was he her right hand, he was accepted throughout the store as a manager who was firm, who would stand no nonsense, but who was fair. It was as if David Hessle had never existed.

Though not for me, Opal thought. She doubted that she would ever see him again but it was impossible that she should ever quite forget him. And there had been good times as well as bad. The last she had heard of him was that Connie was suing him for divorce.

But however pleasing it was that matters were going so well in the store, that the place was once more its clean, attractive, efficient self, that relationships between staff and customers seemed as good as they had ever been, she knew, and so did George, that there were still serious financial problems to be overcome. She did not like to confide them to her staff, other than to exert them to make every economy, and to sell, sell, sell. It would not do for the public, for her customers, to know how difficult it was proving to pay the bills which had been run up in her absence. Sales had increased steadily over the last six months but she had needed ready money for staff commissions and, most importantly, to buy up the two bankrupt stocks which had given them a good July sale. From now until autumn was the quietest time yet she desperately needed money to pay her suppliers so that they would let her have all the goods she needed for a bumper Christmas season. On that she depended to make her solvent for nineteen-thirty-eight.

There was a knock on her door and Daniel came in. When the school year ended she had given him a job in the Packing Department, since he needed to earn pocket money for a trip to Scotland he was taking with Queenie and her family. His cousin, Robert Derwent, was his closest friend. Almost his only friend. He was a solitary boy.

'I know I'm not supposed to invade the Big Chief's office from my humble bench in Packing, but I forgot to tell you that I won't be coming home with you this evening. I'm going to see Robert about the holiday.'

At sixteen he was taller than ever, but too thin, she thought. His voice had long ago settled down to something uncannily like Edgar's. and he had already started to shave. He was like Edgar in manner, too: quiet, reserved, and sometimes just as obstinate.

'Well, give my love to Aunt Queenie and Uncle Mark,' she said. 'Don't be too late home.'

He had, with unconcealed delight, left his boarding school in July and was looking forward to taking his place in the Art school. She was sure that most of his time in Scotland would be devoted to painting and that the pittance he earned in Packing would be spent on paints and brushes. He seemed happy enough most of the time this vacation, except that he still longed for his father. It had grown to be an obsession with him and there was nothing she could do about it. As if reading her thoughts he said:

'If you were to hear from Father while I am in Scotland you would let me know right away?'

She sighed. 'My dear, of course I would. But I don't expect to hear from him. All this time – all the efforts we've made. Daniel, I hate to say it, but wouldn't it be easier for you if you resigned yourself to the facts?'

'You mean give up hope?'

The forward thrust of his chin, the way he spoke, were so like Edgar.

'Do you mean you've given up hope?' he asked.

'Almost,' Opal said quietly. Yet it seemed impossible to her, too, that they would not see Edgar again. He was more alive to her now than David Hessle would ever be.

'I'll never give up hope!' Daniel said passionately. 'And neither should you. Never! When I've finished my art training I shall go to look for him. I don't know where I'll get the money, but I'll get it somehow, and I'll go.'

'Canada is a big place,' Opal said.

'I know. It might take me a long time. But I *shall* go. Perhaps you can give me a whole year's job in Packing or somewhere, so that I can earn the money.'

'I won't condemn you to a whole year in Packing,'

Opal said. 'But when you've finished Art School you can take your proper place in the store, learn all the departments.'

'Mother,' he said patiently, 'I've already told you, and I mean it – I don't want to come into the store with you. Not as a career. It isn't that I hate it. I just don't want to be caught up in it. I want to be a painter. Why can't you resign yourself to that?'

'The store's given you a great deal,' Opal pointed out. 'Almost everything.'

'I know that. I appreciate it. But please don't pretend that you've done it all for me. The store is your world, Mother. It could never be mine. Why can't you accept me for what I am?'

As, perhaps, she had never accepted Edgar. She had not wanted to shut him out but she had wanted him to be part of her world; she had never been prepared to enter his. And now she was doing the same thing with Daniel.

'I'm sorry, Mother!'

'No, don't be,' she said quickly. 'Perhaps it's I who should be sorry. Oddly enough it's the second time today I've been shown that I can't have all my own way! Well, perhaps I'm old enough to accept it now – but if I'd done so when I was younger I wouldn't have had my career. In a way you're really doing what I did then, fighting for what you want. But perhaps you won't hurt as many people on the way.'

'Perhaps I won't need to. Perhaps it will be easier for me than it was for you.'

He leaned across the desk and kissed her on the cheek. It was a rare gesture from her undemonstrative son. It gave her great pleasure.

'Get along with you,' she said, 'or Mr Beecham will

complain that you're not pulling your weight and I shall have to sack you!'

At the end of the first week in November the enlarged Toy Department, its extra territory grabbed from the reluctant buyers of other departments, was ready for the Christmas season. The Wonderland Grotto, to which it led, would in a day or two's time be fit to receive Santa Claus when he arrived, ostensibly from some far-off, cold country.

No-one would ever know, Opal thought, what effort it had cost, what juggling of accounts, what pleading with suppliers, to present this splendid display of toys, games, annuals, puzzles – everything that a child could wish for. Nor how difficult it had been to furnish the Grotto more spectacularly than ever before. Its nurseryland figures, its fairy lights and glitter, its dark, exciting corners and air of magic as well as its sacks of ninepenny parcels to be handed out to the children, had arisen only after a great effort, with small resources, by the staff of the Display Department, and much juggling of finance by Opal and George Soames. Her credit was now stretched to the limit and the bank would allow no further increase in her overdraft. Everything now depended upon the Christmas season.

It was Santa Claus himself who now presented the problem. He hailed, not from the Arctic regions but from the main entrance, where for ten-and-a-half months of the year he was the commissionaire, resplendent in uniform, with medals from the wars in South Africa and France.

'It's hopeless!' George Soames said. 'He's the worse for wear again this afternoon. He sneaks across to the Black Swan at dinner-time and people buy him drinks because he's an old soldier. Potter simply can't be Santa Claus!'

'I know,' Opal agreed miserably. 'Yet I hate to tell him. He so looks forward to it. Well, I'll see to this myself. I've known Sam a long time.'

Sam Potter, sent for, stood to attention in front of Opal's desk and saluted.

'Sit down, Sam,' Opal said. 'You know why you're here, don't you?'

'Of course I do, Miss Opal! Santa Claus time again!'

He was steady enough, but his over-careful enunciation and the powerful smell of whisky which hung around him left no doubt that he was, if only slightly, drunk.

'But not for you, I'm afraid,' Opal said. 'Sam, you must know what I'm talking about. You've been drinking again. It's by no means the first time. And now I have to tell you that you can't be Santa Claus this year. I can't have you breathing whisky all over the children. Their parents would object most strongly.'

She felt terrible, watching this man so proud in his uniform struggle for words to express his shock.

'It's only a little drop I take,' he mumbled. 'Just to keep out the cold. It's a chilly job standing in that entrance.'

'I know,' she said, 'but you can't risk warming yourself up with whisky. I can't prevent you spending your dinner hour in the Black Swan but I have to warn you, Sam, that if you don't put a stop to it then Santa Claus won't be the only job I'll have to take from you.'

He rose to his feet. He was unsteady now and swayed towards her.

'Are you threatening me with the sack?' he demanded.

'Threatening isn't a word I like,' Opal said. 'I'm advising you for your own good.'

He leaned across the desk, his face close to hers so that his drink-laden breath almost choked her.

'You'll be sorry for this,' he said thickly. 'I know all your customers, all the posh people, every one of them. They like me. You'll be sorry for this!'

'And so will you if you don't behave yourself,' Opal said firmly. 'Now take the rest of the day off. Go home, and come back sober in the morning.'

'And if I do, can I have the Santa Claus job?'

'No,' Opal said. 'I'm sorry, I can't risk it.'

In the event a young man from the Stockroom became Santa Claus. He does it very well, Opal thought, watching him, head bent down to a small child confiding its secret wishes. She noted with satisfaction the long queue which wound, caterpillar-like, through the Grotto and out into the Toy Department. It had been like this every minute since Santa had arrived last Saturday, riding through the streets of Leasfield on the back of an elephant which had been hired from a circus in winter quarters on the outskirts of the town. He had left his sledge, he explained to clever children who asked too many questions, with the circus owner.

She walked through the Grotto several times a day since the staircase to her office was at the far end of it. Apart from the business it was bringing in, she enjoyed seeing the children. She must get Mary to bring Emmeline, which would not be difficult for since George Soames had become Store Manager Mary, for one reason or another, visited the store far more often.

Sam Potter had not changed his ways. He was never very drunk but, in the afternoons, never quite sober.

She had put it to him that an indoor job in the Stockroom or in Packing might suit him better but he had refused on the grounds that he would not be able to wear his uniform.

'He'll have to go,' she said to George Soames, 'but it's not something I can do before Christmas. It would be too cruel.'

Working late in her office that evening she thought again about Sam Potter, wished she could do something for him. He was too young to be pensioned off but too old to find another job. He had muttered more threats at her but that did not worry her. He was in no position to do her any harm.

She looked at her watch. Nine o'clock. She must go home. She put on her hat and coat, drew on her gloves, took the car keys out of her handbag, opened her office door – and almost choked.

The narrow staircase was filled with smoke; thick, acrid. It filled her lungs and she coughed and spluttered, tried to hold her breath and could not. Beyond the bottom of the staircase, where a screen divided it from the Grotto, the smoke thickened and glowed red. She was trapped!

She ran back into her office, closed the door, picked up the telephone and rang the Fire Brigade. Then she climbed on to the desk and from there she opened the high window and climbed out on to the steep, frost-covered roof. How long would it be, she wondered, shivering in the night air, trying to keep her footing on the icy slates, before the flames reached her office and licked through to the roof?

'Granted that the Grotto and most of the Toy Department is a write-off,' George Soames said, 'I still say you were lucky. You were fortunate to be rescued in time!'

They were sitting in his office, which she must now share since the fire had burnt out the bottom half of the staircase leading to her own.

'Which is more than can be said for Sam Potter,' Opal said. 'Though thank goodness he *will* recover.'

'To face a charge of arson,' George said. 'There isn't any doubt that he started the fire and if the firemen hadn't come across him quickly he'd have died in it. As might you,' he added soberly, 'had you not decided to go home when you did!'

She was glad to be alive. Every hour since she had been rescued from that icy roof had been like a gift to her. But the joy of living when she might have perished did nothing to solve the problem of what she must do next.

'I'd staked everything on the Grotto and the Toy Department in these six weeks before Christmas,' she reminded George. 'You know that. Now only five weeks to go and nothing left to sell except the fairy cycles and toy motor cars which were at the far end of the department.'

There would be the insurance, of course, when it came through, but she knew she was under-insured and had been for some time. And her credit everywhere was stretched to the limit.

'Even if we had the money,' George Soames said, 'we don't have the time.'

'You're wrong there,' Opal said vehemently. 'If we had the money quickly, we could do it in the time. I know my people. They've already proved themselves. I know they'd work night and day to put everything right. But that's no good unless we have new stock. What can we do, George? What can we do?'

She beat her hands against her head as if she would force some sort of solution from her brain.

George shook his head.

'I have a few hundred pounds, perhaps a thousand. Not being married I've been able to save a bit. It's yours if you want it but it won't go far.'

She looked up quickly, her face suddenly glowing, her eyes alight.

'George, you're a genius! You're an absolute genius!'

'I've only offered you a few hundred pounds,' he said, nonplussed. 'There's nothing especially wonderful about that.'

'Yes there is,' she cried. 'Because it's shown me what I must do! I must do exactly as I did when I needed money to start my store. I went to my richest customer, my darling Miss Taylor, and I asked her to lend me the money.'

She had also asked Queenie but it would not be fair to do that again. Queenie and Mark now had a large family to bring up and educate.

'That's what I shall do,' Opal said. She felt excited, hopeful. 'I shall write to the customers I know best, who know me and, I hope, trust me. I shall tell them the position – they know the kind of year I've had, putting the store to rights again – and I shall frankly ask each one of them for a loan – large or small, according to their means, as long as it's immediate. I shall offer them a good rate of repayment and if I must – if I absolutely must – I'll offer them a share in Opal's. I don't want to go so far, and I'd only do it for a very substantial loan, but if it's the only way then I'll take it.'

'It's impossible!' George protested. 'You can't write and ask customers to lend you money.'

'Yes I can. I'm a woman in trouble, asking for help

263

from my fellow women. I believe I shall get it, at least in some cases. Besides, what's the alternative?'

She rang for her secretary.

'Mrs Sylvester, I have to write a number of letters. No, I don't want them typed. I shall write them in my own hand. But I don't want any interruptions. All these letters must go in today's post. And before I can begin I want the ledgers of all our account customers. It doesn't matter if Accounts Department is working on them; tell them I have to have them.'

While waiting for the ledgers to arrive she drafted out what she would say, writing and re-writing, discarding one attempt after another.

'How will this do?' she said to George at last.

'Dear Mrs So-and-so,

You will doubtless have read of the dreadful fire which destroyed the Wonderland Grotto and most of the Toy Department in Opal's store. Mercifully there was no loss of life and the one person injured is now recovering in hospital. What faces me now is the speedy restoration of those areas, partly because of the great pleasure which they give to the children of Leasfield and beyond, partly – I will be quite frank with you – for the successful continuance of my business.

As you are a regular and valued customer I need not tell you that since my return from my two-year enforced absence I have been fighting a battle to make my store what it once was. That battle was almost over. Had it not been for the fire we should have won through by Christmas. Now we cannot possibly do so without the help of our well-wishers and friends.

I am taking the bold but necessary step of asking you if you would be willing to help me, and Opal's store, by making me a loan. Large or small, it will be welcome, but I need it quickly. I have already been offered several hundred pounds but I need more, much more.

If you are able and willing to help I shall be at your disposal to discuss terms. If you cannot or do not wish to do so I hope that I shall still continue to have your much appreciated custom in my store. Yours sincerely, Opal Carson.

'What do you think, George?'

'Fine, if you think it'll work,' George said doubtfully. 'What can I do to help?'

'Leave me alone to write. Nothing more just now.'

Two days later the replies began to arrive. There were few letters which did not contain money, sometimes in surprisingly large amounts. But even before the letters, on the very day on which they had received the appeal, the customers came in person. Of those who came thus, no-one arrived without an offering of some kind. But from first to last it was not the offer of money which moved Opal most; it was the wealth of good wishes which accompanied it. Mrs Sylvester found her sitting behind a desk spread with letters, tears streaming down her face.

'I can't help it,' she apologized. 'I just had no idea! I had no idea what people thought of us!'

'Of you,' Mrs Sylvester corrected.

'It sounds a terrible thing to say, but it was almost worth having a fire to have this happen!'

She dried her eyes and began to collect the letters together. 'I shall never part with these as long as I live,' she said. 'Now we have to show what we can do with the money. First of all, Mrs Sylvester, I want you to call a special staff meeting. I'm going to need everyone's help.'

Within ten days the Grotto had been rebuilt and the Toy Department was usable again. The display staff, joined by members of the sales staff and office workers who declared themselves handy with paint brushes, hammers and nails, buckets and brooms, had worked around the clock in shifts. Volunteer drivers collected toys from suppliers far and wide; helpers from several departments gave up their lunch hours to price and label them and put them on display.

'It's a miracle,' Opal said when it was finished. 'But no more than I expected!'

'All we want now is the customers,' George Soames said.

'They'll come,' Opal said. 'You watch. They'll come more than ever now, just to see what we've accomplished.'

She was right. When the Toy Department and the Wonderland Grotto re-opened, the smell of smoke still hanging in the air, the crowds of Christmas shoppers flocked in – and continued to do so every day until Christmas.

At closing time on Christmas Eve Opal went to every department in the store, exchanging good wishes, collecting the sales sheets. When the last late customer had left, the last cover been draped over its counter, the last assistant gone home for Christmas, she walked back through the deserted store to George Soames's office.

'You should go home, Opal,' he said. 'You look all in.'

'Not until I've checked the sales sheets,' Opal said. 'Will you give me a hand?'

Long before they had reached the last of the sheets she looked up, smiling. Her eyes were bright, in spite of the fatigue which she knew must soon overwhelm her.

'George, it's far and away the best Christmas we've ever had! We've broken all records and we still have four more departments to check!'

Not long afterwards, the job completed, she took her coat from the closet and he helped her into it.

'Don't be late for Christmas dinner tomorrow,' she said.

'I won't,' he promised. 'I'm looking forward to it. It's a long time since I spent Christmas with a family.'

Chapter Fifteen

The Christmas of nineteen-thirty-seven, as well as being the best ever in the store, was for the most part a happy one at Oak House. When Opal arrived home on Christmas Eve, coming in from the frosty darkness outside to the bright warmth of the hall, Daniel and her father were putting the last touches to the six-foot-tall Christmas tree. Benjamin Derwent stepped back to view the effect.

'I think that's a bit of all right!' he declared. 'Though I say it myself as shouldn't. What do you think, Opal love?'

'It's beautiful,' Opal agreed. 'You two have been really busy.'

She wished, with a pang of remembrance, that Miss Taylor could see her house now. She would surely approve.

'And another thing, our Opal,' her father said, 'I've sawed up enough logs to see us right through Christmas. Now if we had a great big fireplace like your Grandpa Derwent's on the farm we could have a real yule log, big enough to last until New Year.'

Opal shook her head. 'You do too much, Dad. You know you shouldn't overtire yourself.'

'Nay lass, I haven't,' he assured her. 'I'm a very fit man, nowadays, for my age.'

Opal laid a hand on his arm. 'I know you are, love. And now I'll just go up to Emmeline. I wanted to be home before she fell asleep.'

'You are,' Daniel said. 'The little monkey's too excited to sleep.'

As Opal entered the bedroom Emmeline darted back under the bedclothes, bright eyes wide open, determined not to miss a moment of this exciting day. On either side of her a teddy bear, a stuffed elephant and two dolls shared the bed.

'Hey, Miss! You're supposed to be asleep!' Opal said. 'Do you know what time it is?'

'I'm not a bit tired!' Emmeline protested. 'Will it soon be Christmas Day, Mummy?'

'After you've been to sleep. Now you lie still and I'll tell you the Christmas story again, and then you must try to sleep. What if Santa Claus came and found you awake?'

Sitting beside the bed, Opal had hardly begun the story before Emmeline's eyes closed and she was fast asleep. Opal tucked the blankets around the child's shoulders and went back downstairs.

'She was worn out,' she said, laughing. 'But quite determined to stay awake. She'll sleep until morning now.'

On Christmas Day Emmeline delighted, and was delighted by, everyone. In her wonder at the tall tree with its glass baubles, tinsel and fairy lights, in her excited cries as she tore the wrapping from her presents, revealing the spinning top, the toy piano, the dolls, the sweets, they all took pleasure. Benjamin, in particular, watched her with loving eyes.

'Little 'uns are what make Christmas,' he said.

Though he tried not to show it and would never have admitted it, Opal was sure that Emmeline was her father's favourite grandchild.

'Well I must get on,' Mary said, picking up the wrapping paper, smoothing it out to be used again. 'What time do you suppose George will arrive?'

'He said he'd be here at twelve noon,' Opal answered. 'Mary can't you slow down? You've hardly given yourself time to look at your presents!' Her sister was flushed this morning, though whether it was from the heat of the kitchen or from the thought of George Soames's presence at such an intimate family gathering, Opal was not certain.

'Nonsense! I'm thrilled by my presents,' Mary said. 'But I've still got lots to do. The dinner won't cook itself. And I want everything to be just right.'

'I'll help you,' Opal offered.

'Indeed you won't!' Mary retorted. 'If anyone needs a rest it's you!'

In the event, George Soames arrived early, laden with presents.

'I thought if I came in good time I could give a hand,' he said.

'Well if you really mean it you can help me with the table,' Mary said. 'Come along. I'll show you what's to be done.'

With mixed feelings Opal watched the two of them disappear into the dining-room. In the last few months she had sometimes caught herself wondering whether she and George might not come together, make a go of it. In spite of her success in the store she felt herself incomplete, felt, from time to time, an indefinable sadness, an inner loneliness, especially when the day's work was over.

She admired and respected George and she was confident that he was fond of her. It was a good basis for marriage and more might be added to it. But when she observed the meeting between George and her sister on that Christmas morning she knew it was not to be. Mary lit a flame in him so bright and clear that no-one, seeing them together, could miss it. It was a flame she could never have kindled.

After the huge Christmas dinner, when they had pushed back their chairs and George and Mary had gone into the kitchen to make coffee, Opal said, 'I'm going to put Emmeline to bed for a while. She's tired out.'

'I think I'll have a lie down,' her father said. 'I don't want any coffee.' When Opal came down again Daniel was on his own. Sitting at the table, his head in his hands, he did not hear her enter. She put an arm around his shoulders, stroked his hair.

'I know' she whispered. 'I know!'

'If there'd only been a word from him,' he said. 'I thought at Christmas there'd be a word.'

On Boxing Day the word came. Opal and Daniel drove over to Mr and Mrs Carson's to take presents.

'But are you otherwise happier, now?' Opal asked as they sat in the car.

'Of course I am,' he replied. 'I've had a great term at college, doing what I actually want to do. And the new easel you've given me for Christmas is perfect. I'm going to feel really professional using it. I think I shall paint your portrait.' He hesitated. 'It's just . . . well, you know!'

'Let's go by way of Acer Street,' Opal said on an impulse.

It was the first time she had been near the street since they had left to go to Madame Dora's. It was narrower than she remembered it, the houses even smaller. The stonework was still soot black but the net curtains which hung at every window had been newly laundered for Christmas and all along the street the front doors had been painted and glossily varnished in a light oak colour. The mill was doing better now. Most of the families in Acer Street would be in work.

'Do you remember this, Daniel?' she asked.

'Of course I do,' he said. 'I was five when we left here. I didn't want to go.'

She drove slowly down the street. She had passionately wanted to leave it, never to see the place again, but now she could admit that not every day in Acer Street had been a bad one. The first year with Edgar, when Daniel was a small baby, had been happy enough. It was poverty which had changed everything. Though had it not been for poverty, which had relentlessly compelled her to find something better, she would not now be driving along the street (too ostentatiously she thought) in this expensive car.

At the end of the street she turned right into William Street. Her parents-in-law no longer ran the bakery. Percy Carson had been ailing for some years and they had sold the business and moved into a small terraced house near by. By the time Opal stopped the car Mrs Carson was at the front door, waving an envelope.

'It's for you, Daniel love!' she cried. 'It was delivered to the bakery in the Christmas post and they brought it down here this morning. One for me as well. From Montreal!'

'Montreal?'

Daniel tore open the envelope, took out the card, read it while his mother and grandmother watched.

'What does he say?' the old lady asked impatiently. 'Does he give an address?'

Opal knew the answer, read it in the sick disappointment in her son's face.

'I'm afraid not,' he said slowly. 'He just says "Merry Christmas, Son. Merry Christmas to your mother." Nothing more.'

'Aye, that's about all mine says, except that he's well. I hoped he might have let us know where he is.'

Mrs Carson's voice was flat with dejection. Daniel put an arm around her shoulders. Opal looked at the two of them and could hardly bear the sadness in their eyes.

Daniel handed her the Christmas card. The familiarity of the angular handwriting was like a presence. She had not seen it since before she was married, in the days when, between visits, Edgar used to write surprisingly fluent letters to her at Highcliffe. The Christmas card was the first time in three years that he had mentioned her. Did it mean she was forgiven? Perhaps that was reading too much into it, but she would like to think they were no longer enemies.

'Come and see me more often, lad,' Mrs Carson said to Daniel when they were leaving. 'It does me good to see you.'

'I will,' Daniel promised.

The first half of nineteen-thirty-eight brought so much work with it that Opal, except occasionally, had no time for the loneliness she had felt at Christmas. Daniel, though she noticed that he visited his grandmother more often, worked hard and said little. No word came from Edgar.

In the store it was the busiest time Opal had ever known. New housing estates were going up in and around Leasfield – semi-detached houses for a few hundred pounds. As young couples paid the deposit and moved into them, so the demand came for furniture; three-piece suites, kitchen cabinets, curtains – everything (especially if it could be had on hire purchase) to make the new home a palace. Opal quickly had the cellars under the store cleared out and decorated, bright lighting installed, and opened up a basement entirely devoted to everything which could possibly be needed to furnish a home in the latest style.

'Do you realize' she said to George Soames as the store closed on Easter Saturday 'that we've done so well this spring, not only with the new departments but with fashion too, that we're now on an even keel with our suppliers? It even looks as though by the end of the year I'll have repaid most of the loans to my customers.'

'I do realize,' George answered. 'I've sometimes felt this last few weeks that the whole of Leasfield is putting up new curtains and refurnishing! But you deserve the success, Opal. Once again you were quick off the mark.'

And now it was June, and Emmeline's third birthday, and since it was a perfect summer Sunday she and the children were in the garden. George had taken Mary and her father for a drive to Ilkley, promising to be back in time for the birthday tea. Daniel was gently pushing his sister on the swing. From the seat where she watched them Opal smelt the spicy clove scent of the border pinks and the more heady perfume of the roses. The roses, old-fashioned ones which bloomed profusely now and by next month would be gone, had been planted by Miss Taylor.

She watched Daniel. He was so good with

Emmeline, so caring; as if, at seventeen years old, knowing his own loss, he was trying to be the father the little girl did not have. How very much she loved her children! They were the mainspring of her life, more to her than anything in the world, and she wanted the world to be perfect for them.

But people were saying that war would come, that it was inevitable. When she went to the cinema, as she sometimes did with Daniel or her father, the films were full of music and romance but the newsreels showed uniformed men marching across Europe. If war came, what about Daniel? The thought came unbidden and unwelcome into her mind, as it did all too often these days. She pushed it away. It had no place in this perfect June day.

From time to time she closed her eyes, trying to banish all thought, letting the heat soak into her body; sliding towards sleep, so that when the man came towards her she did not see him, or hear his footsteps on the grass. It was only when his shadow blocked out the sun that she opened her eyes and looked up – and believed that she must, in fact, have fallen asleep and be dreaming.

'Edgar!' She managed no more than a whisper.

At the same time as she jumped to her feet, Daniel saw his father. He cried out, and bounded across the lawn, leaving Emmeline to fend for herself. The two men – automatically Opal noticed that Daniel was taller than his father – were locked in an embrace. She stood awkwardly by, not knowing how to act, confused thoughts crowding in on her. It was too sudden. Why had he not warned them?

Emmeline climbed down from the swing, ran across the lawn and took her mother's hand, examining the strange man with a quizzical look. Edgar and Daniel turned to face Opal and she felt herself deeply moved by the luminous joy in her son's face. Edgar made no move towards her, not even holding out his hand. He looked at her with a hard, direct gaze and then from her to the little girl at her side.

'So this is Emmeline,' he said quietly. 'I've seen my mother and she told me about Emmeline. Well, she's a beautiful child, Opal. And the image of you.'

'I was never beautiful,' Opal said nervously. How stupid she sounded, but she could not think of the right words, if there were any for an occasion like this.

'You don't appear to have changed much,' he said.

She could not say that Edgar had not changed. It was not only that he looked older; he was thinner; held himself straighter, like a man who could face the world and take it on. Perhaps the greatest visible change in him was the air of strength, which had nothing to do with physique. It was in his eyes, clear and unafraid; in the firmer line of his mouth, in the confident way he held himself. Here was a man who was in charge of himself and of his life, Opal thought. He had not returned to her cap in hand, she was sure of that. He was as strong as she was.

'I'm sure I *have* changed,' she replied. 'Though perhaps not in looks.' And then she remembered, as she still occasionally did, and lifted her hand to touch the scar which ran down her cheek.

'I heard about your accident from my mother today,' Edgar said. 'I'm sorry. I'd have come back if I'd known.'

'I'm completely recovered,' Opal said. 'What brought you . . . ?' She was interrupted by Daniel.

'This is your new daddy, Emmeline,' he said happily. 'Say hello to your new daddy!'

Opal's eyes, meeting Edgar's, flashed a warning. Don't spoil it for him. For his sake, not yours or mine, don't spoil this moment. She tried to will him to understand but his eyes gave nothing away. She was terrified of what he would say. It seemed an age before he spoke, turning to Emmeline, holding out his hand.

'Would you like me to push you on the swing?' he asked.

The evening, it seemed to Opal, went on for ever, the long northern daylight lingering in the summer sky. She was ill at ease, wanting to be alone with Edgar, knowing that there were things which must be said – yet not wanting to be. She was glad of Daniel's presence long after Emmeline had gone to bed, yet uneasy because of it. Mary and her father, embarrassingly tactful, had gone off to their rooms early, as soon as George had left. In the end Daniel, too, had wished his parents a reluctant 'good night'.

'But you'll be staying, won't you?' he asked his father anxiously.

'I have to go back to your grandmother's,' Edgar said. 'I dare say I'll have to stay there quite a while. Grandad's very ill, you know. But I'll see you tomorrow.'

Opal was grateful for his tact. She felt herself surrounded by people who now saw her future miraculously bright, all problems solved. Daniel saw it that way from ignorance; Mary and her father, she supposed, because they wanted a happy ending. Mary, in the throes of a love which had come suddenly and late, wanted everyone else as amicably settled as she herself would soon be. But it was not so simple, Opal thought. The future was not at all clear to her. It was all too soon. Even if she could sort out her own feelings – which she could not – she had no idea of Edgar's.

One thing was certain, he was not the man who had left her. He was a new man. It seemed impossible that in three years he could have changed so much, but the evidence was there before her and had been constantly reaffirmed in the hours since his arrival. Was it possible that but for the years of unemployment, followed by the third-rate job which he had hated, he would in any case have emerged like this? What part had her own success, at the very time when he saw himself as a failure, played in keeping down this man? She didn't know the answer to that one.

But the success he had won for himself, without help from anyone, had made him into a different person. Whether she would like this new person or not she didn't yet know. Nor could she guess at his feelings for her. The talk over the last few hours, in the presence of the rest of the family, had been general. He had treated her with no more familiarity than he had shown to Mary, and he had shown no eagerness to be alone with her.

When Daniel had finally gone to bed Edgar said, 'Let's go outside again. We don't get midsummer nights like this in Canada. It's one of the things I've dreamed about.'

They walked around the garden. With the setting of the sun the scents of the garden had intensified. The flowers seemed all one pale shade of cream, starkly outlined in the dusk. It was a romantic atmosphere, the last thing she wanted.

'You haven't *really* said what made you decide to come back. I know you never had my letter.'

'No. But then as I've told you, I was never in Toronto after the first year.'

Once in Canada he had quickly found a job, in a new insurance company just starting up. He had done well, grown with the Company, until in three years he had become a senior manager. It had meant, though, that he must move about the country, finding new business, opening new branches.

Was it possible, Opal wondered suddenly, that he had met someone in Canada? A woman he wanted to marry. Had he come to ask her for a divorce?

'I came back because there's going to be a war,' Edgar said. 'I didn't want to talk about it in front of your family, not today. But I reckon it's a certainty. I couldn't stay in Canada with my family in England when there was a war on. At Daniel's age he'll soon be called up. Apart from anything I can do in the war, I had to be here to see Daniel!'

Why must everyone be so sure about war, Opal thought? Did men make war inevitable by accepting it as inevitable? But could she, by refusing to think of it, make it go away?

'You're thirty-nine,' she said. 'Won't you be too old to fight?'

'I didn't come back just to fight,' Edgar said. 'And I have a job here if I want one. My company are only too eager for me to start up here. I may have to fight, of course, though I shall hate it. That's been my trouble. Even for something that meant most in the world to me – you, Daniel – I wouldn't fight. I gave in, ran away. It's not a mistake I shall make again. *You* fought for what you wanted.'

'Is that why you fought for your new company?' Opal asked. 'For your place with them?'

'I didn't fight for the company. I fought for me. For my own self-respect. I had something to prove and I proved it. I assure you, the world looks a very different place to me now! But I also discovered you usually wound someone. I hurt Daniel.'

'Yes you did,' Opal agreed. 'As much by your silence as by your leaving. But Daniel will be all right. He's never doubted that he'd find you again one day, and now he has. Right now, Daniel's world is complete!'

How long it would stay complete if she and Edgar were not to come together was another matter. But Daniel was almost grown up and she must give him credit for understanding. His parents could not build their future on what would please him. Not even Emmeline, she thought, can claim that from me – though my debt to her is greater and will take longer to discharge.

'And you and me?' Edgar asked. 'What did I do to us?'

'We did it to each other. But it appears not to have been all loss for either of us. You found strength and independence. You found that you could survive without me.'

'And what did you find?' he asked.

'Oh quite a lot. Including my weaknesses. I'd been arrogant enough to think that I could run my world single-handed, needing no-one. I was wrong. I've needed – and been given – the help of so many people. I couldn't have survived otherwise.'

It was dark now. The last vestige of colour had faded from the garden and a breeze was beginning to blow.

'I love Emmeline dearly,' Opal said, apropos, it seemed, of nothing.

'And her father?'

'David? I never think of him as Emmeline's father. He's only set eyes on her once, for a few minutes – far less time than you have. He never will again.'

'Where is he?'

'Who knows? Wherever he is I doubt if he'll stay there long. He, at least, is someone I don't have to think about. But Emmeline is another matter.'

They were silent for a while. Then Edgar said, 'She's *your* child. More important, she's a person in her own right. Emmeline shouldn't be punished.'

'And never will be,' Opal said fiercely. 'I wouldn't allow it. As I've told you, I love her dearly.'

'If war comes,' she said after a while, 'Daniel will be involved in no time at all. He'll join the Air Force or something silly like that.'

'We shall all be involved,' Edgar said. 'It will be that kind of war. But Daniel will make out. He has his own strengths. I can see that.'

Opal shivered. 'It's getting quite cool,' she said.

'Yes. And I must be leaving.'

'Would you like a nightcap before you go?'

They went into the house. Watching him as he sipped his drink Opal thought that he was an attractive man. He always had been, but now the bitterness of those years in the 'twenties had left him. He was a man at peace with himself. At peace, but not necessarily acquiescent.

He raised his head, caught her watching him.

'There is the question of you and me, Opal.'

'Not now . . .' she began.

'I agree,' he said. 'It's early days. That was what I was going to say.'

'Unless' Opal said quickly 'there is someone else involved. Someone I don't know about.'

'There's no-one else. There was, but it's over. But you and I are two different people, Opal. We have to get to know each other again. It won't be like it was before.'

'I know.' She knew, too, that if there was to be a relationship between them it would not be on her terms alone. 'We have to be certain,' she said.

'Nothing is certain,' Edgar said. 'But at least let's try to be honest with each other.'

By mutual, unspoken consent, they dropped the subject. It would come up again in its own good time. Neither of them would force it.

'What shall *I* do if war comes?' Opal speculated, turning the conversation. 'Though I refuse to take it for granted that it will. I suppose I'll go on as usual. They say there'd be conscription for women as well as for men so I expect half my staff would be taken. There'd be shortages, rules, regulations – goodness knows what other difficulties. I'd have my battles all right. But the country can't do without retailers so I suppose I'd come through!'

'Oh I know you would,' Edgar assured her. 'I can't see Opal's store going under! I can't see you ever giving up!'

He stood up, ready to leave.

'I'll see you tomorrow, then?' he said.

'Yes,' Opal replied. She was surprised how the thought pleased her.

THE END

THE BRIGHT ONE
by Elvi Rhodes

Molly O'Connor's life was not an easy one. With six children and a husband who earned what he could as a casual farmhand, fisherman, or drover, it was a constant struggle to keep her family fed and raised to be respectable. Of all her children, Breda – the Bright One – was closest to her heart. As, one by one, her other children left Kilbally, Kathleen and Kieran to the Church, Moira to marriage, the twins to war, so Breda, the youngest, was the one who stayed close to her parents. Breda never wanted to leave the West of Ireland. She thought Kilbally was the most beautiful place in the world.

The tragedy struck the O'Connors and the structure of their family life was irrecovably changed. Reeling from unhappiness and humiliation, Breda decided to make a new life for herself – in Yorkshire with her Aunt Josie's family. There she ws to discover a totally different world from the one she had left behind, with new people and new challenges for the future.

0 552 14057 0

THE RAINBOW THROUGH THE RAIN
by Elvi Rhodes

The Brogdens were one of Chalywell's most important families. Old Jacob had started the family antique business when he was nine years old, going round the big houses and buying small items of bric-à-brac for pennies. Now Brogden's was famous for its beautiful furniture and pictures. But the most beautiful – and valuable – thing in Jacob's life was his granddaughter Lois – for Lois reminded him of the daughter he had lost so tragically many years ago.

When Lois fell in love with John Farrar, the whole family were dismayed, for between old Jacob and the Farrars was a deep and abiding feud that could never be mended. Lois, conscious of the storm clouds of war gathering over her future, was determined that nothing and no-one should come between her and her beloved John. But as war broke out, as families were torn apart, Lois found her life changing irrevocably. Loyalty, love, tragedy and hope were to direct her into a future she had never dreamed of.

0 552 13870 3